The way out of tatuksha.

"Tatuksha," the hypnotist said. "Kekkethet. Estittit. What do they mean to you?"

"Nothing."

She put Brodie under again, took him to the high place and the magic carpet, then flew him back beyond his mother's womb. It was a smooth and easy ride.

"Where are you?" she said.

"I . . . I can't describe it. A familiar place. But I can't make it hold still. It all flows. In different directions, all at once."

"What are you doing?"

"Looking at something."

"What are you looking at?"

"Tatuksha."

"What is tatuksha?"

"The place you don't go."

"Why don't you go there?"

"Can't get out."

"Kekkethet," she said. "Estittit." She said the other words.

He nodded as she said them, like a man remembering.

"What do they mean?" she said.

His face brightened. "I have to die."

—from "Timmy, Come Home" by Matthew Hughes

IS ANYBODY OUT THERE?

EDITED BY

Nick Gevers and Marty Halpern

DAW BOOKS, INC.

DONALD A. WOLLHEIM, FOUNDER

375 Hudson Street, New York, NY 10014

ELIZABETH R. WOLLHEIM

SHEILA E. GILBERT

PUBLISHERS

http://www.dawbooks.com

First Printing, June 2010.

1   2   3   4   5   6   7   8

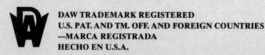

DAW TRADEMARK REGISTERED
U.S. PAT. AND TM. OFF. AND FOREIGN COUNTRIES
—MARCA REGISTRADA
HECHO EN U.S.A.

PRINTED IN THE U.S.A

ACKNOWLEDGMENTS

CONTENTS

Introduction:
Here Comes Everyone

Paul McAuley

One summer day in 1950, at the Los Alamos National Laboratory in New Mexico, four physicists were discussing flying saucers and the probability of faster-than-light travel as they walked to lunch. One, Edward Teller, put the chance that any kind of object would be observed traveling faster than the speed of light in the next ten years at no more than one in a million; another, Enrico Fermi, said that it was more likely to be one in ten. Although their talk turned to other matters, Fermi was still thinking about space travel and life on other planets, and in the middle of lunch startled his companions by exclaiming, "Where are they?"

It wasn't a flippant or trivial question. Fermi was a bona fide genius. He'd won the Nobel Prize at the age of thirty-seven, had helped to design the world's first nuclear pile, and had made significant contributions to quantum theory and nuclear and particle physics. He was also renowned for his ability to work up quick, accurate estimates from first principles and minimal data—back-of-the-envelope calculations dubbed the Fermi Method by his colleagues. During that long-ago lunchtime, Fermi applied his method to the problem of interstellar colonization, and while thinking about the size of the galaxy and life's tendency to spread everywhere it can, he discovered a provocative and fundamental paradox.

The galaxy contains between one hundred billion and four hundred billion stars: even if only a small fraction possess planets capable of supporting life, and technological civilizations arise on only a few of those life-bearing planets, there should still be a large number of civilizations capable of communicating with us. And although the distances between stars are very large, and even if exploration of the galaxy is limited to speeds below that of light, exponential multiplication of interstellar colonies would mean that a determined star-faring civilization would be able to visit or colonize every star in the galaxy within five to fifty million years, a trivial span of time compared to the lifetime of the galaxy. From these basic assumptions and calculations, Fermi concluded that Earth should have been visited by aliens long ago, and many times since. But where was everybody?

The Fermi Paradox is catnip to science-fiction writers. Not only is it an area of scientific enquiry that's directly engaged with one of SF's major tropes, but it's also a debate about a fundamental question—are we alone in the universe?—in which their guesses can be as legitimate as any made by scientists and philosophers. And any answer to the Fermi Paradox *is* no more than a guess: not only don't we know enough about the probability of the emergence and long-term survival of extraterrestrial civilizations, we aren't capable of predicting with any certainty that life could have evolved elsewhere in the universe.

A decade after Fermi's lunchtime eureka moment,

Frank Drake worked up his famous equation that, as he put it, organizes our ignorance. It calculates the number of civilizations in the galaxy with which we can communicate by multiplying the rate of star formation in the galaxy by the fraction of stars with planets, the fraction of those planets that are habitable, the fraction of habitable planets on which life develops, the fraction of biospheres in which intelligent life evolves and develops the ability to communicate over interstellar distances, and the expected lifetime of communicative civilizations. If we could plug the right numbers into Drake's equation, we'd be able to derive a solution to Fermi's Paradox. The problem is, only one of those parameters, the rate of star formation, is known with any degree of accuracy. The rest are wild and hotly contested estimates or best guesses, and the flakiness or absence of hard data is reflected in the wide range of solutions put forward: from Carl Sagan's optimistic statement that there may be a million alien civilizations in the galaxy, to Drake's own calculation of just ten civilizations, and the current consensus that the probability of a technological civilization existing at any particular moment in galactic history is less than one.

We're still no nearer to knowing which of those estimates, if any, is closest to the truth. On the one hand, we now have strong evidence for the existence of liquid water, an absolute requirement for life as we know it, under the icy crusts of two moons, Jupiter's Europa and Saturn's Enceladus. Other moons may possess subsurface oceans, too: Ganymede, Titan, Triton, and Charon, Pluto's co-orbital companion. This not only increases the probability that life could have evolved elsewhere in the solar system, it also suggests that life may not be limited to Earth-like worlds, but could be found in oceans beneath the surface of moons of Jupiter-class gas giants or even on rocky, Earth-like moons of extrasolar gas giants that orbit within their stars' habitable zones. And while no extrasolar planets were known when Drake developed his equation, astronomers have now catalogued almost five hundred, some of them orbiting binary stars, something previously thought unlikely.

But on the other hand, while extrasolar planetary systems are far more common than once believed—one even orbits a neutron star—none of the planets so far detected are likely venues for the evolution of life. Most are ice or gas giants larger than Jupiter or are orbiting very close to their stars—superheated Jupiters boiling away into space or large rocky planets covered in oceans of molten basalt swept by hurricanes of red-hot pebbles. Many orbit red dwarfs, which are the most common stars in the galaxy but are also prone to flares that could sterilize the surface of any planet in the habitable zone. It's true that current techniques for planet spotting, based on observations of minute wobbles in the rotation of stars, favor identification of planets that cause the largest wobbles—big planets or planets that orbit close in. But both kinds of planet seem to be very common, and planets in close orbit around their stars must have migrated inwards, and would have perturbed the orbits of any planets in the stars' habitable zones.

We're left with that intractable question, still hanging in the air sixty years after that otherwise ordinary lunch in the sunny clatter and buzz of a laboratory canteen. Attempts to answer it directly, by searching for signals from extraterrestrial civilizations or signs of stellar engineering, have so far come to nothing. Absence of evidence isn't evidence of absence, of course. Perhaps we haven't been looking for long enough, or perhaps we haven't yet looked in the right place, or listened in to the right frequency. Perhaps truly advanced civilizations surround their stars with constructs—Dyson spheres of Matrioshka brains—that soak up radiated energy. Perhaps there's a universal flaw in the development of technological civilizations that inevitably leads to their downfall. Perhaps they haven't spread to other stars but have evolved into epicurean philosophers uninterested in space travel, or have vanished down the rabbit-hole of virtual reality, or have passed through some kind of rapturous singularity that has rendered them invisible to our slow, meat-bound brains. Perhaps they are deliberately hiding from us. They are out there, but don't want us to know. We're in quarantine, or on double secret probation, or preserved as exhibits in a cage, with the sky all around a sophisticated illusion cloaking a galaxy buzzing with intelligent life of every kind. Or if you believe that intelligence implies ruthless and implacable hostility, perhaps some kind of camouflaged first strike is on its way, triggered by the TV and radar signals we've foolishly radiated to the local group of stars.

Perhaps the answer is as simple as the question. Where are they? They're here. They're us. We're all alone: the only game in this particular galaxy. We haven't found evidence of colonization of the stars because there isn't any—and there won't be, unless we get around to doing it. And if we die out before we tinker up some kind of method of traveling to the stars, if we foolishly squander our unique gift and destroy ourselves, it's extremely unlikely that any other technological civilization will arise.

There's no end to speculation. We don't know if intelligent aliens exist, and if they do exist, it's impossible to predict with any degree of certainty their history and motivations. Think, for a moment, about the eyes of the octopus. Like our own eyes, they gather and transmit images of the surrounding world to the brain, and they are superficially similar to our eyes: in both cases, light passes through the cornea and pupil, which is surrounded by an iris that can expand or contract, depending on light intensity. And in both cases, light entering the eye capsule is focused by a lens onto a layer of photosensitive cells, the retina. But there are also significant differences; our photosensitive cells are on the outside of the retina, overlain by blood vessels and nerve cells, while those of the octopus are on the inside, with the blood supply and nerves behind them: we have a blindspot, where the nerves are bundled together and pierce the retina; octopuses do not. It's a wonderful example of convergent evolution, where two unrelated groups of animals or plants independently develop similar structures to solve the same problem. But while human beings and octopuses share a distant common ancestor and hundreds of millions of years of planetary history, anyone who has looked into the eye of an octopus knows that it's impossible to understand what thoughts or emotions might lie behind its slit-shaped pupils. How much more mysterious, then, must be the thoughts and emotions of aliens with whom we have no common heritage? Even if there are intelligent beings who, by near-impossible accidents of convergent evolution, look exactly like us, they won't think like us. Fictional representations, from green-blooded elf-eared logicians to hoopy froods who always know where their towels are, or even ambulatory gas clouds or nanobot swarms, are all tainted with our anthropocentric assumptions and expectations.

We can, in short, take nothing for granted. The truth is likely to be far stranger than anything we can imagine, and that's why it's important to imagine everything we can. What about the imaginary scenarios in the stories collected here? All of them are bound to be wrong to some degree or another, sure, but we can't ever know exactly how wrong they are until ET finally picks up the phone. Meanwhile, they're more than mere entertainments: they're also informed speculations about unknown unknowns; contributions to an ongoing and important debate; and funny, weird, and thought-provoking explorations of all kinds of answers to Fermi's famous question.

The Word He Was
Looking for Was Hello

Alex Irvine

Because we did not have Us, we invented Them. Then, when They weren't where and when and how They were supposed to be, We castigated Them for it while secretly damning ourselves for fools because We had thought They might be there.

That's what Dalton Topolski told his therapist, anyway.

Dalton's therapist, one Dr. Arvid Lantz, had brought up the topic of alien races because he thought it might give his client—who had previously evinced an interest in science fiction both written and visual—a way to talk about what Dr. Lantz considered a crippling inability to form intimate connections. A loneliness, self-created and -enforced but no less miserable because of its re-flexive origin, pervaded Topolski's life, his work, his (if you could call them that) relationships. Dr. Lantz did some reading, considered the utility of approaching the patient in his own idiom, and decided on the slightly un-orthodox (for a therapist of his theoretical allegiances) tactic of turning his sessions with Topolski into conver-sations about the deep sources of science fiction's most enduring tropes.

Thus, Them. The aliens.

"Where are they?" Dr. Lantz asked on a sunny October Wednesday. "If there are aliens who can travel across galaxies, wouldn't they already be here if they wanted to come?"

"I went to a convention once," Topolski said. "This question apparently comes up a lot. I was there to get an autograph from my favorite writer when I was a kid. He was on this panel and it turned out that the panel discussion was about that question. Everyone just acted superior to everyone else and I never went to another convention. I like the books better when I don't know anything about the people who write them."

"And what was the answer to the question?" Dr. Lantz prompted.

"That there is no answer. Everybody chooses the things they're going to believe in and bases all of their speculations on those. Articles of faith is what they are."

The aliens look like trees, and are biding their time. Or they are microscopic and nobody has ever seen one because they didn't know to look.

On Dalton's way to work, radio signals passed through his body. Next to him on the freeway, people talked on their cell phones. Some of them used hands-free devices and some did not. Each of their conversations, transmogrified into electronic signals, passed through Dalton's body. Radio signals passed through his body. Cosmic rays survived their passage through the Earth's atmosphere and passed through his body. He was at the center of a million conversations and broadcasts that he would never know existed.

Dalton swung off the highway and onto Table Mesa

Drive. He could see NCAR at the top of the afore-
mentioned mesa. In his office, just down the hill from
there, his computer was running a SETI@home helper
program.

The aliens arrive unobtrusively, in twos and threes,
dropping down in entry capsules designed to elude radar detection and aimed at unpopulated areas. Slowly
they work their way into the small towns and farming settlements, traveling strangers taciturn and hard-
working. Over a period of decades they put down roots.
They work their way into the structures of power and
governance. Eventually they are elected to positions in
national governments. When they reveal themselves, it
is too late for anyone to do anything but go along with
their plans.

Dalton debated calling his ex-wife. He felt fortunate
that they did not hate each other. He was lonely without
her, and she without him. Or so she said. Still, they both
knew better than to try a reunion. Some events in every
life leave a permanent mark. Nietzsche's famous formulation, in Dalton's opinion, was flat wrong. That which
did not kill you often just crippled you emotionally to
the extent that you might as well be dead because as
things stood you were just permanently alienated from
the possibility of ever having a reciprocal emotional re-
lationship with anyone. Ever again.
    "Really," asked Dr. Lantz. "Do you really think so?"

The aliens are wavelengths of energy and probability, no
doubt responsible for the timing of those dropped calls
that created a tense miscommunication culminating in a
bitter fight between two people who love each other.

                    *   *   *

The problem was a daughter. Once he had looked at her face. Just once. But he and Marcia had already known they weren't staying together when she got pregnant. She wanted to have the baby, sort of just in case, Dalton thought. He had agreed, sort of just in case ... and then there she was, this tiny girl with dark, dark blue eyes. Dalton looked at her face and wanted to name her.

It wouldn't have been a good idea. They gave her to the social worker, who assured them that she would be adopted into a good home. She was healthy, white, and an infant. In the adoption market, that made her elite.

"I'm glad we did that," Marcia said as the social worker walked away. Then she checked her watch. She had an appointment with her lawyer later that morning, Dalton knew. He had an appointment with his, too. Their court date was coming up.

So long, little girl, he thought. We gave you a start, at least.

A giant disc-shaped spacecraft composed of a metal that returns a highly unusual spectrographic reading appears in the skies over Big Rock Elementary School in central Michigan. A teacher, Roger Flintough, vanishes out of his classroom, disappearing before the eyes of his second-graders. When he reappears in the classroom thirty seconds later, he tells the class to keep working on their art projects; they have been drawing colorful representations of the ecology in a rain-forest canopy. Walking down the hall to the principal's office, Flintough announces that the aliens in the giant spacecraft are offering humanity a bargain. When media crews begin to arrive shortly thereafter, he repeats this. What's the bargain, they want to know.

"Servitude for survival," Flintough says. Then he explodes into a bloody mist.

*   *   *

She was in the face of every girl he saw. Didn't matter what age.

A ridiculous thing happens. Using machines vast and inscrutable, a race of starfaring aliens creates invisible barriers around the great works of humanity, preserving them for interstellar tourism. But the great works of humanity are not what humanity itself might have guessed. Among them are:

a three-year-old girl, running down a beach to stop and gaze out over the Atlantic . . . over and over again . . .

Las Meninas and everything else in its wing of the Prado . . .

the color of five o'clock skies in December along the Continental Divide west of Fort Collins, Colorado . . .

a museum of fish hooks in a tin-roofed shed owned by the fifth in a dynasty of fishermen outside Bolama, Guinea-Bissau . . .

nine hundred and sixty-one square miles of the Mediterranean including two islands of the Peloponnese . . .

a cleared and graded parcel of land outside Shenzhen, China, on which nothing was ever built . . .

a cloud that happened to be hanging over the Grand Canyon the day the aliens arrived . . .

two dead dogs lying nose to tail in a ditch outside Busia, Kenya . . .

a jar of teeth sitting on the bedside table of a dentist in Manila . . .

the first alien to land on Earth, forever waving and motioning toward the forgettable vista of southwestern Minnesota behind him . . .

How the aliens are doing this, no one knows.

We have already killed the polar bears, Dalton was thinking as he sat in traffic on the Boulder Turnpike listening to earnest, pessimistic voices on the radio. Even if they're going to be around another fifty years or so.

Who wouldn't want someone to come and take all this away?

This is what he told Lantz the next Wednesday. Outside, the bushes were flowering and full of bees. "Right? We screwed things up. Time for the *deus ex machina*. Or the alien ex space-ina, or something."

"I can see why difficult times make people want a do-over," Dr. Lantz said. "But why? What good would it do? If you get a do-over, doesn't that just encourage you to make the same mistake again instead of learning how to avoid it?"

"If you're talking about the polar bears, we know how to avoid it. We just didn't." It was almost the end of one of Lantz's fifty-minute hours. Dalton slow-walked the conversation the rest of the way, preferring to keep his thoughts to himself. Lantz knew he was doing it, and let Dalton know in his oh-so-nonjudgmental-therapist kind of way.

Then he went home and flipped through the phone book. She could be anywhere, he thought. Anywhere. I could be putting my finger on her right ... now.

He looked. The name under his index finger was Mahmood Qureishi.

Maybe next time.

"If there are Grays, let them come and get me," he said to his shrink. "I'll even deal with the anal probes. Whatever. Just let me know you're out there."

"Why? Why is it so important to know they're out there?"

Dalton looked out the window. "Jesus, Doctor Lantz," he said. "Don't you ever get lonely?"

* * *

The alien is discovered cold and hungry, dying, in the woods behind an ordinary exurban subdivision. It is killed accidentally—but not really—and when the police arrive, they and the landowner agree that they'll dig a hole and forget the whole thing. On their way home, the police debate whether they should have gotten in touch with the FBI. But who wants the feds involved?

"It's an idea of the human I can't let go of," he said. "I don't think anyone should let go of it."

Silence on the phone as Marcia thought about this. After a while she said, "Dalton, I really never know exactly what you're trying to say."

"What do you think she's doing?" he asked.

There was another long silence.

"Sometimes," Marcia said at the end of it, "I think you sort of died a long time ago."

On Dalton's computer screen, a sinuous graphic told him either that the aliens weren't out there yet or that the SETI people hadn't yet learned how to look.

A nine-year-old boy in South Portland, Maine, looking at the moon through a telescope he got for Christmas, says, "Daddy, there's a building on the moon." His father is looking in another direction, having vaguely untoward and thoroughly unoriginal thoughts about the positioning of the Orion Nebula. "Doubt it, pal," he says. "But let's have a look." The boy's older sister is already looking. "Yep," she says. "There sure is. Who built a building on the moon?" The father looks. Yep. There sure is.

Sometimes he thought Marcia was right, that what he was planning and trying to find a way to accomplish was nothing more than an acknowledgment of something that had already happened. He tried this idea out on Dr.

Lantz, who said, "Listen. It's a big empty universe out there. Right? Except no. It's full of stars and nebulae and dark matter and mystery. Mystery, Dalton! That's what the universe is made of, and it's big enough that no matter how much we learn about it, it will always be made of mystery. If that's what you're having a problem with, stop talking about your ex-wife or this daughter you gave up for adoption."

Lantz flipped through his notes. "Here's what you said about her back when we first started meeting. 'We gave you a start,' you said was your thinking then. And you did. In a way, it's all anyone can ask. So why the guilt?"

"Why the guilt? Do you have kids?"

"I do. But you can't expect that to mean that I understand why you feel the way you do."

Later that day, Dalton stared at his computer screen as his machine sifted through signals. It was inevitable, wasn't it? That a signal would come, or had come, or was coming?

The problem was that time was big, bigger than space, and Dalton Topolski was so, so small. All of the conversations in the universe passed through and around him. He could not stop them, couldn't bend them around to come his way again.

On a September Wednesday, military radars across the world detect a swarm of small vehicles descending into the atmosphere. Efforts to shoot them down are unsuccessful. Spreading out into a flight pattern calculated to overfly the Earth's entire surface in a maximally efficient manner, these drones release an aerosolized nanovirus tailored to interfere with the absorption of oxygen into the blood. After that, there is little to report.

*   *   *

"Ago," he said to Dr. Lantz at the beginning of what he had already decided would be their last visit. "What a word."

Dr. Lantz looked at him. "It is a word that locates an event in time with respect to the speaker's present," he said. "I'm not sure what's exceptional about that."

"How can we exist both now and then?"

"What you mean is how can you still be so convinced that you did the wrong thing giving up your daughter," Dr. Lantz said. "Listen, Dalton. You keep constructing this elaborate superstructure about alien life and time and space and the nature of the universe because you can't face the fact that you're not happy because when you go home at night, you're alone. Until you face that and stop trying to put an extraterrestrial face on it, we're not going to get anywhere."

"The tough-love moment," Dalton said after a pause.

"You leave me no choice," said Dr. Lantz.

"I thought you did that," Dalton said.

"Did what?"

"The superstructure thing,"

"No, Dalton," Dr. Lantz said. "That might be the way you remember it, but it's right here in my notes. That's not how it happened."

"Yeah," Dalton said, looking out the window. He loved spring. The problem with spring was that it turned into summer, which meant that fall was coming.

The aliens are us, and our desire for them is the yearning of any sentient organism to know its origins. Where did we come from? We rode the chariots of the gods across the holographic universe, panspermiatically herding comets toward a universal amnesia that survives only as a longing we get when we look at the stars, for reasons we are never quite able to articulate.

*   *   *

She would be fourteen years old. She would know that she was born in Denver, but she could be anywhere. In four years she might choose to find out who her birth parents are, and she might arrive bright-eyed and curious. Or she might arrive sullen and angry. Or she might not arrive at all. Dalton thought these thoughts while he watched his computer analyze the background noise of the universe. In his head he answered Dr. Lantz's question. So what if I am, he thought.

The mountains were high. The universe was big. The future was too uncertain to endure. Water was wet and prevented the proper function of the lungs. There was a place he knew where people were not supposed to climb near a waterfall because it was dangerous. It was in Boulder Canyon, not far from a sign that said in case of flash flood, motorists should climb to safety.

Dalton Topolski thought that maybe irony was the last straw. The irony of her coming to look and him being gone, the irony of him holding on because she might come to look and then her never doing it....

The next morning he was still staring at his computer screen and it was still doing the same thing and nothing had changed inside Dalton Topolski's head except a modulation of curiosity toward resolution. He thought he had everything worked out. What else was there to say? It was the easiest thing in the world to die. No one was out there who cared.

When they're standing at adjacent urinals in the men's room of a Best Buy on Wadsworth Avenue in Lakewood, Colorado, one man (who is actually not a man) says to another, "I want to tell you a secret."

*   *   *

The word he was looking for was hello. The universe was one big hello, said to everyone else but him.

There are no aliens.
   The aliens are on their way.

Residue

Michael Arsenault

They went outside, lay down on the grass, and looked up at the stars.

Everything was quiet for about a minute, and then:

"So . . ."

"So?"

"So what are we doing out here?"

"We're . . . nothing. We're just out here."

"Why?"

"I don't know. If you really need a reason I guess we could say we're communing with nature. Or something."

"Since when do we do that?"

"Since . . . tonight. Since right now."

"This doesn't sound like you. Why are you being weird?"

"I just want to be outside for a little while, okay? Out of the house and away from distractions."

"What distractions?"

"Lots of things. Television, for instance."

"What's wrong with TV?"

"Nothing, just God forbid it should ever be turned off while we're conscious."

19

"You're touchy all of a sudden."

"Look, I just want to lie here, have a moment of peace, and see if I can connect with something. Stare up into the sky, and, I don't know ... ponder the meaning of the universe. What's so weird about that?"

"It's not like you."

"Fine. It's not like me. I'm different now."

"I think I feel bugs crawling up my legs."

"Maybe you should just go back inside."

"Don't be so—"

"No one's forcing you to stay out here."

"I'm not . . ."

"You're not what?"

"I'm doing my best, okay? I'm trying."

"I guess."

" . . . Do you . . . ?"

"Do I *what?*"

"Don't bite my head off. I was just going to ask if you know any of their names."

"Whose names?"

"The stars. The planets. The ... whatever those patterns are called."

"The constellations?"

"Yeah."

"No. Don't really know their names. I mean, of course I know some of them, but I don't know which is which."

"Me neither. I never really thought much about it before, but now that we're here looking up I feel kind of ignorant."

"You're not ignorant."

"I feel that way. Ignorant. Not to mention insignificant."

"Looking up at the sky can do that to a person."

"It also makes me feel a little weightless. Like gravity doesn't exist and I could just start floating up. Is there such a thing as reverse vertigo? I think I've got that.

The fear of being sucked up into the sky at a moment's notice."

"I don't know if that's a real fear."

"It is, I can promise you. I've got it. It may not have a name, but I'm feeling it right now."

"You're not going to be sick, are you?"

"I don't think so, but it might be time for me to turn my eyes away."

"Here. Hold my hand. Is that better?"

"It's . . . yeah."

"Better?"

"Yeah. Nicer."

"Good."

"Makes me feel a little more . . . rooted, I guess. You make a decent anchor."

"Gee, thanks."

"No, really. That wasn't sarcastic. You really do sort of anchor me. In the good way. Not the 'holding me down' way. And you know what? I hate to admit it, but this actually is kind of . . . okay. The view, the company, this whole thing. Everything considered, maybe it's not so . . ."

"Not so what?"

"Maybe it's not so terrible that you forced me to come out here."

"Well, listen to you. Almost sounds like you're happy."

"Shut up. Don't ruin it."

"Sorry."

"You don't actually have to apologize. I'm not being serious."

"I know."

"Say . . ."

"Yeah?"

"You ever wonder . . . ?"

"Wonder what?"

"Oh, never mind. Just a fleeting thought. And an obvious one."

"What?"

"It's just one of those standard thoughts that goes through your mind while you're looking up at the sky."

"And that is . . . ?"

"Do you think there's anyone out there?"

"Out there . . . you mean like 'other planets' out there? As in 'aliens'?"

"Yeah."

"I don't know."

"Is that your best educated guess?"

"It's my most honest one."

"So don't be honest. Speculate."

"Speculate . . . Speculate. Um, okay. Yes. There are aliens out there."

"It does seem likely, doesn't it? I've heard people say that the odds are good that there's something out there, somewhere."

"It's pretty vast all right. There's certainly room."

"So somewhere, somehow, there's probably life on other planets."

"Probably."

"You ever wonder if we'll see it within our lifetimes?"

"Contact with beings from another world? Once in a while. Mostly I wonder why we haven't seen it already. It gets me thinking . . ."

"About what?"

"You really want to hear some speculation?"

"Sure. You got a theory?"

"Maybe. One or two. You want to hear them?"

"I'm lying here, aren't I?"

"Well how about this . . . maybe they are out there. And not too far away, either. Invisible to detection, of course, but not too far."

"And ... ?"

"And they visit all the time."

"Oh, do they?"

"Yes, but here's how it works: they need to feel a connection in order to come down. They need to home in on a signal."

"What kind of signal?"

"I don't know. Maybe not a technological one. Maybe more of a personal one. A quiet one. Maybe just a person, all by himself. Maybe just the energy a human gives off. Someone who's looking up, just like we are. An individual mind or a force of will, that's what draws them, what they home in on. Maybe to them, a person all alone in the forest looking up is kind of like a beacon. This wouldn't work in the city, where there's so much light and noise, with a dense population, but out there in the quieter parts of the world ... Who knows?"

"So this would explain why all those stories about abductions are always coming from rural areas?"

"Exactly. They don't dare venture into the highly populated places, but one lone human out there all by himself ... it would be hard to pass up on."

"You do realize what you're saying, right? You and I live in a pretty secluded area ourselves. It's hardly like this is the middle of the city."

"Which means you never know. So if you don't see me for a few days ..."

"I'll just assume you're off sightseeing somewhere outside the Milky Way."

"It could happen."

"Oh sure. I won't even go looking for you."

"Suits me fine."

"Well, at least one good thing comes out of this. Now I know what to get you for your birthday."

"Oh, you do? What?"

"A pair of titanium reinforced britches. With a pad-lock. So you can avoid any of that unpleasant probing business."

"Why don't you just get me a chastity belt and be done with it?"

"Don't think I haven't thought about it."

"There you go again. Always trying to stop me from broadening my horizons . . ."

"You think you're funny, don't you?"

"I'm not?"

"You're more silly than funny."

"But I'm a little funny?"

"A little."

"You know, coming from you that's a huge compli-ment. I think I'll take it."

"Let's just lie here and enjoy the view."

"Suits me fine."

"Hmmm . . . you know, I may be mistaken, but I don't think there's a single cloud up there."

"Nope."

"Just a perfect clear sky. Filled with a billion tiny shiny things."

"I like to think of it as the greatest show on Earth."

"Sure. All right, it's the . . . Wait."

"What is it?"

"Wait, if I'm hearing you right, then . . . according to you, the greatest show on Earth . . . isn't actually even *on* Earth?"

"Well, no, technically, I suppose. But it can be seen *from* Earth. That's what counts, right?"

"I don't know. You're working with some pretty skewed logic there."

"Can't we just enjoy it and not pick it apart?"

"I guess."

"Thank you."

"I'll just stare at the moon and let it distract me from all the odd things that keep coming out of your mouth."

"Thanks. Really."

"Wow, it sure is huge tonight. The moon. And then there's also the—*Hey* . . ."

"Something wrong?"

"I think I see a comet."

"Where?

"Straight up. Just a little to the left. See it? That dot moving across the sky."

"No, I don't see it. Anyway, it's probably not a comet."

"It's not? Then what is it?"

"A satellite, most likely."

"Well, isn't that just as good?"

"Why would you say that?"

"It's just as much of a miracle, isn't it?"

"How so?"

"It's an extremely complex man-made machine that gets shot into space and somehow goes into orbit around our world. I'm sure that involves at least one miracle somewhere along the line. Either that or a ton of headache-inducing math."

"Don't ask me. I don't really know how satellites work. I just know they spew out thousands upon thousands of annoying TV channels."

"Not all satellites are for broadcasting sitcoms. You're really down on the whole TV thing tonight, aren't you?"

"It's not like I'm *trying* to be down on TV. Not really. I'm just trying to be up on life. The real world. Sometimes I don't think we spend enough time out in it. So I hope you'll forgive me if I don't see a satellite as being much of a miracle."

"Seems like more of a miracle than just a chunk of rock whizzing through space. At least to me."

"Maybe."

"Do you think you can put aside your disgust with entertainment technology? For a minute? Long enough to tell me another one?"

"Another what?"

"Another one of your theories. On why we haven't seen signs of intelligent life outside our planet. You said you had a few."

"I do."

"So . . . ?"

"Well, there's always the 'They're already here' theory."

"What, like they've integrated into our society and we don't even know it?"

"That's certainly one idea, but I had a somewhat different thought."

"Which is?"

"More of a 'side by side' thing."

"Not sure I follow."

"Imagine this: There's a planet somewhere out there with a very advanced civilization on it. Scientifically advanced. Now, they may look like us or they may not, but—"

"Let's say they don't. Let's say they're like giant bug people."

"Okay, fine, they're giant bug people."

"With six arms."

"Who's telling this story?"

"I'm helping make it more interesting."

"If you say so. Anyway, this scientifically advanced society has gone and perfected space travel."

"Gotcha."

"And all they want to do now is get out there, go exploring and meet some . . . well, aliens, for lack of a better word."

"So in this story, *we* would be the aliens."

"Yes. Good to know you're keeping up."

"I'm quick that way."

"Now, these bug people are on a totally peaceful mission. There's nothing bad here at all. They just want to find some other forms of intelligent life, exchange ideas, and, you know . . ."

"Make friends across the galaxy."

"Yes. Pretty much that kind of thing. Now let's say these six-armed folks have been on this mission—on this ship—for years, maybe decades, searching and searching, coming up with nothing, and they're just about to give up and turn back around . . . when something happens."

"They find Earth."

"They find Earth. Right. Exactly. Our little planet. And it's celebration time. Finally, *finally,* they've found something—someone—they might actually be able to communicate with. There's a banquet on the ship, a great big party, with hats and noise makers, everybody gets drunk, and things couldn't be better. The next day preparations are made for their grand entrance or unveiling or whatever you want to call it. Protocols are followed. They break out their official 'meet new species' uniforms—which are essentially the same as their regular outfits only with multicolored gloves, because of all the extra hands, you know—and then—"

"Get to the point, please."

"Hmm?"

"I get it, okay? They're happy they found us. Then what happens?"

"I'm just trying to set up how big a deal this is for them. How motivated they are for things to go well."

"You've done that. Move on. What happens next?"

"Well, next they fly down, land, exit the ship to come

meet us, and things are looking pretty darn good . . . right up until they realize there's this one little wrinkle."

"Which is?"

"We can't see them."

"We can't?"

"Or hear them. To us, it's like they're not even here."

"We don't even see their ship?"

"Nope."

"Sucky. So why is that happening?"

"Because we're out of phase."

"We're out of what now?"

"It's like this: we're here, and they're here, but all of us are slightly removed from each other. Like two different dimensions partially coexisting at the same time. Overlapping, sort of."

"So what does something like that mean?"

"It means that these bug people are walking around, looking at us, trying to talk to us, but we're just not registering them."

"So why is it they can see us while we can't see them?"

"I don't know. Maybe they're just more advanced. Maybe they have different kinds of eyes than we do or see different spectrums of light. There's endless possibilities."

"But you're saying they could be right here? Standing next to us now?"

"For all I know, they landed ten minutes ago, just behind the house. There could be one of them leaning over you right this second saying, "Hello. Helloooo . . .""

"Not in English, though."

"No, probably not in English. Anyway, after you don't respond, or even blink at him, the first buggy humanoid turns to his buddy and says something like, 'Can you believe this? What the hell? It's like we're invisible to these idiots.' And his buddy just shrugs his many shoulders and says, 'I don't know what to tell you, man.' "

"I bet they're getting exasperated."

"I think they might be. And then the first one says, 'Watch this. I'm going to wave my hand right in front of one of their faces,' and his buddy says, 'Go for it.' And he does, and then, when the human—that's you—doesn't react at all, he says, 'Still nothing. *Nothing*. This is so frustrating,' and then his buddy says, 'I agree. Hey, I think I saw a farm down the road. Let's go mutilate some cows.' And the first one says, 'Awesome idea.' "

"Ohhh . . . groan."

"Don't tell me you doubt my theory."

"No, of course not. But let me see if I understand you correctly. These visitors—these humanoid buggy people—they're not in phase enough for us to see them or hear them, but they're solid enough to go on a cattle mutilation spree?"

"I know. Hard to believe, but that's exactly what happens."

"You're such a goon."

"I can't be held responsible for how this whole dimension overlapping thing works."

"Talk about the dumbest . . . the most absolutely absurd and stupid . . ."

"What? Come on, you said you wanted to hear a theory. You wanted me to speculate. Well, there you go. That's some speculation for you."

"It certainly is."

"And they're not finished, either. Once they've finished up at the farm, they're still pretty angry."

"Slicing up Bessie didn't quite do it for them?"

"Nope, still peeved. So all of them, they hop back in their ship, and fly out over a nearby cornfield."

"Don't say it."

"That's right, they set their ship to spinning round and round and then they grind the hull down into the earth. Because when you're angry and you don't have a proper outlet to express yourself, making crop circles is the alien equivalent of doing donuts in a parking lot."

"I don't believe you just went there."

"You can see it now, can't you? 'Arrrh! God damn humans!' Screech! Crunch! Crrrunnch!!! 'Kill the corn! That'll show 'em!'"

"Oh, you're terrible."

"I know."

"Ohhh . . ."

"Made you laugh, though, didn't I?"

"A little. A tiny little bit."

"Then that's enough."

"Ahem. So . . . According to you, we now have theories which explain—and let's see if I remember them correctly—rural abductions, then cattle mutilations, and finally, crop circles."

"And I'm sure they're all spot on."

"Of course you are."

"I am. I'd stake my world-renowned scientific reputation on it."

"You're not looking, but if you were, you'd see I'm rolling my eyes right now."

"They're lovely eyes."

"Stop it."

"They are. Even if they're right at this moment expressing doubt about my very concrete theories. Still lovely."

"Is this going to become a habit with you?"

"What?"

"This whole 'watching the skies' thing."

"Maybe. What do you think about that?"

"I think I might be okay with it. I might."

"Good."

"You know, it's only going to be warm enough to keep doing this for about another month. What then?"

"I don't know. I guess we could build a skylight in the bedroom."

"How about if we just stick a bunch of those glow-in-the-dark stars up on the ceiling instead?"

"Not quite the same effect."

"But cheaper."

"We can afford it."

"I suppose. Though in all honesty, I was sort of—oh, *hey*."

"What is it?"

"There's that comet again—excuse me—satellite. You know, the one that's definitely not a miracle."

"Right. That one."

"See it? There. Up around . . ."

"No, I—Ahh yeah. I see it now. There it is."

"You know . . . Maybe it's not a satellite. Or even a comet."

"What, then?"

"Maybe it's some . . . visitors."

"You mean . . . other-worldly visitors?"

"Could be."

"I kinda doubt it."

"Why's that?"

"Because of my final theory."

"Oh good. You've got one more?"

"Yes, I do."

"Lay it on me."

"This is the 'Came, saw, tried to conquer, got headed off at the pass' theory."

"You mean the one that's so popular with the kids these days?"

"That's the one."

"I'm all ears."

"Okay, this theory assumes, first of all, that there are tons of aliens out there, on a multitude of worlds, and that all of them are of a certain type. The truly evil, war-mongering, planet-conquering, humanity-enslaving variety."

"So, a bad bunch of eggs."

"One and all. Now, back some time ago—let's say the late 1940s—the first batch of aliens came to Earth and immediately declared war. There was no 'Take me to your leader', no 'We come in peace', they just went straight to trying to blow us up, steal our resources, and generally cause a bunch of mayhem. And after—"

"Sorry, I really don't mean to interrupt, but did you just say the late 1940s?"

"Yes."

"There was an alien attack here in the late '40s?"

"Yes."

"Was this all over the world, or just in one super secret place?"

"All over the world."

"Funny, I don't remember reading about that in history class. Must have been quite the cover-up."

"Shush, I'm explaining. Anyway, like I said, these aliens showed up and suddenly we were at war. Big time. There was a hell of a battle, and it lasted for months. In the end, we managed to fight them off—barely—but we did it. And then, six weeks later, when it finally seemed like everything was getting back to normal . . . the whole thing happened again. A second attack. This time from a completely different race of aliens. And even though it was unconnected to the first invasion, these new aliens had all the same goals: enslave mankind, conquer, pillage, etcetera. Again, we fought them off. It was an even rougher battle, took about a year, but somehow we came out on top. Now . . . as you can imagine, by this point humanity was starting to get pretty wary of visitors from other worlds."

"I bet."

"We began to assemble an army. A really big army. A military initiative like nothing ever dreamed of before. Everyone over a certain age was conscripted. Everyone on Earth."

"What age?"

"Hmm?"

"You said everyone over a certain age got conscripted. What age?"

"I don't know . . . twelve."

"Yikes."

"That's right. Pretty scary, but there you go. Everyone over the age of twelve was now part of the largest military campaign ever devised: Operation Protect the Planet."

"That sounds . . . sorta green."

"Green?"

"Like the name could be a slogan for an environmental movement."

"Sadly, it was anything but that. The O.P.T.P initiative required us to ravage our own world for resources. Everything we had, every industry, every occupation became twisted around defense and tactical planning."

"That can't be *all* there was."

"Well, a small division was put in charge of farming. We had to eat, of course, but other than—"

"So it was all . . . what? Guns and food? That's all anybody did anymore?"

"Pretty much."

"That's horrible."

"Humanity struggled for a while to try to hold on to even a scrap of its culture, but eventually everything got erased. Art, music, diversity of language—all gone. Everything became homogenized. We became a people obsessed with a single goal: survival."

"Again, that's just ... horrible. Were there more attacks?"

"There were lots and lots of attacks. They kept coming in waves, year after year. These alien species would show up one after another, decide they wanted what we had, and try to take it from us by force."

"That is so sucky."

"I know. But it kept happening. By the year 2200, things were pretty grim. The battles had been so constant—so ceaseless—that humanity had known nothing but warfare for generations. Many generations. Even the memory that we had ever lived any other kind of existence was fading. The ironic thing, of course, is that we were slowly turning into the same kind of creatures who kept invading our planet. We started to thrive on war. Hunger for it ourselves."

"This doesn't sound like it's going anywhere happy. I don't know if I want to hear any more."

"Sweetie ..."

"Yeah?"

"You trust me, right?"

"Sometimes."

"Sometimes?"

"Of course I trust you."

"Then just listen for a teensy bit longer, okay?"

"Okay."

"All right, so humanity was in a bad place. Little by little they were transforming into one of the same kind of bloodthirsty races they'd been fighting against for so long. And they'd learned quite a bit in the two-hundred-and-fifty-plus years they'd been battling through this new way of life. And so, using captured and co-opted alien technologies, they'd just finished developing their own interstellar warships. They had built an entire fleet. Sadly, this was no longer just for defense, but to begin launching their own attacks on other worlds. Things were looking dark, very dark indeed. Everything was coming to a head, and it was on the eve of the big launch when it happened."

"When what happened?"

"Someone invented time travel."

"You're kidding."

"It was an accident, of course. They'd been trying to design a new weapon, hurrying to get it ready before the launch. It was a heavy-duty plasma cannon, something like that. But in the rush to get it finished, some slight miscalculations were made and the first time the weapon was test fired, it ripped a small hole in the fabric of time."

"I'm listening . . ."

"They sent some probes through the rip and learned that this was indeed a doorway to the past. And after conducting a variety of experiments, it was discovered that with slight adjustments, they could use the device to pick exact points in time and space to travel to. This led to a great deal of debate. What should they use this for? Should they use it at all? And why were they even bothering to discuss it when there was war to be fought somewhere? And then, from somewhere in the back of the room, this one guy spoke up. He wasn't too high in the chain of command, just a sergeant, but he had this bright idea . . ."

"Which was?"

"Instead of sending their brand-spanking new fleet out to other worlds to wage war, why not send them back in time instead? Back to the very first alien attack against Earth."

"You mean . . . a preemptive strike?"

"They promoted that sergeant to general, and he led the fleet through the rip and thwarted the aliens just before they were about to attack. It was easy enough to do. Their technology was two-hundred-and-fifty years ahead of the enemy's. Taking them down was child's play."

"Good for them."

"Emboldened by their victory, they went on, continuing to travel through time and fought off every alien invasion that was ever to be. They cleared the path, allowing human history to progress without any outside interruptions."

"That's kind of . . . cool."

"I think so."

"One thing though . . ."

"Yes?"

"Well, if they changed the past, wouldn't that affect them? They were from the future. Wouldn't they cease to exist?"

"Time travel is a lot more complicated than that. And by traveling through it themselves, the fleet came to exist outside of time. This freed them up to continue protecting the Earth. To act as unseen guardians."

"And so . . . that's it? That's the reason why we've never had contact with aliens?"

"And why we never will."

"It was all just . . . erased."

"Yes—well, yes and no."

"Yes and no?"

"Nothing can ever be *completely* erased. You see, time traveling prevented the invasions, but those events *did* happen. And it left something hanging over us. Like a faint echo in our shared consciousness. A kind of residue."

"What does that mean?"

"Well, in the 1950s there was suddenly this huge glut of science fiction movies that started to pop up one after another. This was followed by comics, television shows, and more. There'd long been stories written about visitors from other worlds, but the '50s saw such an explosion of that kind of material that it makes one wonder if there wasn't something more at work here than just a trend. Maybe those stories needed to be told. Maybe there was an underlying urge to get them out there."

"Huh."

"Do you have a comment?"

"That's a . . . That's a pretty complex theory. Did you just come up with that?"

"Yeah."

"Really? The whole thing? Just now?"

"Yeah, it kinda popped into my head."

"That's a little hard to believe."

"Not if it's true."

"Excuse me?"

"If it's true, then I didn't make it up. I remembered it."

"That's a little eerie."

"Also, if everything I said was right, then that dot you saw moving in the sky might not be a satellite after all. Or a comet, or even some aliens."

"You're saying it might be the fleet."

"That's right."

"What was it you called them again? The O.P.T.P.?"

"I believe so."

"It's a funny name."

"I guess."

"Say . . ."

"Yes?"

"I'm definitely okay with it."

"It?"

"This. Doing this regularly from now on. Looking up at the sky, holding your hand. It feels good to me. Does it feel good to you, spending time this way?"

"I think so. I just know you're the one I want to spend that time with."

"Will you look at me when you say that?"

"Hmm?"

"You're looking up. Look at me when you say that."

"You're the one I want to spend that time with."

"Good. Better."

"Yeah?"

"Yes. It's all in the eyes, you know."

"I know."

They stared at each other in silence for a little while, then stood together and went back inside.

Good News from Antares

Yves Meynard

The El makes the same racket it always did, a tortured shriek as it slowly rounds the corner of the track between Van Buren and Quincy stations. Alone in his room, Gerrard feels the sound pulling him backward in time, like a wondrous device from one of his own stories, back to a year when all of space-time had lain wide open, for himself as well as the whole of humanity. In that year he attained the zenith of his career, at the ripe age of twenty-five. It might even have been in this very hotel; he doesn't remember which one it was, but of course people would know. Long ago he tore up all the zines he had accumulated and threw them into the trash without regret, but in the hoards of collectors some must survive. Certainly there are many who would consider it a privilege to let him look at a copy of *Second City Fandom*. They'd treat him to dinner in the bargain, and spend the entire night drunk on nostalgia, trying to evoke a world lost forever. He'd rather get mugged.

Downstairs, in the reception room that may or may not be the very one where he came close to the ultimate glory, his daughter is waiting for him. She is wearing the eggplant dress he loathes; her husband Walter will be hovering at her elbow, simpering and nattering, drinking too much. People must be crowding Alice, trying to let her success wash over them, just as Walter is doing. Many will be waving copies of *Dark Nocturne* brazenly in her face. Some may even be asking about her father, who was a writer too, wasn't he, isn't it marvelous how talent runs in the family. Gerrard wishes he could go down now and tell them all what he really thinks of his daughter's writing, how mocked he feels that all she can offer the world is adolescent feel-good fantasy, dripping with just the right amount of simulated blood and fake angst. This, this is all that the world really wants: sparkly tales of blissful undeath, a retreat into its own navel.

Gerrard feels himself settling down into the armchair, growing heavier by the second. He will not rise; maybe he will stay here the whole night, let himself fall asleep with the drapes drawn and the lights on. He isn't asleep yet, but his eyes have closed. He dreams, aware that he dreams, able to nudge the dream along but no longer to control it.

In Gerrard's dream he leaves his room, walks along the corridor to the elevator. It strikes him how the art deco ornamentation on its doors gleams in the neon light. This is not the illumination the gilding was conceived for, yet the electrum glow is soothing to his eyes. There is no one about; the silence fills his ears like cotton. When the bell signaling the elevator's arrival rings, it feels like a weapon cutting into him.

The doors open and he steps inside the cabin. Next to the doors, the twin columns of buttons extend further down than he had noticed previously. After the numbers come M, L, LL; symbols he is familiar with. But there are further buttons: G, G1, G2 he can guess at, but what of that last one, square where all the others are round, stamped with a glyph that Gerrard cannot recognize as a letter? He pushes it, the doors slide shut and the elevator descends so swiftly that his stomach rises against his throat. He feels a touch of fear, but then he recalls he is dreaming.

When the doors open (this time without a bell), a strange and dark vista is revealed. The elevator has reached into tunnels dug into the rock beneath Chicago, below the level of the subway. Gerrard can hear the roar of a train passing; it comes from far above rather than in front of him. Slowly, he steps out of the elevator cabin. Behind him the doors remain open, promising a safe haven; he does not look back, but walks forward into the dim, steam-wreathed region. Lights shine somewhere in the distance, and shed just enough illumination for him to move about. He holds his arms forward, groping for obstacles, clutching nothing but moist air.

After a time comes the awareness that he is no longer alone; looking to his left, he glimpses a half-familiar shape in the dimness. He moves forward, and the shape follows silently. Soon lights from ahead kindle a blue gleam on the figure's swollen forehead, and he recognizes Exben the Antarean. Gerrard's heart leaps painfully; he does not know if he is glad or horrified. Exben turns its head towards him, and Gerrard heaves a strangled sigh. Even now, even in his dream, he sees Exben as it was portrayed on the screen for twenty-five embarrassing episodes of *Mission: Universe*. Beneath the caked blue makeup, the pasty features of a character actor well past his prime, whose name always escapes Gerrard's memory, twist in a leering smile.

"Stars bring greetings, my friend," says Exben, and Gerrard answers with the trite response heard on every episode: "And the Universe is one." Long, long ago, he opened a story in this way. He was so young then that the words seemed fresh and full of wisdom to him. He thought he was spelling out a view of a glorious future, and thousands of others thought so too. They were even younger than he was, barely out of childhood; they, at least, had the excuse of innocence.

For a minute Gerrard remains mute and motionless; Exben matches him. There is a faint hiss from the prosthetic nose's thin nostrils as the actor breathes in and out. Finally Gerrard gives in; it's his dream, after all. "It's good to see you, Exben," he says finally, and is surprised to realize he means it. "How . . . how are you?"

"I am quite well," answers Exben. "But I am concerned about you, my old friend. You are definitely not well."

"Stop it," whispers Gerrard. "This is wrong. You're speaking to me as if I was Major Vance. I'm . . . just the man who invented both of you. I'm dreaming all this."

"I am fully aware that you are not Major Vance," says Exben, taking Gerrard's hand. Exben has three digits only, long and many-jointed. In the television series he was given human hands, though he always wore gloves with odd markings, as a cheap token of alienness. These hands are not gloved. "As I am aware of your status. You grieve, friend Gerrard, so terribly."

Exben pulls him forward now, until they come to a better-lit area; a trio of parallel tubes hanging from the distant ceiling casts a bubble of radiance within the fog. Here Exben pauses and turns to face Gerrard fully. Gerrard can see, distinctly, the line where the rubber prosthetic skull meets the actor's skin; here, on the jaw, a cluster of acne scars blotted with concealer still reveal themselves under the layers of makeup. Yet the fingers that grip his hand wrap themselves all the way up his wrist; the alien skin is cool, finely textured like chamois cloth.

"I have spent many years among humans," Exben says. "You cast me among your species and gave me a mission; do you remember it?"

Of course Gerrard remembers. It was in his second story of Exben and Vance that he came up with the idea: an alien given an all-important mission that, for once, wasn't about war, about conquest or enslavement. The mission had been to understand humanity, because—how had he put it?—nothing could be more meaningful in the universe than to understand one another. Something like that. He should remember the sentence better, since it almost won him the Gernsback. That is what people vote for, he later came to understand: slogans, catchphrases, expressions of neat ideas that respond to their own prejudices. That year, it had been in fashion to seek fellow-feeling and understanding, because America was terrified of the Soviets and friendship seemed like an easy solution. But decades later, by the time the Caucasus oil-fields had collapsed and Andropov had been overthrown, the country felt invincible. No one cared for Exben's mission anymore; not even Gerrard himself, truth be told. And soon after that had come the Clarke theorem and its implications, and the old universe had died.

"I remember," says Gerrard. "I gave you the mission and I saw you through it, until the last story."

Ten stories. This is his legacy to the defunct world of scientifiction, according to Chalmers in his *Encyclopedia;* the rest of Gerrard's work dismissed in one word as "forgettable." But the Exben sequence, *that* warrants a whole paragraph. Ten stories about an alien, and a human astronaut who endeavors to show him what it means to be human. Collected together in the late-seventies by an amateur press as *Exben from the Stars*, provided with appalling cover art and poorly distributed. Written over a span of twenty-five years, the stories improve greatly from first to last, says Chalmers. And Gerrard is forced to agree. The first one he can no longer stand to even glance at; only the last three, for him, hold any value anymore. Yet their popularity went steadily downhill after the second one. By the time of the last story, Gabriel Enders at the *Magazine of Scientifiction* was doing an old hack a favor, and made sure Gerrard knew it. And yet, and yet! That last story was far more ambitious, far more subtle and wise than any of Gerrard's previous work. He has reread it, more than once, always after a long interval, and been surprised that he was the one to write it. It is something any writer of scientifiction could be satisfied with.

Exben is speaking. Atop its skull, its antennae are curling and extending, no longer waving haphazardly like the painted twin rubber whips they are. "According to you, my mission was finished long ago, my friend. You claimed that I had fulfilled it, that I could go home."

"Maybe that was why the story failed," says Gerrard. "You can't win hearts by telling stories that end. You have to open doors and stop as your character passes through. No one liked 'End of the Mission' because no one wants things to end. All the hard work I put in to become a better writer; what did they care about that? They didn't want to see things as they are, they wanted magic and fun. They didn't want people to grow old and die, they wanted spaceships and explosions. They didn't want the universe to end."

"I have not gone home," Exben says. "My mission is not complete. I have stayed for your sake, my friend."

"What do you mean?"

With its left hand, Exben reaches into its clothing and pulls out an intricate device from an inner pocket. "Look," it whispers, and at the touch of one of its spider-leg fingers, a three-dimensional image appears above the projector. It is a small cluster of brilliant points, a few hundred at most. "The universe," says Exben.

"No, don't show me," begs Gerrard. "I never understood it, I just know the results . . ."

"The shape of space as well as the basic properties of matter are bound up with the structure of Galois symmetry groups," says Exben. "Light rays emitted from stars do not move only in straight lines, but simultaneously along multidimensional geodesics . . ."

"Please, Exben, stop it. I know what it boils down to, that's all that matters."

Above the 3D projector the cluster of stars is reflected and distorted, again and again, in a dizzying progression. Mathematicians claim it all makes perfect sense, that nothing about the process is arbitrary. To Gerrard, it looks as if someone is madly placing mirrors by the hundreds all about the small cluster, some straight, most of them curved. And on and on the process goes, the initial bubble of points swelling until stars by the millions merge into folds and whorls of light, which are themselves repeated and reflected. At the end of it all there is a colossal mass of lights spinning slowly above the projector: the universe as it appears to the telescope, the great cosmic lie, the artifact of higher mathematics.

There are no spiral arms, no galaxies, no superclusters. There are only a few, a very few stars; all the rest are illusions, artifacts of the structure of space. Ghosts from the distant past, a thousand thousand images of the same few stars endlessly repeated and distorted, reddened by the light's passage along exotic geodesics, swollen by gravitational lensing . . . Sometimes Gerrard tells himself he understands it, but he's lying to himself. All he knows is what everyone knows, the truly important result: that there is no great infinite universe awaiting them out there. That there is, really, almost nowhere to go.

Antares is probably a real star; that is, the image of it that impinges upon the telescopes of Earth is probably the most authentic one. And for this single authentic image, there are thousands and millions of others, ghosts of Antares that appear much farther away, far beyond the actual bounds of space as it exists. Gerrard isn't sure if he has understood that part of it correctly, but he thinks to remember that at least one of the distant galaxies Edwin Hubble thought he saw is in fact nothing more than a hundred billion distorted copies of Antares.

Scientifiction was bound up with the dream of space. Once mankind awoke from that dream, it was all over. Not everyone understood it at first, and for maybe ten years some authors struggled on. But the invisible hand of the market is too strong to resist, especially when it makes a fist and smashes your editor into the dust.

"This is the great discovery of your age," says Exben. "Clarke's theorem has elucidated the basic structure of the cosmos. Humankind has come to a better understanding of its place among the universe. The understanding of this reality has provided an answer to some of your most pressing questions. And yet, my friend Gerrard, instead of reveling in triumph, you grieve. How can that be? You must help me understand."

Its voice has a buzzing tone it lacked before; lifting his gaze from the mockup of the universe, Gerrard is surprised to see sideways mandibles about Exben's mouth, astonished when he notices the faceted eyes. Exben is now as he imagined it at first in the early stories, no longer the feeble copy prescribed by the constraints of television, but the insectoid alien he conceptualized, the strange and coherent form that dwelled within his mind, beyond his ability to ever fully describe.

"What . . . what's there to understand?" he stammers. "Haven't you learned everything by now?"

"I cannot fathom why you are not happy. You wanted answers. How many times did Major Vance say this? Humans want answers. They want to know the truth; it is this insatiable curiosity that makes your race so great. But you grieve; you grieve because you know. How can that be?"

"Shit; shit! I was wrong, Exben, that's all. I was young and stupid. We *don't* want to know and we certainly don't want the truth. We want the lies, we want the mystery. We want infinite fields, we want things that make us feel important. Not this! Not this sad joke. We can't deal with the truth."

"Yet many of you are happy. I saw how so many of your fellow humans were delirious with bliss once the Clarke theorem was proven and its implications had sunk in."

"Because they think it vindicates what they've always believed. They think Clarke proved God exists, and so they'll live forever in Heaven."

"And you don't. Is that the answer, then?"

"How the hell should I know? When I was young I thought humanity wanted to learn the truth, because *I* wanted to learn the truth. Later I thought humanity was defined by religion, because I had lost my faith and I wanted to feel superior to those who still had theirs. Now I don't have anything anymore. No faith, no knowledge."

For a long moment Exben is silent. Gerrard, in the throes of the dream, feels powerless to escape it, nailed into this half-world by the alien's thoughtful silence.

"Then, my friend, I shall make you an offer," it says, the fricatives and sibilants almost dissolving into buzzes.

"What offer? What do you mean?"

"You yourself brought me into being as the emissary of truth. Every time you read the article about yourself in the *Encyclopedia*, you sneer at Chalmers because he describes me as a religious figure; whereas you no longer believe. Yet I *am* a religious figure—among other things. How could I not be? And in this capacity I now offer redemption."

Gerrard says nothing. Exben's chitin-sheathed, mottled blue face is unreadable. It continues.

"You desire infinity. I shall grant it. I can prove the Clarke theorem is flawed. A simpler lemma does hold, but the overall conclusion is too restrictive, and it just so happens that this makes it inapplicable to the universe as a whole. The demonstration does not involve any transcendent insight; there is in fact a fairly simple counterexample any serious mathematician can understand. Once this counterexample is discovered, the current cosmological model will fall. Space-time will be revealed as stranger and more complex than was realized and far, far bigger. You will have a vast cosmos once more. Future historians of science will marvel at the mass insanity that led the whole community to believe in the current model for so long, when the evidence was almost staring them in the face."

"Such a little thing!" comments Gerrard. "And what do you want in return? Do I have to die? Is that it? This is how stories are written, you know. When a character is offered a great wish, there's always a terrible price to pay. Every beginner comes up with this idea that you have to die to make the wish come true, so you never get to enjoy it. And then the little bastards write it, send it in, and get rejected, and they don't know why."

"I am far more than a beginner's dream, my friend Gerrard. You do not have to die to receive this. There is no payment to be made. This is not a bargain, it is a gift. And if endless space is not what you want, I can offer you endless time. Your mortality weighs on you; would you rather have endless life? That also lies within my power."

"Endless life!" Gerrard snorts in derision. "You've got the wrong person, Exben. It's my daughter you want for that. She's the one writing about bloodsucking immortals and raking in the cash. I'm sure she would be happy to take you up on the offer."

He feels his throat tighten as he says this, and falls silent for a moment. Then he says, in a low voice: "I don't want any great and wonderful gifts. Chalmers is full of crap; you're not a religious figure, you're not God or Jesus, you're just a grownup's version of an imaginary friend. I made you up because I didn't want to be alone."

"Nor were you ever," says the alien before him, its voice charged with potency, and Gerrard knows a flash of an emotion he could not name, like a pang of love mixed with bowel-churning terror. Breaking the grip of the three-fingered hand on his, he steps backwards, faster and faster, until Exben's blue form is lost in the mist. Then he turns around and runs for the still-open elevator. Once the doors close on him, once he has pushed the button for his floor, he begins to calm down. The doors open, he stumbles out into the corridor, reaches his room, collapses at the foot of the armchair where he fell asleep, raises his head, unsure for an endless moment whether he has awakened.

He goes to the sink in the bathroom and splashes water on his face, roughly towels it dry. On the countertop next to the sink, he finds the copy of *Dark Nocturne* his daughter gave him, inscribed to him in her hand; he wipes a few drops of water from the dust jacket with a corner of the hand towel. He picks up the book and exits his room. He will go down and join the well-wishers and sycophants, he will join his daughter and her husband and the rest of humanity, huddled together in the bright reception room to keep the cold and empty universe at bay.

The door snicks shut behind him; he walks along the corridor and, having reached the elevator doors gleaming electrum in the neon light, turns aside and walks down the stairs.

Report from the Field

Mike Resnick and Lezli Robyn

To Galactic Coordinator Ryllf:

Day 1, Year 403,772,109 of Project Earth

I can't begin to tell you how thrilled I am to receive this assignment. We have been observing the planet the inhabitants call "Earth" for more than four hundred million years now. At first we couldn't understand why they would not respond to our signals, which was the reason for the First Expedition, but what we discovered was that evolution seemed to be occurring at a much slower rate here than in neighboring systems. We returned sporadically, and although a race known as Man had finally developed sentience, it did not have the technological wherewithal to receive our signals or send any of its own, so we passed word to our member worlds not to bother trying to contact Earth until we informed them that the inhabitants were capable of capturing and interpreting our signals.

It was less than a century ago that our observation post in the Spiral Arm observed a marked increase in Earth's level of neutrino activity; we have given them these few extra years to develop before telling the Galactic Community at large that it is acceptable to make contact with them. We never want to be guilty of rushing things; I'm sure we're all painfully aware of the unfortunate situation on Blarnigog IV. (Well, on what used to be Blarnigog IV, anyway.)

I will be using our standard procedures to monitor their transmissions and get a better idea concerning how best to alert them that a vast and long-established Galactic Community has been observing them for almost half a billion years, just waiting to welcome them into the fold.

I am both proud and honored that you have chosen me to be the one to make the initial contact.

Day 2, Year 403,772,109 of Project Earth

I am truly impressed by this gritty little race. Most of them live in cities, all concrete and steel and glass, and some of these cities hold ten million or more inhabitants. All right, that's insignificant compared to some of *our* megalopolises, but a million years ago, on our last visit here, their progenitors were living in trees.

They are centuries, perhaps a millennium, away from fast and inexpensive forms of transportation such as teleportation, but they have developed mass travel on land, on sea, and in the air. They have created written languages, eliminated most disease, have invented a remedial (but functional) form of computer based on, of all things, the silicon chip, and have even managed to construct an orbiting space station.

I am sure I will report that they are ready for membership in the Galactic Community—and oh, the things we can teach them! I hate it when we offer to initiate a race such as the Breff and they arrogantly claim to need none of the myriad benefits we can bring them. The people of Earth still die of old age, they haven't yet discovered even the simplest means of exceeding the speed of light, their medical science hasn't yet mastered the brain transplant, and their agriculture is so backward that there are actually hungry people on the planet. In a week's time we can show them how to feed everyone on a continent with the food that is produced on only six square *pryllches,* and with a simple injection at maturity no one will ever show the effects, visual or internal, of age.

This world has been isolated long enough. I will monitor its transmissions for a few more days, making notes on all the areas in which we can bring our expertise to bear, but there is no question in my mind that it is time to invite Earth into our community and give it the full range of benefits that accrue to all our members.

Day 4, Year 403,772,109 of Project Earth

I may have spoken a bit too soon.

I saw some disturbing transmissions today. I am not sure that I fully understand them, but they have convinced me that the situation bears further study before we make too hasty a decision.

There seems to be a small round creature, relatively helpless, without any discernable means of locomotion. It is spherical in shape, white, clearly defenseless, resembling in almost every way the adorable *quiblit* of Altair IV. You might remember that more than a million *quiblit* were slaughtered on their home world when one race from the Galactic Community first colonized their planet an eon ago, not realizing that they were sentient—or even alive. I have not as yet been able to determine the genus or species of *this* white sphere, but I feel I must do so with some degree of haste, for clearly its existence on Earth is otherwise of limited duration.

I was subjected to the appalling spectacle of Men taking turns beating these poor creatures with elongated clubs in the most sadistic possible displays. Not only that, but literally tens of thousands more Men cheered lustily every time one of these creatures was struck with a club.

The worst part? Many of the creatures somehow survived, and their reward was to be pummeled by the club-wielding Men again and again.

Such public displays of brutality are not readily discerned except in select locations, but that they exist at all gives me a very uneasy feeling about this race.

Clearly a certain degree of sadism exists just beneath the surface. When I could no longer force myself to watch the endless torture of the round creatures, I sought other transmissions to see if this was an aberration I had uncovered, or if I had not previously been looking deeply enough into the race's motivations.

And what I found was a transmission labeled "Late Night Entertainment," depicting a confrontation between a male and a female of the species. The lighting was poor, even after I internally adjusted my optical lenses, but I was able to make out most of their actions. At first I thought they were simply practicing a new means of sharing their food supply, because they kept pressing their mouths together—but then (and I am not fabricating this, bizarre as it seems) the larger of the two began peeling layers of skin from the smaller! A moment later the instigator was running his manipulators and mouth all over what was left of the smaller one's body; she was clearly too terrified to contemplate escaping, and her moans and screams were so horrifying that I fear I shall hear them to my dying day.

"Entertainment"? What kind of race can possibly find this entertaining?

Day 8, Year 403,772,109 of Project Earth

It may be noted that it has been some time since my last report. It took longer than expected for me to be able to purge the negative emotions I experienced when watching the last transmissions I reported on; and this was necessary for me to objectively consider the latest revelations of this complicated race. I was determined to discover some more positive aspects of Man, and I did indeed do so—at least initially.

Man has a rather remarkable ability to empathize with creatures of limited intelligence, which I find puzzling when I consider how I've just seen him treat his own kind. They even call one species that often cohabits with them "Man's best friend," and can be heard cooing to it in high-pitched tones, thereby causing the creature's nethermost appendage to spasm uncontrollably. For reasons unknown to me this seems to be a desirable response. So is allowing these four-footed creatures to drag their owners around the city, usually before the sun has arisen, just so they can defecate on the very objects Man seems to take such pride in building. And here is the most puzzling part of all: the creatures—their most common identifications seem to be Pookey, Cuddles, or Fluffy—are often being overfed to death in the name of love.

Is this another example of cruelty (albeit a passive version) on the part of Man? I was not sure, so I decided to investigate how they treated their own young. The transmissions I found on the subject were, in a word, astonishing.

First I saw something termed a "documentary" on water births, which is apparently a modern way of helping the females expel their offspring. However, I couldn't see how it could possibly help the female, who alternated between screaming incoherently and yelling "I will never let you touch me again!" to her mate during the final stages of the process.

It should also be noted that once the offspring is born it is immediately turned upside down and pelted sharply on its waste conductor—an unnecessary torture that caused the offspring to cry in agony and begin gasping for air.

And this barbaric ritual is not confined just to water births. Indeed, many human medics (the ones I had previously praised for eradicating many diseases) seem to take great pleasure in pelting a newborn infant immediately after it is born in a hospital, just to hear it scream in pain, before returning it to the mother so they can move on to pelt the next one.

I am at a loss to discover the purpose of this ritual, other than to introduce the offspring to violence at an early age, and I am starting to strongly suspect that this sentient race is not as evolved as I initially thought. In fact, I am beginning to have considerable doubt as to Man's ability to interact and work with the civilized races of the Galactic Community. How could this race have made such huge scientific advancements in such a short time, and still exhibit such obvious signs of barbarism? Clearly I will have to study them further.

Day 9, Year 403,772,109 of Project Earth

For today's research I decided I needed to determine how Man instinctively perceives himself before I can fully understand how *we* should perceive them as a race. So I looked for transmissions that focused on the race's artistic development to see what I could glean from their use of creative mediums.

Again, I was surprised. For a sentient race, they seem to have very primitive means of expressing themselves. While I discovered some simply beautiful art pieces, such as the statue of *David,* generally Man seems to have an inclination to revere the more flawed pieces of creation, perhaps as a metaphor for how he sees himself. The armless *Venus de Milo* and the headless *Winged Victory* are held in no less esteem than the complete *David*.

There is a museum in Amsterdam that showcases the art of one Vincent van Gogh, who by all accounts was a mentally disturbed being, mutilating one of his own auditory appendages before self-terminating more than a century ago. For reasons that elude me, members of his own species *still* revere the paintings he created, calling them "cutting edge." (I haven't been able to adequately translate that term, though I suspect it may refer in some obscure way to the removal of his auditory appendage with a sharp object.) The proportions of the various structures depicted in his "paintings" are clearly mathematically inaccurate, and yet it is that very inaccuracy that seems to inspire the most admiration. So I decided to look at the work of more recent artists on the assumption that Man's creative ability must surely have evolved in the intervening century. After determining only to research artists whose work is respected by a large percentage of the population (thus ensuring I would have a more complete understanding of Man's perceptions in general), I discovered the paintings of Pablo Diego José Francisco de Paula Juan Nepomuceno María de los Remedios Cipriano de la Santísima Trinidad Ruiz y Picasso—an impressive name, to be sure— and was shocked to discover that this man, probably the most revered artist of the past millennium, had such a distorted vision of humanity. He often painted faces in which both optical lenses were on the same side of the olfactory appendage, or in which the skin—which comes in various shades of black, brown, tan, red, yellow, and pink among Man's sub-races—was *blue*. In fact, he frequently painted contorted images of both the male and female members of his species, their forms brutally mutilated and twisted almost beyond recognition.

I must conclude that if this is what is praised above all other artwork, Man is still a barbarian at heart—even his depictions of himself are violent. However, just to be certain, I examined the works of one other highly respected artist, Salvador Dali, but words are inadequate to describe the endless aberrations I encountered in painting after painting.

At this moment, based on these observations, I am leaning toward the conclusion that Man is not ready to be offered membership at this time. However, before I make my final decision and formally submit my findings, I feel I must determine if there is a *potential* in Man that outweighs what I have seen to date.

Day 12, Year 403,772,109 of Project Earth

It occurred to me, as I again consigned myself to watching more of Earth's transmissions, that the two genders of this race—so different as to almost be considered separate species—do not appear to have equal status on their world. It is clear to me that the female gender of the race is weaker in physical proportions, so I sought out transmissions that focused on the limitations of the female form—and what I unearthed appalled me. I discovered that, as small as they already are, it is an accepted notion in their society for females to deny themselves the necessary nutrients to be physically healthy, because apparently starving their form makes them more attractive to their potential mates.

Yes, I know this sounds absurd, but the evidence is overwhelming. In fact, females who obtain the truest form of Man's desire are designated by the term "models." So using that word I intercepted a transmission depicting "catwalk models," to see what represents perfection in Man's eyes. To say that I was shocked is actually understating the case. The transmission displayed females whose skeletal structures often showed through various points of their skin, their fragile frames encased in uncomfortable-looking coverings that appeared to limit their movement.

And they did not look like happy specimens of their race. All of the females exhibited unresponsive—one might even say lifeless—facial conformations, clearly to mask their pain as they strode down the "catwalk" wearing long-spiked torture devices on the bottoms of their locomotive appendages.

They would not even react when the spectators surrounding them started banging their manipulators together (to keep them submissive with the threat of violence, perhaps?) as they reached the end of the "catwalk." Instead each model would turn this way and that with that soulless look to her face, pause as if stunned to realize she was trapped, and then turn around and retreat the way she had come—only to repeat the torture encased in another more uncomfortable contraption not five minutes later.

Not only this, but in transmission after transmission I find that females, and to some extent males as well, mutilate their flesh, piercing auditory and olfactory appendages and even more personal body parts with everything from metal to superhardened carbon, evidently on the assumption that such displays of courage in the face of senseless pain find favor in the eyes of the opposite sex.

I was utterly confounded. I had to discover if the threat of violence was the underlying reason females mutilated various body parts and deprived themselves of life-sustaining nutrients in order to attract a mate, or whether there was a deeper psychological reason that could explain such unnatural acts. So I began to research what females desired in a mate to better understand their mentality, and quickly discovered there were many mating manuals on the subject, all helpfully categorized (and thus easily researchable) as "romance novels."

To make sure I was getting an accurate perception of the female mind in general, I read only the manuals that were considered the most popular of their kind—and there I made the most horrifying discovery. It appears that there is a sub-species of Man that Earth females are unable to resist. This object of lust is always "tall, dark, and handsome," exhibiting "bedroom eyes" (which I assume are carried in with them and donned only within the confines of the sleeping quarters) and a "silken touch" (incomprehensible) that can immediately mesmerize the female when employed—and once mesmerized, *he actually drinks their blood!*

Yes, you read correctly. This sub-species of Man practices a form of barbaric cannibalism that either kills the victim to unnaturally sustain his own violent existence or infects them so they devolve to also live the "tortured life of the undead." And for some baffling reason, the females of Earth find it wildly pleasing when a vampire (the designation of this violent sub-species) tells them that their blood is so desirable to him that he has to fight not to "drain her dry," which I have since discovered is a euphemism for killing them.

How could *any* sentient creature find the threat of death attractive? That they willingly put themselves in violent life-threatening situations, declaring their (ironically) undying love for these dangerous and dominating Vampires, leads me to the conclusion that this race is instinctively drawn to violence on nearly all levels of their collective psyche.

And if Man's propensity for violence could possibly deny him a position in the Galactic Community, I believe the presence of Vampires (even if they are just a minority) requires that First Contact be made by a member of our Interplanetary Relations Division that is from a race without a bloodstream. We don't want to risk spreading such an insidious disease throughout the galaxy until a vaccine can be successfully created and tested and/or the Vampires are completely exterminated.

My last chance to determine if Man has any potential to evolve past his current self-destructive tendency lies with his spiritual beliefs—but that is a task for tomorrow. I have spent several days poring over these mating manuals, and desperately need to purge the violent images before I can begin to continue this report with any degree of impartiality.

Day 13, Year 403,772,109 of Project Earth

I never thought I would be the one who could potentially deny a sentient race's entrance into the Galactic Community, but it is becoming more and more likely.

Today I endeavored to discover this race's spiritual underpinnings. I elected to study only the most popular and well-known beliefs to get the clearest picture of the race as a whole. What I discovered was nothing short of appalling.

Man is a race of death worshippers!

There can be no mistake about it. At least a third of Earth's population, a staggering two billion beings, practices a religion that is based on the death of one man some two millennia ago. Although there appears to be some discrepancy between the texts of the various sects practicing this religion, the violent nature of the man's death is beyond dispute. There are literally tens of thousands of graphic representations in museums around the world, depictions of how his manipulators and motor appendages were "nailed to the cross" preceding his death, a procedure whereby spiky objects were inserted *through* the flesh of the victim to forcibly affix him to an artificial structure.

Coming from an enlightened race that believes all sentient life is sacred (well, all that they know about, anyway), I was shocked to discover that instead of *saving* this man from such a violent death, his friends stood by and *watched* him die, then created a religion that postulates the theory that it is acceptable for an innocent being to die in order to atone for someone else's crimes—someone he did not even know.

Followers of this religion wear replicas of the instrument of his death—the cross—around their necks, and more than half of them practice symbolic cannibalism in their designated buildings of worship, drinking his blood and eating his flesh (well, artificial substitutes for them) as a way of spiritually connecting to his violent murder. They even go so far as adorning their own burial sites with representations of this instrument, a clear statement that they admired a brutal and violent death, even if their own leave-taking was peaceful.

I would veto Earth's membership right now, except for this one fact: the object of their worship seems to have been imbued with an inexplicable power to heal all pain and cure all suffering—true acts of kindness. If that is so, it may well be that he was an early mutation, that Man is still capable of evolving as a race, and this endless violence I have catalogued is merely an adolescent stage through which the race is passing. It is with that single hope that I will put off my decision for another day, while I scour the planet to see if there are any other heretofore overlooked forms of benevolent mutation.

Day 14, Year 403,772,109 of Project Earth

Yesterday I was appalled. I mean, here was a race, clearly in its adolescence, a race that hadn't yet outgrown sadism, brutality, ignorance, even death worship.

But that was yesterday. Today I am terrified.

I began my search for the advanced members of the race, the possible mutations, those who demonstrated those qualities and abilities that would reassure the Council that Man indeed deserved to be invited into our vast community of civilized worlds.

Where does one look for such beings? In the most popular transmissions, of course. And so I did.

And yes, they exist.

Very few of them represent themselves as they truly are to the rest of their race. At first I thought it was because they are *so* advanced it would generate feelings of inferiority in those who interact with them. It turns out that the truth is much more diabolical.

For you see, Man's mutations are not mental, not spiritual, but physical. They hide behind what they call "secret identities," though the reasons for this are vague, since they are clearly impervious to permanent injury. Most of them wear colorful, form-fitting costumes. Many wear capes, which seem to hinder movement and I suspect serve the same purpose as brightly colored feathers in avian species: to attract the opposite sex for procreative activities.

They have not all evolved in the same ways. One has blinding (and I mean that literally) speed. One morphs into a muscular giant of a color not seen on any other member of the species. One stretches almost to infinity. One female is equipped with phenomenal strength and a set of artificial implements that are little short of magic. One climbs walls. One's manipulatory appendages actually become sharp-edged metal weapons, his every injury healing instantaneously. And the most revered of them all has every physical asset of the others: invulnerability, unlimited strength, the ability to levitate at phenomenal speeds, and even the ability to see through solid objects.

And what do they do with these attributes?

They fight.

Whom do they fight?

Another class of costumed mutants, clearly for dominance in the power structures of Earth.

I have observed only a few such encounters in public transmissions, but the collateral damage must be almost unimaginable.

I am forced to the following conclusions:

1. There *are* physical mutations in the race of Man, and there is no reason to think they will not continue to increase in numbers, as clearly these particular mutations are survival traits.

2. Based on my observations, the fact of the mutation does not cause a diminution of aggressive behavior.

3. We in the Galactic Community have no defenses and no weaponry capable of dealing with the most powerful of these mutants.

4. Based on everything I have learned about Man during the past fourteen days, it would be foolhardy, indeed suicidal, to assume they will be content to be a small cog in the galactic machine, or that they will not look farther afield for additional conquests once they have pacified their enemies on their home world.

Therefore, it is my recommendation to the Galactic Coordinator that Earth be isolated for another hundred millennia. There must be no contact, no radio or microwave transmissions, no attempt at communication of any kind. I further recommend that the entire Sol system be placed off limits for that same duration.

It's a pity. It seemed such a promising little planet when we discovered it four hundred million years ago. Perhaps if the Neanderthals had won that first great war. . . .

Permanent Fatal Errors

Jay Lake

Maduabuchi St. Macaria had never before traveled with an all-Howard crew. Mostly his kind kept to themselves, even under the empty skies of a planet. Those who did take ship almost always did so in a mixed or all-baseline human crew.

Not here, not aboard the threadneedle starship *Inclined Plane*. Seven crew including him, captained by a very strange woman who called herself Peridot Smith. All Howard Institute immortals. This was a new concept in long-range exploration, multi-decade interstellar missions with ageless crew, testbedded in orbit around the brown dwarf Tiede 1. That's what the newsfeeds said, anyway.

His experience was far more akin to a violent soap opera. Howards really weren't meant to be bottled up together. It wasn't in the design templates. Socially well-adjusted people didn't generally self-select to outlive everyone they'd ever known.

Even so, Maduabuchi was impressed by the welcome distraction of Tiede 1. Everyone else was too busy cleaning their weapons and hacking the internal comms and cams to pay attention to their mission objective. Not him.

Inclined Plane boasted an observation lounge. The hatch was coded "Observatory," but everything of scientific significance actually happened within the instrumentation woven into the ship's hull and the diaphanous energy fields stretching for kilometers beyond. The lounge was a folly of naval architecture, a translucent bubble fitted to the hull, consisting of roughly a third of a sphere of optically corrected artificial diamond grown to nanometer symmetry and smoothness in microgravity. Chances were good that in a catastrophe the rest of the ship would be shredded before the bubble would so much as be scratched.

There had been long, heated arguments in the galley, with math and footnotes and thumb breaking, over that exact question.

Maduabuchi liked to sit in the smartgel bodpods and let the ship perform a three-sixty massage while he watched the universe. The rest of the crew were like cats in a sack, too busy stalking the passageways and one another to care what might be outside the window. Here in the lounge one could see creation, witness the birth of stars, observe the death of planets, or listen to the quiet, empty cold of hard vacuum. The silence held a glorious music that echoed inside his head.

Maduabuchi wasn't a complete idiot—he'd rigged his own cabin with self-powered screamer circuits and an ultrahigh voltage capacitor. That ought to slow down anyone with delusions of traps.

Tiede 1 loomed outside. It seemed to shimmer as he watched, as if a starquake were propagating. The little star belied the ancient label of "brown dwarf." Stepped down by filtering nano that coated the diamond bubble, the surface glowed a dull reddish orange: a coal left too long in a campfire or a jewel in the velvet setting of night. Only 300,000 kilometers in diameter, and about five percent of a solar mass, it fell in that class of objects ambiguously distributed between planets and stars.

It could be anything, he thought. Anything.

A speck of green tugged at Maduabuchi's eye, straight from the heart of the star.

Green? There were no green emitters in nature.

"Amplification," he whispered. The nano filters living on the outside of the diamond shell obligingly began to self-assemble a lens. He controlled the aiming and focus with eye movements, trying to find whatever it was he had seen. Another ship? Reflection from a piece of rock or debris?

Excitement chilled Maduabuchi despite his best intentions to remain calm. What if this were evidence of the long-rumored but never-located alien civilizations that should have abounded in the Orion Arm of the Milky Way?

He scanned for twenty minutes, quartering Tiede 1's face as minutely as he could without direct access to the instrumentation and sensors carried by *Inclined Plane*. The ship's AI was friendly and helpful, but outside its narrow and critical competencies in managing the threadneedle drive and localspace navigation, was no more intelligent than your average dog, and so essentially useless for such work. He'd need to go to the Survey Suite to do more.

Maduabuchi finally stopped staring at the star and called up a deck schematic. "Ship, plot all weapons discharges or unscheduled energy expenditures within the pressurized cubage."

The schematic winked twice, but nothing was highlighted. Maybe Captain Smith had finally gotten them all to stand down. None of Maduabuchi's screamers had gone off, either, though everyone else had long since realized he didn't play their games.

Trusting that no one had hacked the entire tracking system, he cycled the lock and stepped into the passageway beyond. Glancing back at Tiede 1 as the lock irised shut, Maduabuchi saw another green flash.

He fought back a surge of irritation. The star was *not* mocking him.

Peridot Smith was in the Survey Suite when Maduabuchi cycled the lock there. Radiation-tanned from some melanin-deficient base hue of skin, lean, with her hair follicles removed and her scalp tattooed in an intricate mandala using magnetically sensitive ink, the captain was an arresting sight at any time. At the moment, she was glaring at him, her eyes flashing a strange, flat silver indicating serious tech integrated into the tissues. "Mr. St. Macaria." She gave him a terse nod. "How are the weapons systems?"

Ironically, of all the bloody-minded engineers and analysts and navigators aboard, *he* was the weapons officer.

"Capped and sealed per orders, ma'am," he replied. "Test circuits warm and green." *Inclined Plane* carried a modest mix of hardware, generalized for unknown threats rather than optimized for anti-piracy or planetary blockade duty, for example. Missiles, field projectors, electron strippers, fléchettes, even foggers and a sandcaster.

Most of which he had no real idea about. They were icons in the control systems, each maintained by its own little armies of nano and workbots. All he had were status lights and strat-tac displays. Decisions were made by specialized subsystems.

It was the rankest makework, but Maduabuchi didn't

mind. He'd volunteered for the Howard Institute program because of the most basic human motivation—tourism. Seeing what was over the next hill had trumped even sex as the driving force in human evolution. He was happy to be a walking, talking selection mechanism.

Everything else, including this tour of duty, was just something to do while the years slid past.

"What did you need, Mr. St. Macaria?"

"I was going to take a closer look at Tiede 1, ma'am."

"That *is* what we're here for."

He looked for humor in her dry voice, and did not find it. "Ma'am, yes ma'am. I . . . I just think I saw something."

"Oh, really?" Her eyes flashed, reminding Maduabuchi uncomfortably of blades.

Embarrassed, he turned back to the passageway.

"What did you see?" she asked from behind him. Now her voice was edged as well.

"Nothing, ma'am. Nothing at all."

Back in the passageway, Maduabuchi fled toward his cabin. Several of the crew laughed from sick bay, their voices rising over the whine of the bone-knitter. Someone had gone down hard.

Not him. Not even at the hands—or eyes—of Captain Smith.

An hour later, after checking the locations of the crew again with the ship's AI, he ventured back to the Survey Suite. Chillicothe Xiang nodded to him in the passageway, almost friendly, as she headed aft for a half-shift monitoring the power plants in Engineering.

"Hey," Maduabuchi said in return. She didn't answer, didn't even seem to notice he'd spoken. All these years, all the surgeries and nano injections and training, and somehow he was still the odd kid out on the playground.

Being a Howard Immortal was supposed to be *different*. And it was, when he wasn't around other Howard Immortals.

The Survey Suite was empty, as advertised. Ultra-def screens wrapped the walls, along with a variety of control inputs, from classical keypads to haptics and gestural zones. Maduabuchi slipped into the observer's seat and swept his hand to open the primary sensor routines.

Captain Smith had left her last data run parked in the core sandbox.

His fingers hovered over the purge, then pulled back. What had she been looking at that had made her so interested in what he'd seen? Those eyes flashed edged and dangerous in his memory. He almost asked the ship where she was, but a question like that would be reported, drawing more attention than it was worth.

Maduabuchi closed his eyes for a moment, screwing up his courage, and opened the data run.

It cascaded across the screens, as well as virtual presentations in the aerosolized atmosphere of the Survey Suite. Much more than he'd seen when he was in here before—plots, scales, arrays, imaging across the EM spectrum, color-coded tabs and fields and stacks and matrices. Even his Howard-enhanced senses had trouble keeping up with the flood. Captain Smith was far older and more experienced than Maduabuchi, over half a dozen centuries to his few decades, and she had developed both the mental habits and the individualized mentarium to handle such inputs.

On the other hand, *he* was a much newer model. Everyone upgraded, but the Howard Institute baseline tech evolved over generations just like everything else in human culture. Maduabuchi bent to his work, absorb-

ing the overwhelming bandwidth of her scans of Tiede 1,
and trying to sort out what it was that had been the true
object of her attention.

Something *had* to be hidden in plain sight here.

He worked an entire half-shift without being disturbed,
sifting petabytes of data, until the truth hit him. The
color-coding of one spectral analysis matrix was nearly
identical to the green flash he thought he'd seen on the
surface of Tiede 1.

All the data was a distraction. Her real work had been
hidden in the metadata, passing for nothing more than
a sorting signifier.

Once Maduabuchi realized that, he unpacked the la-
beling on the spectral analysis matrix and opened up an
entirely new data environment. Green, it was all about
the green.

"I was wondering how long that would take you,"
said Captain Smith from the opening hatch.

Maduabuchi jumped in his chair, opened his mouth
to make some denial, then closed it again. Her eyes
didn't *look* razored this time, and her voice held a tense
amusement.

He fell back on that neglected standby, the truth. "Interesting color you have here, ma'am."

"I thought so." Smith stepped inside, cycled the lock
shut, then code-locked it with a series of beeps that
meant her command override was engaged. "Ship," she
said absently, "sensory blackout on this area."

"Acknowledged, Captain," said the ship's puppy-
friendly voice.

"What do you think it means, Mr. St. Macaria?"

"Stars don't shine green. Not to the human eye. The
blackbody radiation curve just doesn't work that way."
He added, "Ma'am."

"Thank you for defining the problem." Her voice was dust-dry again.

Maduabuchi winced. He'd given himself away, as simply as that. But clearly she already knew about the green flashes. "I don't think that's the problem, ma'am."

"Mmm?"

"If it was, we'd all be lining up like good kids to have a look at the optically impossible brown dwarf."

"Fair enough. Then what *is* the problem, Mr. St. Macaria?"

He drew a deep breath and chose his next words with care. Peridot Smith was *old,* old in a way he'd never be, even with her years behind him someday. "I don't know what the problem is, ma'am, but if it's a problem to you, it's a command issue. Politics. And light doesn't have politics."

Much to his surprise, she laughed. "You'd be amazed. But yes. Again, well done."

She hadn't said that before, but he took the compliment. "What kind of command problem, ma'am?"

Captain Smith sucked in a long, noisy breath and eyed him speculatively. A sharp gaze, to be certain. "Someone on this ship is on their own mission. We were jiggered into coming to Tiede 1 to provide cover, and I don't know what for."

"Not me!" Maduabuchi blurted.

"I know that."

The dismissal in her words stung for a moment, but on the whole, he realized he'd rather not be a suspect in this particular witch hunt.

His feelings must have shown in his face, because she smiled and added, "You haven't been around long enough to get sucked into the Howard factions. And you have a rep for being indifferent to the seductive charms of power."

"Uh, yes." Maduabuchi wasn't certain what to say to that.

"Why do you think you're *here?*" She leaned close, her breath hot on his face. "I needed someone who would reliably not be conspiring against me."

"A useful idiot," he said. "But there's only seven of us. How many *could* be conspiring? And over a green light?"

"It's Tiede 1," Captain Smith answered. "Someone is here gathering signals. I don't know for what. Or who. Because it could be any of the rest of the crew. Or all of them."

"But this is politics, not mutiny. Right . . . ?"

"Right." She brushed off the concern. "We're not getting hijacked out here. And if someone tries, I *am* the meanest fighter on this ship by a wide margin. I can take any three of this crew apart."

"Any five of us, though?" he asked softly.

"That's another use for you."

"I don't fight."

"No, but you're a Howard. You're hard enough to kill that you can take it at my back long enough to keep me alive."

"Uh, thanks," Maduabuchi said, very uncertain now.

"You're welcome." Her eyes strayed to the data arrays floating across the screens and in the virtual presentations. "The question is who, what and why."

"Have you compared the observational data to known stellar norms?" he asked.

"Green flashes aren't a known stellar norm."

"No, but we don't know for what the green flashes are normal, either. If we compare Tiede 1 to other brown dwarfs, we might spot further anomalies. Then we triangulate."

"And *that* is why I brought you." Captain Smith's

tone was very satisfied indeed. "I'll leave you to your work."

"Thank you, ma'am." To his surprise, Maduabuchi realized he meant it.

He spent the next half-shift combing through comparative astronomy. At this point, almost a thousand years into the human experience of interstellar travel, there was an embarrassing wealth of data. So much so that even petabyte q-bit storage matrices were overrun, as eventually the challenges of indexing and retrieval went metastatic. Still, one thing Howards were very good at was data processing. Nothing ever built could truly match the pattern recognition and free associative skills of human (or post-human) wetware collectively known as "hunches." Strong AIs could approximate that uniquely biological skill through a combination of brute force and deeply clever circuit design, but even then, the spark of inspiration did not flow so well.

Maduabuchi slipped into his flow state to comb through more data in a few hours than a baseline human could absorb in a year. Brown dwarfs, superjovians, fusion cycles, failed stars, hydrogen, helium, lithium, surface temperatures, density, gravity gradients, emission spectrum lines, astrographic surveys, theories dating back to the dawn of observational astronomy, digital images in two and three dimensions as well as time-lensed.

When he emerged, driven by the physiological mundanities of bladder and blood sugar, Maduabuchi knew something was wrong. He *knew* it. Captain Smith had been right about her mission, about there being something off in their voyage to Tiede 1.

But she didn't know what it was she was right about. He didn't either.

Still, the thought niggled somewhere deep in his mind.

Not the green flash *per se,* though that, too. Something more about Tiede 1.

Or less.

"And what the hell did that mean?" he asked the swarming motes of data surrounding him on the virtual displays, now reduced to confetti as he left his informational fugue.

Maduabuchi stumbled out of the Survey Suite to find the head, the galley, and Captain Peridot Smith, in that order.

The corridor was filled with smoke, though no alarms wailed. He almost ducked back into the Survey Suite, but instead dashed for one of the emergency stations found every ten meters or so and grabbed an oxygen mask. Then he hit the panic button.

That produced a satisfying wail, along with lights strobing at four distinct frequencies. Something was wrong with the gravimetrics, too—the floor had felt syrupy, then too light, with each step. Where the hell was fire suppression?

The bridge was next. He couldn't imagine that they were under attack—*Inclined Plane* was the only ship in the Tiede 1 system so far as any of them knew. And short of some kind of pogrom against Howard immortals, no one had any reason to attack their vessel.

Mutiny, he thought, and wished he had an actual weapon. Though what he'd do with it was not clear. The irony that the lowest-scoring shooter in the history of the Howard training programs was now working as a weapons officer was not lost on him.

He stumbled onto the bridge to find Chillicothe Xiang there, laughing her ass off with Paimei Joyner, one of their two scouts—hard-assed Howards so heavily modded that they could at need tolerate hard vacuum on their bare skin, and routinely worked outside for hours with minimal life support and radiation shielding. The strobes were running in here, but the audible alarm was mercifully muted. Also, whatever was causing the smoke didn't seem to have reached into here yet.

Captain Smith stood at the far end of the bridge, her back to the diamond viewing wall that was normally occluded by a virtual display, though at the moment the actual, empty majesty of Tiede 1 localspace was visible.

Smith was snarling. " . . . don't care what you thought you were doing; clean up my ship's air! Now, damn it."

The two turned toward the hatch, nearly ran into Maduabuchi in his breathing mask, and renewed their laughter.

"You look like a spaceman," said Chillicothe.

"Moral here," added Paimei. One deep black hand reached out to grasp Maduabuchi's shoulder so hard he winced. "Don't try making a barbecue in the galley."

"We'll be eating con-rats for a week," snapped Captain Smith. "And everyone on this ship will know damned well it's your fault we're chewing our teeth loose."

The two walked out, Paimei shoving Maduabuchi into a bulkhead while Chillicothe leaned close. "Take off the mask," she whispered. "You look stupid in it."

Moments later, Maduabuchi was alone with the captain, the mask dangling in his grasp.

"What was it?" she asked in a quiet, gentle voice that carried more respect than he probably deserved.

"I have . . . had something," Maduabuchi said. "A sort of, well, *hunch*. But it's slipped away in all that chaos."

Smith nodded, her face closed and hard. "Idiots built a fire in the galley, just to see if they could."

"Is that *possible?*"

"If you have sufficient engineering talent, yes," the captain admitted grudgingly. "And are very bored."

"Or want to create a distraction," Maduabuchi said, unthinking.

"Damn it," Smith shouted. She stepped to her command console. "What did we miss out there?"

"No," he said, his hunches suddenly back in play. This was like a flow hangover. "Whatever's out there was out there all along. The green flash. Whatever it is." And didn't *that* niggle at his thoughts like a cockroach in an airscrubber. "What we missed was in here."

"And when," the captain asked, her voice very slow now, viscous with thought, "did you and I become *we* as separate from the rest of this crew?"

When you first picked me, ma'am, Maduabuchi thought but did not say. "I don't know. But I was in the Survey Suite, and you were on the bridge. The rest of this crew was somewhere else."

"You can't look at everything, damn it," she muttered. "Some things should just be trusted to match their skin."

Her words pushed Maduabuchi back into his flow state, where the hunch reared up and slammed him in the forebrain with a broad, hairy paw.

"I know what's wrong," he said, shocked at the enormity of the realization.

"What?"

Maduabuchi shook his head. It couldn't possibly be true. The ship's orientation was currently such that the bridge faced away from Tiede 1, but he stared at the screen anyway. Somewhere outside that diamond sheeting—rather smaller than the lounge, but still substantial—was a work of engineering on a scale no human had ever contemplated.

No *human* was the key word.

"The brown dwarf out there . . ." He shook with the thought, trying to force the words out. "It's artificial.

Camouflage. S-something else is hidden beneath that surface. Something big and huge and ... I don't know what. And s-someone on our ship has been communicating with it."

Who could possibly manage such a thing?

Captain Peridot Smith gave him a long, slow stare. Her razored eyes cut into him as if he were a specimen on a lab table. Slowly, she pursed her lips. Her head shook just slightly. "I'm going to have to ask you to stand down, Mr. St. Macaria. You're clearly unfit for duty."

What! Maduabuchi opened his mouth to protest, to argue, to push back against her decision, but closed it again in the face of that stare. Of course she knew. She'd known all along. She was testing ... whom? Him? The rest of the crew?

He realized it didn't matter. His line of investigation was cut off. Maduabuchi knew when he was beaten. He turned to leave the bridge, then stopped at the hatch. The breathing mask still dangled in his hand.

"If you didn't want me to find that out, ma'am," he asked, "then why did you set me to looking for it?"

But she'd already turned away from him without answering, and was making a study of her command data.

Chillicothe Xiang found him in the observation lounge an hour later. Uncharacteristically, Maduabuchi had retreated into alcohol. Metabolic poisons were not so effective on Howard Immortals, but if he hit something high enough proof, he could follow youthful memories of the buzz.

"That's Patrice's forty-year-old scotch you're drinking," she observed, standing over the smartgel bodpod that wrapped him like a warm, sticky uterus.

"Huh." Patrice Tonwe, their engineering chief, was a hard son of a bitch. One of the leaders in that perpetual game of shake-and-break the rest of the crew spent their time on. Extremely political as well, even by Howard standards. Not someone to get on the wrong side of.

Shrugging off the thought and its implications, Maduabuchi looked at the little beaker he'd poured the stuff into. "Smelled strongest to me."

Chillicothe laughed. "You are hopeless, Mad. Like the galaxy's oldest adolescent."

Once again he felt stung. "I'm one hundred forty-three years-subjective old. Born over two hundred years-objective ago."

"So?" She nodded at his drink. "Look at that. And I'll bet you never even changed genders once before you went Howard. The boy who never grew up."

He settled further back and took a gulp from his beaker. His throat burned and itched, but Maduabuchi would be damned if he'd give her the satisfaction of choking. "What do you want?"

She knelt close. "I kind of like you, okay? Don't get excited, you're just an all right kid. That's all I'm saying. And because I like you, I'm telling you, don't ask."

Maduabuchi was going to make her say it. "Don't ask what?"

"Just don't ask questions." Chillicothe mimed a pistol with the fingers of her left hand. "Some answers are permanent fatal errors."

He couldn't help noting her right hand was on the butt of a real pistol. Fléchette-throwing riot gun, capable of shredding skin, muscle and bone to pink fog without damaging hull integrity.

"I don't know," he mumbled. "Where I grew up, green light means go."

Chillicothe shook him, a disgusted sneer chasing across her lips. "It's your life, kid. Do what you like."

With that, she stalked out of the observation lounge.

Maduabuchi wondered why she'd cared enough to bother trying to warn him off. Maybe Chillicothe had told the simple truth for once. Maybe she liked him. No way for him to know.

Instead of trying to work that out, he stared at Tiede 1's churning orange surface. "Who are you? What are you doing in there? What does it take to fake being an entire *star?*"

The silent light brought no answers, and neither did Patrice's scotch. Still, he continued to ask the questions for a while.

Eventually he woke up, stiff in the smartgel. The stuff had enclosed all of Maduabuchi except for his face, and it took several minutes of effort to extract himself. When he looked up at the sky, the stars had shifted.

They'd broken Tiede 1 orbit!

He scrambled for the hatch, but to his surprise, his hand on the touchpad did not cause the door to open. A moment's stabbing and squinting showed that the lock had been frozen on command override.

Captain Smith had trapped him in here.

"Not for long," he muttered. There was a maintenance hatch at the aft end of the lounge, leading to the dorsal weapons turret. The power and materials chase in the spine of the hull was partially pressurized, well within his minimally Howard-enhanced environmental tolerances.

And as weapons officer, *he* had the command overrides to those systems. If Captain Smith hadn't already locked him out.

To keep himself going, Maduabuchi gobbled some prote-nuts from the little service bar at the back of the lounge. Then, before he lost his nerve, he shifted wall hangings that obscured the maintenance hatch and hit that pad. The interlock system demanded his command code, which he provided with a swift haptic pass, then the wall section retracted with a faint squeak that spoke of neglected maintenance.

The passage beyond was ridiculously low-clearance. He nearly had to hold his breath to climb to the spinal chase. And cold, damned cold. Maduabuchi figured he could spend ten, fifteen minutes tops up there before he began experiencing serious physiological and psychological reactions.

Where to go?

The chase terminated aft above Engineering, with access to the firing points there, as well as egress to the Engineering bay. Forward it met a vertical chase just before the bridge section, with an exterior hatch, access to the forward firing points, and a connection to the ventral chase.

No point in going outside. Not much point in going to Engineering, where like as not he'd meet Patrice or Paimei and wind up being sorry about it.

He couldn't get onto the bridge directly, but he'd get close and try to find out.

The chase wasn't really intended for crew transit, but it had to be large enough to admit a human being for inspection and repairs, when the automated systems couldn't handle something. It was a shitty, difficult crawl, but *Inclined Plane* was only about two hundred meters stem to stern anyway. He passed over several intermediate access hatches—no point in getting out—then simply climbed down and out in the passageway when he reached the bridge. Taking control of the exterior weapons systems from within the walls of the ship wasn't going to do him any good. The interior systems concentrated on disaster suppression and anti-hijacking, and were not under his control anyway.

No one was visible when Maduabuchi slipped out from the walls. He wished he had a pistol, or even a good, long-handled wrench, but he couldn't take down any of the rest of these Howards even if he tried. He settled for hitting the bridge touchpad and walking in when the hatch irised open.

Patrice sat in the captain's chair. Chillicothe manned the navigation boards. They both glanced up at him, surprised.

"What are you doing here?" Chillicothe demanded.

"Not being locked in the lounge," he answered, acutely conscious of his utter lack of any plan of action. "Where's Captain Smith?"

"In her cabin," said Patrice without looking up. His voice was a growl, coming from a heavyworld body like a sack of bricks. "Where she'll be staying."

"Wh-why?"

"What did I tell you about questions?" Chillicothe asked softly.

Something cold rested against the hollow spot of skin just behind Maduabuchi's right ear. Paimei's voice whispered close. "Should have listened to the woman. Curiosity killed the cat, you know."

They will never expect it, he thought, and threw an elbow back, spinning to land a punch on Paimei. He never made the hit. Instead he found himself on the deck, her boot against the side of his head.

At least the pistol wasn't in his ear any more.

Maduabuchi laughed at that thought. Such a pathetic rationalization. He opened his eyes to see Chillicothe leaning over.

"What do you think is happening here?" she asked.

He had to spit the words out. "You've taken over the sh-ship. L-locked Captain Smith in her cabin. L-locked me up to k-keep me out of the way."

Chillicothe laughed, her voice harsh and bitter. Patrice growled some warning that Maduabuchi couldn't hear, not with Paimei's boot pressing down on his ear.

"She tried to open a comms channel to something very dangerous. She's been relieved of her command. That's not mutiny; that's self-defense."

"And compliance to regulation," said Paimei, shifting her foot a little so Maduabuchi would be sure to hear her.

"Something's inside that star."

Chillicothe's eyes stirred. "You still haven't learned about questions, have you?"

"I w-want to talk to the captain."

She glanced back toward Patrice, now out of Maduabuchi's very limited line of sight. Whatever look was exchanged resulted in Chillicothe shaking her head. "No. That's not wise. You'd have been fine inside the lounge. A day or two, we could have let you out. We're less than eighty hours-subjective from making threadneedle transit back to Saorsen Station; then this won't matter any more."

He just couldn't keep his mouth shut. "Why won't it matter?"

"Because no one will ever know. Even what's in the data will be lost in the flood of information."

I could talk, Maduabuchi thought. *I could tell. But then I'd just be another crazy ranting about the aliens that no one has ever found across several thousand explored solar systems in hundreds of lightyears of the Orion Arm.* The crazies that had been ranting all through human history about the Fermi Paradox. He could imagine the conversation. *"No, really. There are aliens. Living in the heart of a brown dwarf. They flashed a green light at me."*

Brown dwarfs were *everywhere*. Did that mean that

aliens were *everywhere,* hiding inside the hearts of their guttering little stars?

He was starting to sound crazy, even to himself. But even now, Maduabuchi couldn't keep his mouth shut. "You know the answer to the greatest question in human history. 'Where is everybody else?' And you're not talking about it. What did the aliens tell you?"

"That's it," said Paimei. Her fingers closed on his shoulder. "You're out the airlock, buddy."

"No," said Chillicothe. "Leave him alone."

Another rumble from Patrice, of agreement. Maduabuchi, in sudden, sweaty fear for his life, couldn't tell whom the man was agreeing *with.*

The fléchette pistol was back against his ear. "Why?"

"Because we like him. Because he's one of ours." Her voice grew very soft. "Because I said so."

Reluctantly, Paimei let him go. Maduabuchi got to his feet, shaking. He wanted to *know,* damn it, his curiosity burning with a fire he couldn't ever recall feeling in his nearly two centuries of life.

"Go back to your cabin." Chillicothe's voice was tired. "Or the lounge. Just stay out of everyone's way."

"Especially mine," Paimei growled. She shoved him out the bridge hatch, which cycled to cut him off.

Like that, he was alone. So little a threat that they left him unescorted within the ship. Maduabuchi considered his options. The sane one was to go sit quietly with some books until this was all over. The most appealing was to go find Captain Smith, but she'd be under guard behind a hatch locked by command override.

But if he shut up, if he left now, if he never *knew* ... *Inclined Plane* wouldn't be back this way, even if he happened to be crewing her again. No one else had reason to come to Tiede 1, and he didn't have resources to mount his own expedition. Might not for many centuries to come. When they departed this system, they'd leave the mystery behind. *And it was too damned important.*

Maduabuchi realized he couldn't live with that. To be this close to the answer to Fermi's question. To know that the people around him, possibly everyone around him, knew the truth and had kept him in the dark.

The crew wanted to play hard games? Then hard games they'd get.

He stalked back through the passageway to the number two lateral. Both of *Inclined Plane*'s boats were docked there, one on each side. A workstation was at each hatch, intended for use when managing docking or cargo transfers or other such logistical efforts where the best eyes might be down here, off the bridge.

Maduabuchi tapped himself into the weapons systems with his own still-active overrides. Patrice and Chillicothe and the rest were counting on the safety of silence to ensure there were no untoward questions when they got home. He could nix that.

He locked down every weapons system for 300 seconds, then set them all to emergency purge. Every chamber, every rack, every capacitor would be fully discharged and emptied. It was a procedure for emergency dockings, so you didn't come in hot and hard with a payload that could blow holes in the rescuers trying to catch you.

Let *Inclined Plane* return to port with every weapons system blown, and there'd be an investigation. He cycled the hatch, slipped into the portside launch. Let *Inclined Plane* come into port with a boat and a crewman missing, and there'd be even more of an investigation. Those two events together would make faking a convincing log report pretty tough. Especially without Captain Smith's help.

He couldn't think about it any more. Maduabuchi

strapped himself in, initiated the hot-start preflight sequence, and muted ship comms. He'd be gone before Paimei and her cohorts could force the blast-rated docking hatch. His weapons systems override would keep them from simply blasting him out of space, then concocting a story at their leisure.

And the launch had plenty of engine capacity to get him back to close orbit around Tiede 1.

Blowing the clamps on a hot-start drop, Maduabuchi goosed the launch on a minimum-time transit back toward the glowering brown dwarf. Captain Smith wouldn't leave him here to die. She'd be back before he ran out of water and air.

Besides, someone was home down there, damn it, and he was going to go knocking.

Behind him, munitions began cooking off into the vacuum. Radiations across the EM spectrum coruscated against the launch's forward viewports, while instrumentation screeched alerts he didn't need to hear. It didn't matter now. Screw Chillicothe's warning about not asking questions. "Permanent fatal errors," his ass.

One way or the other, Maduabuchi would find the answers if it killed him.

Galaxy of Mirrors

Paul Di Filippo

Silent and observant, Fayard Avouris clustered with his fellow chattering tourists at the enormous bow-bellied windows constituting the observation deck of the luxury starliner *Melungeon Bride*. Their lazy, leisurely, loafers' ship had just taken up orbit around the uninhabited wilderness world dubbed Youth Regained. Soon the cosseted and high-paying visitors would be ferried down to enjoy such unspoiled natural attractions as the Scintillating Firefalls, the Roving Islands of Lake Vervet, and the Coral Warrens of the Drunken Monkey-mites. Then, before boredom could set in, off to the next stop: the hedonistic casino planet of Rowl.

Contemplating the lovely, patchwork, impasto orb hung against a backdrop of gemlike stars flaring amber, magenta, and violet, Fayard Avouris sighed. This trip had failed, so far, either to re-stimulate his sense of wonder or replenish his intellectual pep.

A fellow of medium height and pudgy girth, Avouris did not necessarily resemble the stereotypical professor of anthropology, but neither did he entirely defy such a status. He looked rather too louche and proletarian to be employed as an instructor by such a famous university as the Alavoine Academy of Durwood IV. His style of dress was humble and careless, and his rubicund countenance marked him as a fan more of various weathers than of library interiors. But a certain pedantic twist to his lips, and a tendency to drop the most abstruse and aberrant allusions into mundane conversation betrayed his affiliation with the independently thinking classes.

A proud affiliation of many years, which he had routinely cherished up until his nervous breakdown some six months ago.

The unanticipated mental spasm had overtaken Avouris as he lectured a classroom full of graduate students, his remarks also being streamed onto the astromesh for galactic consumption. His theme that day was the explicable exoticism of the several dozen cultures dominant on Hrnd, ranging from the Whitesouls and their recondite taxonomy of sin to the Gongoras and their puzzling paraphilias. As he recounted a particularly spicy anecdote from his field studies among the Gongoras, involving an orgy featuring the massive "walking birds" of the Faraway Steppes, an anecdote that could always be counted on to hold the audience spellbound, he suddenly felt his own savor for the tale evaporate.

And then his hard-won mental topography of galactic culture instantly flattened.

Ever since his own undergraduate days, Fayard Avouris had painstakingly built up a multidimensional mental map of the hundreds of thousands of human societies and their quirks. Useful as an aide-mémoire, this metaphorical model of the Milky Way's myriad ethnographical topoi resembled a mountain range of human diversity, a splendid chart of mankind's outré customs.

But all of a sudden, his laboriously honed virtual creation deflated to a thin pancake of dull homogeneity.

Whereas previous to this moment Avouris had always seen humans, the only sentients in all the vast galaxy, as creatures exhibiting a practically infinite range of behaviors, suddenly his species seemed to resemble paramecia in their limited repertoire. Like some star collapsing into a black hole and losing all its unique complexion in darkness, all the manifold variations of human behavior born of chance, circumstance and free will now imploded into a kernel of mere instinctual responses to stimuli. Humanity seemed no more than hardwired automatons. Sentience itself, so precious and unique amidst all the organisms in a life-teeming galaxy, appeared more like a curse than a gift. All of humanity's long variegated history appeared bland and predictable.

Avouris slammed to a stop in mid-sentence and froze in place, hands clamped on the podium. A hastily summoned EMT crew had been required to remove him from behind the lectern.

Alavoine Academy had been very understanding and sympathetic. The tenured holder of the Stridor Chair of Anthropology simply needed a sabbatical; he had been working too hard. A university-sponsored ticket for the next cruise of the *Melungeon Bride* would solve everything. He'd return invigorated and in top-notch mental health.

But now, three planets into the cruise, as Fayard Avouris contemplated more sightseeing—this time, thankfully, on a world devoid of humans—any such recovery seemed increasingly problematical. The matter of how he could ever reawaken his quondam fascination with the antics of his race plagued him. Moreover, he had begun to suspect that his own dalliance with neurosis was not unique—that this affliction was becoming widespread, and that his own anticipatory bout with it reflected merely a greater sensitivity to the zeitgeist.

On this cruise, Avouris had discreetly probed his fellow passengers, seeking to ascertain their level of excitement regarding their itinerary. The first three stops had occurred at worlds that boasted supremely exotic cultures that deviated far from the galactic norm, a consensual baseline of behaviors continually updated by astromesh polling.

On the world known as Karoshi, people vied to perform the most odious jobs possible in order to attain the highest social status. The most admired and rewarded citizens, virtual royalty, were those who applied medicinal salves to the sores of plague victims via their tongues.

On Weebo III, exogamy was enforced to the exact degree that no two citizens could enjoy intercourse unless a different stranger was invited into the affair each time.

And on Tugnath, a booming trade in afterlife communications involved the perilous enactment of near-death experiences among the interlocutors.

And here they were now at the edenic Youth Regained, afterwards to be visiting Rowl, Lyrely, Ahab's Folly, Zizzofizz and Port Canker. Surely, an itinerary to feed a lifetime of vibrant memories.

And yet Avouris's companions manifested little real excitement. They seemed bored or apathetic, no matter how bizarre their encounters with oddball races. Why? Not because they were all jaded cosmopolites; many of the travelers aboard the *Melungeon Bride* were entirely new to starfaring. No, the only explanation that Avouris could sustain involved immunization to the limited ideational space of human customs and beliefs.

No matter how strange a culture looked initially, upon closer contemplation it became merely one more predictable example of a general class of human behaviors. Death, sex, piety, hedonism, sports, procreative ardor, fashion sense, artistic accomplishment—these few motivators, along with a couple of others, constituted the entire range of determinants for human culture. True, the factors could be combined and permuted in a large number of ways. But in the end, a discerning or even a naïve eye could always unriddle the basic forces at work.

This sense of a limited ideational space constraining the potentials of the species was what had brought Avouris down with a crash. And he suspected that some of the same malaise was beginning to afflict the general populace as well, a millennium into the complete expansion of humanity into the peerless galaxy.

If only other modalities of sentience had presented themselves, mankind could have had various educational windows to look through, rather than an endless hall of mirrors. But galactic evolution had been cruel and parsimonious with regards to intelligence. . . .

Flatscreens across the observation deck and on various personal devices came to life with the voice and face of Slick Willywacker, the ship's obnoxious tummler. Fayard Avouris experienced a crawling dislike for the clownish fellow.

"Hey-nonny-nay, sirs and sirettes! Prepare to embark for a glamorous groundling's go-round! We'll be loading the lighters with the guests from cabins A100 through A500 first. Meanwhile, have a gander at these little imps cavorting in realtime down below!"

The screens filled with Drunken Monkey-mites at play in the surf. The tiny agile beings seemed beguilingly human, but Avouris knew that they were in reality no smarter than a terrestrial gecko.

Sighing deeply, Avouris turned toward the exit. Perhaps he'd just sit at the bar and drink all day. . . .

Startled exclamations and shrieks caused the anthropologist to whirl around and face the windows again.

In the moment of turning his back upon Youth Regained, the planet had changed radically.

Where before empty plains and coasts and mountain ranges had loomed, there now reared vast conurbations, plainly artificial in nature. From this low-orbit vantage, Avouris could even make out extensive agricultural patternings.

Avouris inquired of a stranger, "What happened?"

The elderly woman replied in a dazed fashion. "I don't know. I just blinked, and life was altered!"

The screens had gone blank during this inexplicable and impossible transition. But now they flared back to life.

A single Drunken Monkey-mite face dominated each display. But this creature resembled the little imps of a minute past only insofar as a lemur resembled a human. This evolved being wore clothing, and stood in a room full of alien devices.

The Monkey-mite spoke in perfect astromesh-standard Galglot.

"Hello, ship in orbit. Who are you? Where do you come from? We have never had visitors before!"

Fayard Avouris felt a big smile crease his face.

Life had suddenly become vitally interesting again.

The stark and cheerless offices of the Okhranka on Muntjac in the Al'queem system had not been designed to coddle visitors. Generally speaking, the only types who visited the Okhranka willingly and via the public entrance were vendors of spyware and concealed weaponry; informers either vengeful or altruistic; errant politicians being called out to correct their views; and kooks with sundry theories regarding infernal dangers and utopian opportunities.

Fayard Avouris knew without a doubt that the officials of the galactic security apparatus would certainly place him in the last-named category. An academic from a small institution, however respectable, purporting to hold unique insights regarding the biggest conundrum of recorded history, a puzzle which had kept all the best minds of the galaxy stymied for the past six months— well, how else could he appear to them, other than as one of those eccentric amateurs who claimed to hold the answer to the fabled disappearance of the *Pitchforth Lady,* or the key to the unbreakable ciphers of the Neo-Essenes?

Knowing how he must appear to these bureaucrats, who were probably observing him in secret even now, Avouris strove to maintain his dignity, composure and respectability, even as he tallied his third excruciating hour of waiting in this uncomfortable chair. For the twentieth time he paged through a hardcopy leaflet entitled *A Field Agent's Best Practices for Intra-urban Rumor Quelling* without seeing a word of the text, all the while revolving in his mind the most compelling way to deliver his pitch.

Ever since making his discovery some five weeks ago, Avouris had striven to reach someone in the government who would pay heed to his findings. After many futile entreaties, this appointment with a mid-level apparatchik had been the best meeting he could secure. He wondered now what I. G. Narozhylenko would look like, how receptive he would be. Avouris had tried searching the astromesh for details of the man, but as an Okhranka functionary, the fellow was almost nonexistent so far as public records went. Avouris hoped he would be neither too apathetic nor too closed-minded to listen to an unconventional theory.

Just as the anthropologist was about to peruse the old leaflet for the twenty-third time, an inner door opened and Narozhylenko's personal assistant appeared. Avouris instinctively admired the young woman's grace and shape and modest yet stylish fashion sense. Short hair the color of a raven's wing, arrayed in bangs across an intelligent forehead, nicely framed alert, inquisitive features.

"You may enter now, Professor Avouris."

Inside the office, Avouris dropped down into a guest chair microscopically more comfortable than his previous seat. To his astonishment, the woman took up a desk chair on the far side of a nameplate scribed AGENT I. G. NAROZHYLENKO.

"You are I. G. Narozhylenko?"

"Yes, Ina Glinka Narozhylenko." The woman smiled wryly. "You had a pre-formed conception of me at variance with reality?"

"No, of course not! That is, I—" Avouris gave up apologies and explanations as a waste of time. Luckily, Narozhylenko did not seem put out or inclined to pursue the embarrassing matter. Indeed, Avouris seemed to detect a small smile threatening to escape bureaucratic suppression.

"Let's get right to your business then, Professor. I won't apologize for keeping you waiting so long. As you might imagine, our agency has been stressed beyond belief in dealing with the advent of these nonhuman sophonts. Not only must we manage the pressing practical issues involved in fitting them into galactic culture, but the implications of their instant creation carry even more disturbing challenges. The past six months have overturned so many paradigms that we can barely get our heads above the wreckage. Galactic culture is churning like a Standeven milkmaid on the eve of the springtime butter-sculpting festival."

Avouris appreciated the clever metaphor. It seemed to bespeak learning, humor and broad-mindedness: three qualities he could appeal to in his pitch.

"I agree absolutely. Out of nowhere, our age has become a revolutionary era."

The miraculous and instantaneous transformation of Youth Regained from a wilderness planet into the seemingly long-established homeworld of the first nonhuman civilization ever encountered had been merely the opening note in a bizarre symphony of spontaneous generation.

Shortly thereafter, the world known as Pronk-Kissle had instantly flipped from uninhabited desert wastes to the thriving techno-hives of giant talking sand fleas.

Voynet VII suddenly sported a global culture of stratospheric sentient gasbags.

Spaethmire now hosted a single group intelligence distributed across billions of individuals resembling both sessile and mobile slime molds.

Los Caminos now featured continent-spanning burrows populated by sensitive and poetical beings who resembled naked mole-rats crossbred with whales, each one large as a subway car.

And so on, for another two dozen transformed worlds scattered across the formerly humans-only galaxy, with fresh instances occurring at regular intervals.

All these new alien civilizations had just two things in common.

They all claimed to have arisen naturally over geological timespans on their native planets.

None of them had ever encountered humans before.

These mutually exclusive assertions—each tenet impossible in its own way, given humanity's long acquaintance with these worlds—had engendered scores of theories, none of which had yet been proven to represent the truth.

Ina Glinka Narozhylenko regarded Avouris sternly. "You're not here to tell me you have the answer to these manifestations, are you, Professor? Because I do not believe that your field of expertise—anthropology, is it not?—could feature insights unavailable to our best quantum physicists and plectic fabulists."

Momentarily distracted by the deep grey eyes of the attractive Okhranka agent, Fayard Avouris hesitated a moment before saying, "Oh, no, Agent Narozhylenko, I don't pretend to know the origins of these aliens. However, I do believe that I can predict with some degree of accuracy where the next such outbreak will occur."

Narozhylenko leaned forward intently. "You have exactly fifteen minutes to justify this bold assertion, Professor."

"I have here a memory stick. If you would be so kind as to plug it into your system, Agent Narozhylenko . . ."

The woman did so.

On a large screen popped up a navigable simulacrum of the galaxy. Avouris rose to stand beside the screen where he could interact with the display.

"Here are the recorded outbreaks." The map zoomed and shrank across several scales, as Avouris called up the locations of the alien worlds as he had plotted them earlier. "Do you see any pattern to their distribution?"

"No. And neither did any of several thousand experts."

"Ah, but that is because you do not have a solid theory that would allow you to examine and compare the relevant data sets."

Avouris went on to explain about his personal disillusionment, his dismal anti-epiphany regarding human limitations and sameness, and how he believed that such a malaise was now a general, albeit unrecognized, condition across the galaxy.

"I call this spiritual ailment 'Mirror Sickness.' Perhaps you've seen symptoms of it around you, or even in yourself . . . ?"

Agent Narozhylenko sat pensive. "Yes . . . yes . . . I recognize the feeling. Proceed with your presentation."

"I have spent hundreds of hours since the first alien incursion performing astromesh polling across thousands of worlds on the phenomenon of Mirror Sickness." The screen came alive with animated histograms. "Sifting the results involved the employment of a number of expert machine systems, or I would not have finished for years. In any case, here is a map of the neurosis, graded by severity of symptoms."

Avouris overlaid his findings atop the display of alien outbreaks.

Agent Narozhylenko rose slowly to her feet. "They match . . . they match exactly! Aliens are appearing at equidistant loci relative to those human worlds most despairing of the limitations of our species."

"Let's call them 'the loneliest worlds,' for convenience's sake. And you'll note that the manifestations are precisely encoding the severity gradient of Mirror Sickness, from worst case downward."

Narozhylenko approached the screen and magnified a sector of the galactic map. "Wustner's Weatherbolt should display the next outbreak then. In just a week's time." She turned to Avouris. "Are you currently free from teaching duties, Professor Avouris?"

"Now, and perhaps for the rest of my life!"

Agent Ina Glinka Narozhylenko manifested superior piloting abilities at the helm of her little space clipper, the

Okhranka-supplied *Whispering Shade*. Fayard Avouris felt utterly safe in her hands, although her extremely speedy and cavalier passage through the Oort Cloud on the extremes of the Sockeye star system where the world called Wustner's Weatherbolt revolved had induced a little transient anxiety in the anthropologist.

But now, as the homely little ship floated serenely and safely above the rondure of the planet where—if Avouris's theory and calculations were correct—a miraculous transformation from nescient virgin mudball to home of another unprecedented alien civilization was about to occur, Avouris could not fully relax. Unable to quell a griping sense of injustice, he felt compelled to speak.

"I still can't believe that you and I were deputed alone to affirm my theory. Are your superiors insane or merely mingy, that they could not devote more resources than this to such a potentially lucrative information-gathering expedition? Where is the vast armada of research vessels that should have accompanied us?"

Across the cabin from where Avouris sat, Agent Narozhylenko fussed with the craft's small food reconstituter, preparing a meal. Avouris admired her efficient, graceful movements. He only wished the woman would open up and discuss personal matters with him. The social ambiance during their journey of three days had been rather more arid and formalistic than Avouris could have wished. But so far, Agent Ina Glinka Narozhylenko had maintained a scrupulously businesslike demeanor. After his one attempt to call her by her given names and to probe into her familial background had been met with silence and a frosty stare and the subliminal threat of esoteric martial-arts dissuasions, he had refrained from any further pleasantries. So now all he could do by way of conversation was complain.

"The Okhranka Directorate," said the agent in response to his gripe, "are not fools or gamblers. And their resources are always limited, never more so than at present. Oftentimes only a single agent is tasked with a complex assignment. We are highly competent and trained across a broad number of surprising disciplines. The *Whispering Shade* boasts all the sensors of a larger craft, so more vessels would be superfluous. And the satellites I've launched give us complete telemetric coverage of the planet. Believe me, if we witness the fulfillment of your prediction, the next such occasion will merit a fuller contingent."

Avouris grumped before responding. "Well, I suppose you people know what you're doing."

Narozhylenko cocked one eyebrow. "A very generous allowance on your part, Professor Avouris. Now, would you care for some shabara filets?"

After eating they rested in their separate berths, under a programmed bout of artificial sleep. The guardian machines triggered wakefulness well in advance of the projected time for the planetary transition. Then commenced the nerve-wracking waiting.

"What do you see as the probable cause of these eruptions of nonhuman sentience, Professor?" Narozhylenko asked, while she fiddled with the satellites' feed. "Of the theories so far proposed, I place Planck-level punctuated equilibrium first, global de-masking of long-established hidden worlds second, and mass mind-tampering third."

Avouris shook his head thoughtfully. "No, no, none of those explanations appeal to me as sufficiently comprehensive. Whatever the answer, it will be more complex than any scenario so far advanced. And then we have the question of motive. I can't believe this is a natural phenomenon. A prime mover is implied. Who and why? And why now?"

"Perhaps your own theories about the spatial distribution of the changes will contribute to an ultimate solution, Professor."

"So I hope. Now, let us focus on these screens. The change is imminent, I believe."

Agent Narozhylenko moved to magnify the image of Wustner's Weatherbolt on one display, but even as she did so the planet vanished, to be replaced by an edgeless curving wall bristling with dangerous-looking protrusions.

Avouris could merely gasp and say, "What the—?" before Narozhylenko had moved to step down the scale of the display.

Interposed between the *Whispering Shade* and the altered planet was a space-going vessel that had appeared from nowhere. So enormous as to render the Okhranka ship a pea next to a prize-winning pumpkin, the alien craft radiated martial prowess and a defiant hostility.

Narozhylenko's frantic fingers found an active communications channel.

A separate panel showed a being that resembled a bipedal lobster colored fungal white. Its stubby midriff legs wiggled angrily. It occupied a command center bustling with others of its kind.

Avouris had time only to say, "That's plainly an evolved form of the Ghost Crawdad of Miravalle Caverns." Then the lobster was speaking.

"You are friends of the World Thinker, or enemies?"

"Who is the World Thinker?" asked Narozhylenko.

"Wrong answer. Now you must die."

A coruscating sphere of blue-gold energy bloomed from the ship of the Ghost Crawdads, but the *Whispering Shade* was already curving and jinking away. The ball of destruction missed them and decohered violently but uselessly, flooding space with radiation. On the communications channel, the lobster captain gestured silently with his antennae, audio transmissions temporarily suspended at Narozhylenko's behest.

Sweating yet composed, Narozhylenko said, "We have to get well beyond the mass of the planet before I dare kick in the superposition drive. Even then it's extremely dangerous. Stall these angry arthropods somehow! Go!"

She flicked the audio back on, and Avouris began to babble.

"Sweet saltworms to you, my hardshell friends! May all your mates molt most enticingly! You mistake us for enemies? We are not! This World Thinker you mention is unknown to us. Please enlighten us poor, exoskeleton-bereft, leg-deficient beings."

The lobster captain made no reply, but evidently shut off his own audio to consult with his officers. Narozhylenko evoked a tithe of additional power from the *Shade*'s engines. Avouris felt his own shirt pasted to his wet armpits.

"That's it, keep it up! Just another five minutes . . ."

The lobster's idiosyncratic but intelligible Galglot resumed. "You must know the World Thinker, source of all intelligence. His gift is a poisoned one, though. Admit it! Don't you wish his destruction, impossible as that might be?"

"Oh, of course! Death to all World Thinkers! Free the sentients!"

The lobster captain performed what could only be interpreted as a disdainful arthropodic glare. "Your protestations are insufficiently sincere. Goodbye."

Several more deadly rosettes of energy bloomed, converging rapidly and ineluctably on the human ship, just as Narozhylenko shouted, "Now!"

The *Whispering Shade* juddered, leaped, its metal

bones ringing with one tremendous *bong!* then settled down into easy superposition travel outside the relativistic universe.

Agent Narozhylenko jumped up from the controls and flung herself at Fayard Avouris. He hardly knew how to react, half-expecting chastising corporal punishment for his diplomatic incompetence. But the agent's kisses and caresses soon allayed that fear. Avouris returned them heartily.

In the interstices, the anthropologist whispered, "Oh, Ina Glinka . . ."

"No," she whispered lusciously, "call me Rosy. . . ."

The armada amassed around Wangba-Szypyt IX would have caused the Ghost Crawdads to shed their tails and flee. The Okhranka Directorate was taking no chances on the arrival of another belligerent space-faring set of aliens. The human ships were porcupined with weaponry.

On the command deck of the lead cruiser, Rosy and Fayard occupied a rare position of civilian perquisite. Agent Narozhylenko was discussing tactics with a dour silver-haired soldier named Admiral Leppo Brice, while Avouris speculated with a team of academics about which species native to Wangba-Szypyt IX would be the candidate for uplift by the mysterious World Thinker.

"I like the odds on the Golden Dog-Snails. They already exhibit complex herd behaviors. . . ."

After their safe return from the Sockeye system, Rosy and Fayard had been thoroughly debriefed by the Okhranka. The telemetric records of their encounter with the Ghost Crawdads and the transformation of their planet had proven illuminating. Physicists were still analyzing the instantaneous phase-change the planet had undergone, but no final theories about the methodologies or technics employed by the enigmatic prime mover referenced by the Ghost Crawdads were forthcoming as yet. Of course, researches among the more placid alien races also continued apace.

The success of Fayard's prediction and the strategic resourcefulness of Agent Narozhylenko naturally ensured that both would be invited to witness the next eruption of sentience.

As for their personal affairs—well, Fayard often caught himself whistling tunelessly and wearing the broadest of grins. All his old anomie derived from Mirror Sickness had been dispelled like mist before a tornado. Such was the power of Rosy's affections.

Additionally, Mirror Sickness itself seemed to be abating as a cultural wavefront. The arrival of these new sophonts into the formerly homogenous galactic milieu was having a stimulating positive effect.

Avouris had taken this change into account in his calculations, redoing his astromesh polling to reflect the changed gradients of Mirror Sickness. His old predictions, in fact, had nominated the world of Bricklebank as the next candidate for change after Wustner's Weatherbolt. But the new dynamics had brought them here instead.

And now the predicted moment was nearly at hand.

Hemmed in by taut-nerved military personnel, Fayard and Rosy intently observed the big screen dominated by a view of the mottled sapphire that was Wangba-Szypyt IX.

The anticipated moment came—

—passed—

—and passed again, with no evident change.

Admiral Brice demanded, "Status groundside!"

"No alterations, sir!"

Avouris began to feel sick. "What of Bricklebank?"

The communications officer reported no relevant news from that world, then hesitated at fresh data.

"Admiral Brice, a mining colony in the Furbini system reports an uplift outbreak there!"

"Belligerents?"

"No, sir. The new aliens appear to be vegetative in origin."

A grim-faced Rosy clasped the hand of her lover in support. His voice weakly solicitous, Fayard Avouris contributed: "That would probably be the Hardaway Pitcher Plants. They already employ their vines like tentacles. . . ."

Admiral Brice glared at the hapless anthropologist. "Luckily, Professor, your incompetence has resulted in no harm to any innocents."

"I assure you, Admiral, the next time—"

But the next predicted occurrence likewise failed to meet Avouris's specifications.

And after that, his services were no longer valued at a premium.

What damnable factor had thrown off his careful plot of the contingent uplift instances? Avouris sensed that the errors were down to a faulty map of the Mirror Sickness. But his polling techniques and data-mining were watertight, as evidenced by his success at Wustner's Weatherbolt.

Therefore, he must be getting bad inputs. Could some cultural force manifesting only in the portion of the galaxy currently under examination be responsible?

Avouris began a mental tour of his restored virtual topography of human culture.

The Leatherheads of Xyella would speak truth only to fellow clansmen, but his polling of them had enlisted such informers.

The Mudmen of Bitterfields offered the reverse of what they believed. A transparent fix.

The Pingpanks of Stellwagen V radically modified all their speech with a complex vocabulary of mudras. Trivial to interpolate those gestures.

The Perciasepians of Troutfalls—

Some trained intuition made Avouris re-examine what he knew about this culture.

Six months ago, unknown to an otherwise preoccupied Avouris, a prophet named Hardesty had manifested among the Perciasepians. Hardesty's rubric? Simplicity itself!

Optimism trumped reality!

Archived news reports revealed that the faddish ethos had spread like a plague, to the point that no Perciasepian nowadays would ever admit to any despair.

Here was the blot in his calculations! The Perciasepians had denied any Mirror Sickness among them.

Hastily, Avouris took his Perciasepian datapoints from half a year ago, prior to Hardesty's advent, added in some compensatory factors, and reformulated his maps.

Eureka!

The office of Ina Glinka Narozhylenko had never witnessed such an intemperate visitor. Bursting into Rosy's inner sanctum, Avouris found the agent occupied with the minor and semi-humiliating tasks she had been assigned since the debacle of sponsoring Avouris.

"Bofoellesskaber! Bofoellesskaber!"

"Fayard, please. What does that nonsense mean?"

"It's the place where the next uplift outbreak will happen! You've got to tell the Directorate!"

"They want no part of you or me."

"Then we'll just have to go alone to prove we're right."

"I cannot secure a ship from the Okhranka this time."

"We'll rent one! What good are my savings now? Are you with me?"

Rosy sighed. "Who would take care of you otherwise?"

Once more, Rosy kicked at a plant resembling a green hassock. The vegetable furniture emitted a squeak from its punctured bladders, and collapsed fractionally into itself.

"Damn that cheating shipyard! And damn me for trusting them!"

Sitting on another living ottoman, Fayard nursed his contusions and sighed. "Please, Rosy, no more self-recriminations. Your skills are the only reason we are still alive."

Some yards distant, the crumpled hulk of an old Pryton's Nebulaskimmer still exuded vital fluids into the lush turf of Bofoellesskaber, at the terminus of a mile-long gouge in the planet's rich soil. The rental craft would never journey from star to star again.

Rosy plopped down beside Fayard. "Granted. But I should have done a better pre-flight inspection. It's just that we were in such a hurry—"

"My fault entirely. But look at the bright side. We're unharmed for the moment. When the uplift happens, chances are good that the new aliens will be benevolent. Their presence will register on the Directorate's desktop, an expedition will arrive, and we'll soon be safely home."

"I suppose . . ."

"Let's brace ourselves now. We can expect the change soon."

Fayard and Rosy hugged each other as they tried to anticipate what the uplift experience would feel like from planetside. Would the unknown phenomenon have any effect on their own constitutions? Might they be mutated in fast-forward fashion?

A subliminal shiver like the kiss of a ghost resonated through them. The moment must have come! But outwardly, nothing had changed.

"We must be distant from any new alien settlement on this world . . ." ventured Avouris.

"Fayard, look!"

Rosy was pointing skyward.

Bofoellesskaber's single sun had been replaced by three.

A voice spoke in their heads: *Welcome to your future. I am the World Thinker, humanity's final heir.*

As the World Thinker patiently explained things to his accidental visitors, his work was practically child's play, here in a period some two billion years removed from Fayard and Rosy's time.

Viewing the past and selecting a planet with the best potential for uplift, and in a galactic location where it would subsequently do the most good to mitigate Mirror Sickness, this demiurge would abstract the world entire from its native era. Brought forward to the far future and installed in this artificial star system whose three suns could be modulated to provide just the right spectrum that would mimic the original stellar environment, the world was ready for development.

The World Thinker next approached the species chosen for uplift treatment, tinkered with its genome to foster sentience, and then simply allowed Darwinian evolution to take its course over a few hundred or thousand millennia. No acceleration necessary. The alien culture would develop naturally in situ. When judged ripe, the whole world would be translated back to Fayard and

Rosy's era without more than a single unit of Planck time having ticked by in the eyes of the human observers in the past, thus making a whole race appear to arise instantaneously out of nowhere.

"But why?" asked Avouris. Despite receiving no visible sign of the World Thinker, Fayard had conceived an image of the being from its mental projections, an image which consorted nicely with a fussy old neurotic and knowledge-heavy librarian from his own undergraduate days.

A note of resigned sadness filtered into the World Thinker's speech. *To render myself nonexistent.*

The native timeline known to the World Thinker had never exhibited any sentience save humanity. The cosmic human civilization had succumbed to wave after wave of Mirror Sickness, resulting in myriad ugly apocalyptic crashes and warped resurgences, an endless cycle of inbred frustration and soul miasma that had culminated in the World Thinker's own lonely damaged birth at the end of human history.

I am an imperfect thing, half mad and so much less than I could have been. I bear within me the entire record of humanity's bitter isolation. But it occurred to me that I could remake the past, to engender a better scenario. So I chose your era as the pivotal moment to install change, and began to seed it with alien sentience.

Rosy interrupted. "But if you still exist, then your plan did not work. Your seeding occurred two billion years ago, and yet you remain. You should have vanished instantly upon first conceiving of your scheme."

A faint sense of laughter seemed to permeate the next words of the World Thinker.

But then how would the scheme ever have been carried out to result in my vanishing? No, the chronal paradoxes are unresolved. Am I operating across multiple timelines, living in one and tinkering with another, or do all my actions occur only in one strand of the multiverse? Maybe I am improving the continuum next door to mine. Is that yours or not? In any case, I have no choice but to continue. Humanity cannot develop in a healthy manner without alien peers. I am testament to that premise.

The three suns of Bofoellesskaber were now setting, and the air grew chill. Fayard and Rosy held each other more tightly.

"What's to become of us?" Avouris asked.

Your presence will allow me to fulfill one last seeding, the most crucial of all. Don't worry: I will visit you from time to time with aid.

Realization struck Avouris like a blow. "Surely such a sophisticated entity as yourself will not endorse such a cliché!"

No reply was forthcoming. Instantly their surroundings had altered.

The air, the light, the smells, the sounds—all possessed a primeval rightness, an ancestral gravity.

Rosy laughed with a touch of grimness. "Earth? Would you care to guess the date?"

Avouris sighed, then chuckled. "Far enough back, my dear, that there will be no constraints on our family size whatsoever, I imagine."

Where Two or Three

Sheila Finch

The charge nurse barely paused in her fast trot down the hospice hallway. "Seventeen needs his water jug refilled. Can you get it?"

"I'll get it." Maddie turned back the way she had come. It was her second day as a volunteer—what a joke! she hadn't volunteered for anything—but already she was getting the routine. Here, the charge nurse was boss.

She picked up a full plastic jug of ice water from the kitchen and walked back to room seventeen. Like most of the other rooms, it contained a hospital bed with a white coverlet, a straight-back visitor's chair, a battered chest of drawers that had hosted too many patients' belongings. Unlike the others, the occupant or his family hadn't made an effort to personalize the room with family photos, artwork, or flowering plants. They hadn't replaced the old 2-D, which probably didn't work any more, with a newer Tri-D either. The hospice cat, a large orange tabby, jumped off the bed when she came in as if his shift was over once a volunteer showed up.

"Hi," she said. "I'm Maddie. I brought your water."

The skinny old man on the bed didn't open his eyes. "Haven't seen you before."

"Only my second day."

He had the most wrinkled skin she'd ever seen, and his face was blotchy as if he'd had a bad sunburn and skinned recently. He had to be at least a hundred, she thought. There was a smell in the room too, not really bad but odd, sort of baby-powdery and musty at the same time. She picked up the empty jug. She definitely did not want to spend time in here.

"Why're you here if you don't like it?"

Maddie jumped. "Would I be here if I didn't?" Lying again, she thought. One of these days she was going to have to break the habit.

He turned his head away from her. The back of his neck was scrawny as a chicken's, and the skin was patchy here too. "Sit and visit."

She sat gracelessly on the edge of the chair by the wall and stared at the old man's neck. "So, what did you used to do?" she asked brightly. Most of the older ones liked to talk about the old days, the younger ones not so much.

"Astronaut," he said.

"Astronaut? You mean, like space and stuff?"

"Space," he said to the wall. "And stuff."

"Have I heard of you?" she asked cautiously.

"Probably not. Name's Sam." He rolled back to face her, surprisingly agile for someone who looked so old. His eyes were a pale, washed-out blue, same color as the jeans she was wearing. "And how did you get sentenced to this place?"

Maddie felt her cheeks grow warm. "I'm a volunteer."

"Crap. Person your age has better things to do than visit old coots like me."

"All right. Here's the truth. I got busted for doing drugs at a party. One rotten joint—and if I'd been eighteen already like everybody else it would've been legal anyway. So the judge gave me community service."

"Good," Sam said. "I don't have time for lies. What would you rather be doing—besides being stupid?"

"You really are unpleasant, know that?" she snapped.

He chuckled—at least she thought that was what he was doing. Maybe he was choking or something. "Didn't they tell you you're supposed to humor me?"

"I'm in high school. I'll be a senior starting next month. I don't get much time to do what I'd rather be doing. But when I do, I play the flute."

"A musician," he said. "Will you play for me?"

"I didn't bring it with me."

"How about next time you come?" He gazed at her with the washed-out eyes. The edges of his lipless old mouth creased up. "Please?"

Why not? The staff encouraged volunteers to entertain the residents any way possible. "Well, maybe when I come back on Friday."

"And maybe I'll tell you about space. And stuff."

Maddie got out of the room before he could say anything else. In the hallway, she passed the charge nurse again.

"Glad to see you spent some time with Mr. Ferenzi. He never gets any visitors." The charge nurse smoothed the pink tunic over her white slacks. "He used to be famous. But something happened to him, and he was never quite right afterwards."

Even if it wasn't true, she thought, it beat spending time with the old biddies here who only wanted her to play cards with them.

*   *   *

Maddie had been ready to finish her monthly mandated hours at the hospice yesterday, but Mom wanted to take her back-to-school shopping. She would've been happy with the Gap, but Mom insisted on heading down to the OC and taking all day. At least that was better than the virtual house arrest Daddy had put her on. So now she had to make it up by wasting Saturday afternoon at the hospice.

It was a fine late summer day, the sky an almost transparent blue as if she could see through to the other side if she squinted hard. The neighbor's gardener was mowing, filling the air with the sweet green smell of cut grass. At the last minute, she remembered her promise to bring the flute. She slid the flute into its case and stuffed it into the canvas shoulder bag with her house keys and purse, and headed out to grab her bicycle.

Sam Ferenzi looked as if he hadn't moved an inch since the last time she was here. If anything, he looked skinnier than ever, as if he might shrivel up and blow away once the desert Santa Ana started blowing.

She flopped in the visitor's chair. "I brought the flute."

"Play." His voice rasped.

She opened the case, then lifted the flute to her lips. She loved the flute and didn't mind practicing, in contrast to her rebellion against all other forms of homework. When she was younger, she'd thought about becoming a professional musician and playing with the L.A. Phil. But that would take years at the university and Maddie had had enough of school and no idea what she was going to do with her life. She began to play a section of a flute solo.

"Mozart, Concerto Number Two," Sam said when she stopped. "Fine, but thin."

"Of course it is! It needs an orchestra to make it whole—"

"And meaningful."

"—but I'm just me."

"Exactly."

"All right," she said, exasperated. "I did what you asked. Now it's your turn."

He scared her by sitting up so suddenly she was afraid he was going to lose his balance and tumble off the narrow bed. His green pajama sleeves with hideous pink hearts flapped back, revealing skinny arms covered in the same white blotchy patches she could see on his face and neck. He raised an arm and pointed the remote at the small 2-D set perched on the scratched chest of drawers.

The screen brightened, then revealed a lone squiggle of electric-bright color, red shading into purple on a black background. The line looped across the screen slowly, endlessly, hypnotically. A second line, blue-indigo this time, braided itself in and under and over the first one. She waited. Nothing else happened.

"What's that supposed to mean?"

He lowered his arm and the screen went dark. "That's the question, isn't it?"

"Okay." She blew her breath out in a long sigh. "I'm leaving now."

"I'm trying to tell you something."

"Well, you're not doing too good!" She stood up, and put the flute in her shoulder bag.

He lay back against the pillows. "Sorry."

She thought he sounded tired, but also something more—sad, maybe. As if no matter how hard he tried he just couldn't get something right and was fed up with trying. For a moment, he reminded her of her grandfather who'd died when she was only ten. Even now, she missed him. He must've been something like this tired, lonely old man at the end. She sat down again.

"Your nurse says you did some amazing things once."

"All useless."

"I wouldn't say that!" she protested. "I'm impressed."

"You're a musician. Makes a difference."

It was really difficult to hold a conversation with him. She changed the subject. "Don't you get bored in this room? I could take you outside in a wheelchair."

"Where would we go?"

"The garden's nice."

He shook his head.

"Where then?

"Hat Creek would be good, Northern California. But the desert'll do."

"Oh, right!" Maddie laughed. "I'm sure they'd let me take you to the Mojave! 'Specially this time of year."

"Don't you have a driver's license?"

"Of course I do. But I don't have a car." Actually, she thought, that was another lie—or at least a near one. Daddy had taken away the keys to the used Tesla her parents had given her for her birthday when she'd got caught with one joint at that stupid party.

Sam was silent so long she was afraid he'd died on her. She stared at the white sheet covering his bony old chest, willing it to rise and fall. It didn't move. What was she supposed to do now? Finally he let some air whistle out from his mouth.

"Why do you want to go to the desert, anyway?" she asked

He didn't answer. She glanced at her watch. Ten more minutes and the aides would be bringing round the dinner trays. If she stayed much longer, they'd put her to work.

She stood up. "I have to go now. I'll see you in a couple of days."

"You ever read the Bible?" he asked suddenly.

"No. My dad's a scientist at JPL. We aren't superstitious."

"Pity. You should try Matthew 18: verse 20."

She couldn't stop thinking about Sam. Of course Daddy would find out if she took him for a ride in the car! And even if she did get the keys, she certainly shouldn't be driving all the way to Palm Springs, the only part of the desert she knew how to get to. By Monday morning she was roaming around the silent house as antsy as if it were the first day of school in a new place.

Who did that old guy think he was, anyway?

That was a question she could find the answer to.

Daddy had gone to the airport on his way to a two-day SETI conference on the east coast; Mom had driven up to Santa Barbara to see Grandma, who'd suddenly taken ill, and she planned to stay the night. Maddie was on her own.

She went into the study to use the computer. It didn't take long to learn that Samuel Coulter Ferenzi had once been famous. And that there was something really odd about the dates.

He'd been the first astronaut to rendezvous with an asteroid, she read, a feat no one else had repeated in the twenty years since. She skipped over the voyage and its mission. When the crew came back to Earth, there'd been a huge welcome parade. Ferenzi had given speeches at universities. He'd cut the ribbons opening air & space museums. The tabloids had buzzed over his romance with a movie star. Then things had apparently gone wrong.

The phone beeped. She touched the pad for the study extension. "Parker residence."

"What're your plans for today, Madison?" her father's voice asked.

Just like that, she thought. No *how are you, sweetie?* No *I hope you're not bored all by yourself?* that anybody else's dad might've asked. Sounded like he'd given up on her already; she really resented that. "I'm putting in my hours at the hospice like I'm supposed to!"

He'd taken her cell too, as if he thought she'd be putting in a call to her supplier.

"Don't get snarky with me, young lady!" Daddy said. "Be home before dark."

"Sure."

"My plane's boarding. See you in a couple of days."

Maddie turned the phone off before he put any more conditions on her. It wasn't fair. Maybe she should've done something that would really deserve it, not just a couple of puffs off a joint someone handed her. And it hadn't even given her much of a buzz!

She turned her attention back to the monitor. Ferenzi had started acting strangely. Several hospital stays had followed; one article mentioned psychiatric care. On the tenth page of citations, she found a tabloid headline: *Spaceman sees aliens. Bride calls off wedding.* The date was puzzling, only a little more than twenty years ago. Too recent to fit the old man in the hospice bed.

Maddie exited the program and thought about what she had just read. Chances were, Sam was crazy. Why did he want to go to the desert? And more important, why should she risk being grounded for the entire school year to take him there? She'd be as crazy as he was to do it.

A flicker of movement on the computer's monitor attracted her attention; the screensaver had activated. She stared at the ballet of spinning galaxies and soaring cloudlike nebulae her father had installed. He was involved with the SETI program at JPL, but it wasn't something he talked about much. Not because it was secret, Maddie knew, but because the results were so disappointing. She wondered if he knew about Sam Ferenzi. Her father thought people who claimed to have seen aliens cheapened the real search for extraterrestrial intelligence.

The old man seemed so lonely. At least she could take him for a short drive around Pasadena. Maybe the change of scenery would do him good.

She knew where her father had put her car keys. He never locked his desk drawer, trusting the members of his household. She felt a twinge of guilt as she retrieved her keys.

"I'm taking Mr. Ferenzi out for a drive," she told the charge nurse as she pushed the empty wheelchair past the nurses' station. "That okay?"

The charge nurse today, a young dark-skinned man in green scrubs, looked up from the charts he'd been studying. "How long you planning on keeping him out?"

She hadn't expected to be asked. "Umm ... we shouldn't be too long."

The charge nurse rubbed his eyes as if he'd put in a long shift. "He'll need his meds again in a couple of hours."

No way she could've gone to Palm Springs and back in a couple of hours! Sam would just have to take the disappointment. If he even remembered.

But the moment she stepped into his room, she knew he'd remembered. He was sitting on the edge of his bed, dressed in maroon sweats several sizes too large, one bony hand holding a scruffy olive-green duffel bag, the other stroking the hospice cat.

"Want to go for a ride around town?" she asked brightly.

"Stop worrying about the meds," he said. "I don't need them. Only take them to shut the nurses up."

"Are you reading my mind?"

"Obvious they'd tell you when I'm due for the next dose. Where's the car?"

"Around the corner," she said. Where—she hoped—no one who knew her would notice it.

"Good. Let's go."

Resentment at the way he ordered her around welled up, sharp and hot. She was a volunteer, not a servant. As if sensing her mood, the cat hissed at her and jumped down from the bed. She held her arm out for support as Sam maneuvered himself into the wheelchair. He huffed and wheezed and settled cautiously, then indicated she should put the duffel bag on his lap.

"You're not as old as you look, are you?" she said spitefully. "I looked you up."

The face he turned to her was open, stricken, like a flower pelted by a sudden, hard rain. She regretted her words instantly, but there was no way to take them back. She wheeled him in silence down the hall, past the charge nurse who was too busy to glance up, and out the automatic door at the front of the building.

Sam didn't say anything when they reached her silver Tesla, and he managed to get into the passenger seat without much help, never letting go of the duffel bag. But she heard him gasp with pain as he landed heavily on his thin hips. She slid in behind the wheel and passed the electronic key over the sensor. Only the red lights on the dash confirmed the electric motor was ready to roll.

They drove east through Pasadena in silence. She thought about pointing out some of the lovely old houses, but he'd closed his eyes as if he was bored already.

After a while he said, "You need to take Interstate 10 east."

"We're not taking the freeway at all."

"You want to hear my story? Then we do it my way."

She glanced at him. "No way! I'd be in a lot of trouble if I did that."

"Me too." The old man rummaged in the duffel, then held out a disk. "Put this in your CD player."

"Cars don't have CD players any more. Everybody has their own—"

"Yours does."

He pointed to the slit low on the dash where she'd never needed to notice it before. Steering with one hand, she slipped the disk into the player.

After a moment's silence, a low, sustained note came out of the speakers, like an oboe, she thought, or a bassoon. The sound undulated in dark, thin loops. Once in a while, the loops were punctuated with a single higher note that died away as it fell. There was something lonely in the sound as if it spoke of enormous distance and the vast passage of time. Then it changed—or was replaced—by another, higher voice, this one mournful, with the suggestion of an echo over a frozen sea. Spooky!

She listened for a while, trying to guess what she might be hearing. Then it hit her so suddenly she felt ice pour through her veins. "Aliens?"

"Nope. But not a bad guess," he said. "Whales. Humpback whale songs."

"I suppose next you're going to tell me they make up symphonies and operas!"

"I doubt it. But we don't know, do we? And that's the problem. *We don't know.*"

"We're going back!" she decided.

"I'm trying, Maddie," Sam said. "But I haven't got the right words. I'm going to have to show you."

"Maybe I'm just a dumb kid and I don't care."

"You *have* to care," he said. "Somebody must! There's the on-ramp."

Obviously, she hadn't been paying enough attention to the road. She slowed the Tesla, a block before the interstate on-ramp. Overhead, the unfinished span of what was going to be the high-speed monorail from Pasadena to Los Angeles, which they'd been building ever since she could remember, looked like a casualty of the terrorist attacks on London and Paris.

She was aware of car horns, a car alarm going off, the ululation of a police siren. Familiar urban sounds, she thought, and remembered the waves on the oscilloscope when the technician tuned the grand piano at home. It had picked up her voice too, and displayed its peaks and valleys in a running line. Insight struck.

"Your vid. That was the sound wave of a whale's song, wasn't it?"

"Two of them."

Something about this strange old man held her, like he was some kind of modern wizard or something. Whatever his secret was, she believed him that it was important. "But what does it all *mean?*"

"I'm going to show you."

If her father found out she'd taken her car keys, she was going to be in a lot of trouble anyway. Driving a bit farther wasn't going to make it much worse. And she resented being treated like some delinquent kid.

The clock on the dash read two thirty-three already. She fingered *Palm Springs* into the GPS pad and the readout told her *ETA three hours twenty minutes due to heavy traffic.* Even if she could hurry Sam along once they got there, it would probably be midnight before they were home again. The hospice would've missed Sam and called the police by then.

"Sam, I can't do this."

"Do it!" His voice was suddenly strong and compelling like the young man he once must've been. She stared at him. Then he added in his normal, old man's voice, "I'm going to show you what happened. Maybe you'll understand."

She thought of her father, frustrated because decades of SETI had revealed no messages. It was weird to believe this old man knew something no one else did. But something had happened to Sam Ferenzi in space, and though he looked a hundred years old, she knew from the biography she'd read he couldn't be much older than sixty.

"There must be hundreds of scientists who'd like to know!"

"Tried it. Many times. Got sent to a psych ward."

"But why *me?*"

"Because you're a musician, and the young aren't so prejudiced against new ideas," he said. "And I don't have much time left."

She gave up worrying about what she was doing or the consequences. What was the use? There was no question Daddy would find out. She risked taking her eyes off the crowded interstate to glance at her passenger.

"Just trying to figure out the best way to tell it," he said.

"Starting at the beginning's good."

"I was born. I grew up. I went into space." He closed his eyes.

"You are really the most annoying—"

"Don't be so impatient." He opened his eyes and peered out the window to see where they were. "NASA planned the mission to the asteroid when there was no budget for Mars. Doesn't matter which asteroid. You wouldn't know anyway. We hadn't paid much attention to it, but it was in a near-Earth orbit. So we took the opportunity and went. Routine mission so far."

He paused, and Maddie prompted, "And you walked on it."

"Euphemism. You couldn't properly walk anywhere on it. It was too small and had no gravity. It was like standing on the surface of a giant stone potato. I had a tether to the excursion module—I wasn't going anywhere."

Maddie listened without interrupting as he described space from the vantage point of a small asteroid. In her imagination she saw the deep, cold blackness studded with unwavering stars, the regular flare of the sun as the asteroid rolled in its orbit. Earth was a small, bright dot in the distance.

"Weren't you afraid?"

He turned his scrawny neck and stared at her. "The astronaut who's never afraid is a liar or a liability. The one who lets his fear rule is a disaster."

"Tell me about seeing the aliens."

"*National World Enquirer* said that. Not me."

He took a moment, then continued. "I'd been on the asteroid for almost the full time for EVA, and the shuttle's commander radioed to remind me. Then a sudden burst of light blinded me—and a strong carrier wave knocked out my headset."

He fell silent again.

"Go on," she prompted. "What was it like?"

"The worst pain you can imagine. Like being a T-bone steak plopped onto the hot grill and not being able to get off. Like all your skin is scorched and peeling. Like being knocked out by a high-voltage wire. Like having your eyelids ripped off and being forced to watch a nuclear explosion. Like going blind and stark raving mad at the same time."

That explained his blotchy skin, she thought: radiation burns. The long outburst seemed to have tired him again. He rested his head on the seat-back and went to sleep.

At least, she hoped he was only sleeping.

The sun was setting as they entered the outskirts of Palm Springs, a fuzzy red beach ball sinking into hazy waves of low-lying smog. Maddie was tired from driving in heavy traffic. Sam had slept most of the way. Now he woke and struggled upright.

"You want to eat something?" she asked as they passed a coffee shop.

"No. Go on through the city."

"How much farther are we going?" The Tesla was new enough to have an efficient fuel cell system, but there was still a limit on how far it could go without a recharge. Since she'd never had the chance to drive it this far, she had no idea what that limit was. The battery's indicator bars remained in the safe zone, but for how much longer?

"Just outside the city, you're going to make a left."

And then what? She kept the thought to herself because he obviously wouldn't answer anyway. She gazed at the people strolling from boutiques where golden light spilled out onto the sidewalk to restaurants whose banners pronounced them award-winning. Maddie retracted her window and the car filled with the aroma of barbecue and garlic and the faint sounds of music. Her stomach rumbled.

"Oblivious," Sam said. "All of them. It's going right through them and they're oblivious!"

"What?"

"You too. And me. And worst of all, NASA and SETI. Turn left at the next light."

The lights and sounds of Palm Springs fell away as they took the narrow dirt road across the desert floor rising slowly toward the nearby hills. The sky was filled with misty rose and lavender light, and the tops of the Little San Bernardinos looked as if they'd been draped in glowing chiffon.

"Pull off here."

Tiredness flooded through her. This was without question the stupidest thing she'd done in her life. Sam scrambled out of the car without help, yanking the duffel bag behind him. In the twilight, he looked spidery and strange, like an alien himself. She yawned and reached to turn off the engine.

"Leave it running," he said. "I need a power supply."

He rummaged through the bag, pulling objects out and setting them down on the sand. She got out of the car.

"Here." He handed her a pair of field glasses. "You might as well look at the stars while I'm getting set up."

She took the glasses out of their case. She could see Venus in the west already, and other pinpricks of light were beginning to show against the rapidly darkening sky. Her father had taught her to recognize the major constellations and nebula clusters and most of the minor ones too.

"Easier at night," Sam said.

"What is?"

"Listening."

Did he mean the kind of signals SETI was listening for? That would be dumb, she thought; the stars were there even when we didn't see them. "What difference does darkness make to messages coming from way across the universe?"

"I meant for us!" he said testily. "Fewer distractions."

Arms folded tightly across her chest, Maddie stepped

away from the car. The sky glittered overhead but she'd lost interest. The desert night was already much cooler than the day and if they stayed here too long she'd regret not bringing a jacket. Somewhere in the hills, a coyote yipped. A large bird flew past her on silent wings.

"Look," he said suddenly.

On a flat-topped boulder he'd set up the contents of the duffel bag. She saw a small oscilloscope with the regular undulation of a carrier wave passing over its screen. Beside it was something that looked like a really old cell phone, bulky, with an antenna poking out; cables ran between them and a metal box, also small. He was really nuts if he thought that contraption was going to capture alien signals. Daddy had taken the family on a vacation trip to see the Allen Array in Northern California; it looked nothing like that.

"You forgot to bring a dish!" Her voice added its own snaking wave to the screen.

The coyote gave a full-throated howl this time and was joined by another. The lines on the oscilloscope jumped into peaks and valleys. He bent over the rig he'd assembled, cocking his ear and turning dials. The night air filled with the eerie whale song he'd played for her in the car. An owl hooted. The screen became a jumble of snaking lines.

"I don't get it."

"You need a symphony. At least—" He hesitated as if trying to find the words to explain a difficult concept to a kindergartner. "You need to learn how to *listen* to a symphony. Too bad you didn't bring your flute."

She jumped as if he'd poked her. "I think I might have—it's still in my shoulder bag."

He nodded. "Get it."

No point in arguing with him. She found her flute in

the car and put it to her lips. The instrument added its own line to the undulating patterns of the oscilloscope.

"A symphony not made up of our instruments," he said.

In the dark, his eyes glittered like the stars. She glanced up. Somewhere, in all that magnificent light show, there were other intelligent beings. She believed that, even though scientists like her father had spent more than seven decades trying to capture a message from just one, and failing absolutely. But what Sam was trying to do wasn't science.

"You saying that *whales* could help SETI listen for alien signals?"

"Don't be stupid!" the old man scolded. "Sentient creatures that've been on this planet maybe longer than we have. What might they know? Trees too. Thousand-year-old sequoias—centuries to process the hormonal messages in their cells! And creosote bushes—there's a budding hive mind for you! Ravens and crows. Even coyotes. We don't have the first idea how to listen to the intelligence on our own planet, yet we think we'd recognize an alien message if it hit us!"

A light breeze came up, carrying the scent of wild sage. She shivered. Fine sand particles coated her face.

"We're never going to get the message until we understand that the voice of the universe is a symphony," Sam said. He turned away from her and stared up at the brilliant tapestry of the desert sky. "Doesn't mean the message isn't there. But right now we're searching for the flute part all by itself."

"My father says—"

"We have to learn how to get more out of the carrier wave. Background radiation of the universe. Whatever scientists want to call it."

Mad, she thought. Totally mad. "Well, I'm not a scientist, so why me?"

"No!" he shouted at her. "I can't read it yet—nobody can! But *somebody* has to understand what the problem is, or we'll never even work on it!"

She gazed at the oscilloscope again. The coyotes were singing, a whole pack by the sound of it. The owl hooted from the arms of a nearby cottonwood. The oscilloscope was alive with their combined voices. She didn't know enough to say Sam was wrong, but she knew stranger things had turned out to be true.

"They're out there," he said quietly. "But I've run out of time to find a better apprentice."

Glancing at him in surprise, she saw he was bent over his weird contraption again. She lifted her face to the stars and was immediately bombarded by a huge cold light that overwhelmed her optical nerves. She shrieked.

Sam chuckled. "Just the full moon rising."

She was trembling uncontrollably. "We have to get back."

"I'm done, anyway," he said. "You were just my last chance."

He started packing his things back into the duffel bag, slowly as if the effort exhausted him. She got into the driver's seat. Fine volunteer she was, she thought; she didn't even offer to help him into the car. All she could think of was starting the heater. She heard the old man stumble into the passenger seat and close the car door, sighing with pain, or sadness perhaps. She listened for the familiar click of the seat web locking into place. Then she thought of something.

"It was the messages that hit you, wasn't it, on that asteroid? Even though you couldn't understand them, they were there?"

He didn't reply.

Yawning, she touched the heater's sensor. Nothing happened. She glanced at the battery gauge.

Zero bars.

"Umm, Sam? I think we're stuck."

He seemed to have gone to sleep already.

Well, what difference did it make? she thought. She was already in trouble for driving out here. But it was cold in the car without the heater and she started to worry. How low did the night temperature drop in August? She looked over at the skinny old man, slumped in his seat. Too cold for him, in any case.

Wasn't there an old ratty blanket in the Tesla's trunk? She'd thrown it in there after Junior Class Day at the beach and didn't remember taking it out again. She got out of the car and raised the trunk lid. Yes. She shook sand out of it, smelling the faint trace of ocean as she did so. Maybe there'd been whales passing by, far out in the water, that day she'd played volleyball with her friends. Whales making up songs that humans didn't understand.

An awful lot that humans didn't understand!

She draped the gritty blanket around the old man's shoulders, and he muttered in his sleep. No way she was going to get any sleep. It was going to be a long night till someone came to rescue them. The coyotes were still singing; she could hear them—nearer now—even with the windows closed. Weird to think of the noises animals made as music, but then maybe they thought the sounds humans made were weird too.

And maybe Sam was right and the universe was streaming with messages we didn't know how to listen to just yet.

On impulse, she reached into the back seat and retrieved her flute. She cracked the window, letting the coyotes' song enter, and put the flute to her lips to join them.

She heard Sam sigh, and glanced over at him. He seemed to be smiling in his sleep.

The sheriffs her father summoned found her at dawn by tracking the Tesla's GPS. She woke to the sound of a helicopter's rotors beating the desert air. She was cold, hungry, otherwise unharmed.

Sam Ferenzi wasn't so lucky. Or maybe that's what he'd wanted from the start, she thought, as the sheriff's paramedics loaded her into the chopper for the flight home. Dying like a shriveled up insect in a hospice bed after you've been into space and experienced the tsunami of alien communication, even if you can't understand a word of it and nobody believes you: she could understand how he might've felt. Going in his sleep was a mercy.

She watched the medics carrying Sam's body, reverently. He'd found the clue to a puzzle her father would give anything to solve.

"What were you doing out there?" one of the paramedics asked.

"Just stargazing," she said. It was only a half lie.

The paramedic handed her a juice box as the chopper lifted off the desert floor. The sun flooded in through the east-facing port. A star, only one among billions in the known universe. A symphony of star voices that someday somebody was going to learn how to hear. Somebody who loved both the stars and music.

She drifted off to sleep, thinking of what that might mean for her future.

Graffiti in the Library of Babel

David Langford

"There seems to be no difference at all between the message of maximum content (or maximum ambiguity) and the message of zero content (noise)."
—John Sladek, "The Communicants"

As it turned out, they had no sense of drama. They failed to descend in shiny flying discs, or even to fill some little-used frequency with a tantalizing stutter of sequenced primes. No: they came with spray cans and felt-tips, scrawling their grubby little tags across our heritage.

Or as an apologetic TotLib intern first broke the news: "Sir, someone's done something nasty all over Jane Austen."

The Total Library project is named in homage to Kurd Lasswitz's thought experiment "Die Universal Bibliothek," which inspired a famous story by Jorge Luis Borges. Another influence is the "World Brain" concept proposed by H. G. Wells. Assembling the totality of world literature and knowledge should allow a rich degree of cross-referencing and interdisciplinary . . .

Ceri Evans looked up from the brochure. Even in this white office that smelled of top management, she could never resist a straight line: "Why, congratulations, Professor. I think you may have invented the Internet!"

"Doctor, not Professor, and I do not use the title," said Ngombi with well-simulated patience. "Call me Joseph. The essential point of TotLib is that we are *isolated* from the net. No trolls, no hackers, none of what that Manson book called sleazo inputs. Controlled rather than chaotic cross-referencing."

"But still you seem to have these taggers?"

"Congratulations, Doctor Evans! I think you may have just deduced the contents of my original email to you."

"All right. All square." Ceri held up one thin hand in mock surrender. "We'll leave the posh titles for the medics. Now tell me: why is this a problem in what I do, which is a far-out region of information theory, rather than plain data security?"

"Believe me, data security we know about. Hackers and student pranksters have been rather exhaustively ruled out. As it has been said, 'Once you eliminate the impossible, whatever remains, no matter how improbable, must be the truth.'"

"'Holmes, this is marvelous,'" said Ceri dutifully.

"'Meretricious,' said he." Joseph grinned. "We are a literary team here."

Ceri felt a sudden contrarian urge not to be literary. "Maybe we should cut to the chase. There's only one logical reason to call me in. You suspect the Library is under attack through the kind of acausal channel I've discussed in my more speculative papers? A concept, I should remind you, that got me an IgNobel Prize and a long denunciation in *The Skeptic* because everyone knows it's utter lunacy. Every Einstein-worshipping physicist, at least."

A shrug. "'Once you eliminate the impossible . . .' And I'm not a physicist. Come and see." He was so very large and very black. Ceri found herself wondering whether his white-on-white decor was deliberate contrast.

The taggers had spattered their marks across the digital texts of TotLib: short bursts of characters that made no particular sense but clearly belonged to the same family, like some ideogram repeated with slight variations along the shopping mall, through the car park and across the sides of subway carriages. Along Jane Austen, through Shakespeare and underground to deface Jack Kerouac and the Beats. After half an hour of onscreen examples Ceri felt the familiar eye glaze of overdosing on conceptual art.

"The tags," she said cautiously, *"never* appear within words?" This is a test. Do not be afraid of the obvious.

"We decided all by ourselves to call them tags." The faint smile indicated that Joseph was still in a mood for point-scoring.

"Okay. I see." She didn't, but in a moment it came. "Not just graffiti but mark-up, like HTML or XML tags. Emphasis marks. You think they're not so much defacing the texts as going through them with a highlighter. Boldface on, It is a truth universally acknowledged, boldface off."

"Congratulations! It took our people several days to reach that point."

Ceri drummed her fingers irritably against the TotLib workstation. "The point seems to be that it's already been reached. So why me?"

"I saw a need for someone who can deal with the implications. If this tagging is coming in through your acausal channels—and we truly cannot trace any conventional route—and if that *New Scientist* piece on you was not too impossibly dumbed down . . ."

"Oh God. It was, but never mind."

" . . . the origin of the transmission would necessarily be something in the close vicinity of a supermassive black hole?"

"Well. That assumes the channel source is in our universe in the first place. The IgNobel presenter was very funny about Dimension X and the Phantom Zone." Another memory that clung and stuck, a mental itch she couldn't stop scratching.

"So many times it has been said, 'They laughed at Galileo.' "

"And sometimes it's also been said that they laughed at nitrous oxide."

Again Joseph smiled hugely. "Would you care for lunch?"

"Let me have another look first. Let me plod my slow way to some other plateau your staff reached last week. Boldface on, instruments of darkness, boldface off. Did that make you think of my black hole? Masters of the universe. God's quarantine regulations. These things need to be grouped or sequenced—no, both."

The TotLib interface was easy enough to use. Ceri backtracked, paused, went forward again through lexical chaos. "The structure of those tags . . . there's a flavor of inversion symmetry . . . suppose ON has a group identifier wrapped around a sequence number and OFF is sequence around group? Or the other way around, of course. That would sort your grab bag of quotes into chunks and give the chunks an internal order. Oh bugger, I'm biting my nails again. Sorry. Have we caught up with your clever staff yet?" She hadn't meant to get hooked on the dizzy rush of problem-solving. But, she thought, be glad it still comes.

The big man seemed perceptibly less smug. "My clever staff will catch up with you . . . maybe next week.

Ceri—if I may—I am impressed. It is most definitely time for lunch."

The meal was inoffensive and the wine better, if only by about ten per cent, than you'd expect from an institution in a secure vault under a dour Swiss alp. As her host explained: "The Scientologists are working to preserve their founder's teachings for all eternity, and our sponsors feel there should be an alternative view."

At first Ceri had felt obscurely prickly about Dr. Joseph Ngombi, and she tried now to be a little friendlier: mustn't let him think a good Welsh girl like herself had a streak of racism. Part of her mind was elsewhere, though (structured tags, that kaleidoscope of quoted fragments), and her vague attempts at friendly signals led to some carefully placed mentions of his dear wife and children. Earlier that day she'd thought she was looking good, with a new dark-red hair rinse; now she wondered whether Joseph saw her as a dyed and predatory hag. What were the chances of making sense of graffiti from some distant supermassive black hole when communications went astray across the width of a restaurant table?

"No, thanks," she said, protecting her wineglass from the waiter's menacing pass. "I'll need a clear head." Or maybe just an empty one. The trouble with an open mind, the saying went, is that people come along and put things in it.

Ceri liked the idea of TotLib staff handling the boring rote-work, but didn't want to get too far away from that tagged text. Layers of abstraction are great in software but tend to blur the focus of real-world problems. They compromised on a multi-view workstation: defaced ebooks here, grouped and sequenced tags there, and the clear light of understanding in the window that for a long time stayed dismally blank.

Clearing away the relentless tag repetition through multiple editions, critical cites and anthologies of quotations, there were just 125 tagged phrases in all. "Five to the third power," Ceri muttered. "The science fiction writers would say straight away that our friends must count to base five, meaning they have five limbs or five tentacles or . . ." She stared moodily at the significant number of jointed manipulators on her left hand. "Or not."

Joseph spread out a hand that proved to be missing one finger. "Just an old accident, but I would seem to be ruled out. Perhaps, though, that is merely my cunning."

The first of the eleven sequences, or maybe the last ("Has it never occurred to you that the ancient Romans *counted backwards?*" Ceri quoted), ran a gamut of fuzzily resonating phrases from "It is a truth universally acknowledged" through Hazlitt's "How often have I put off writing a letter" to E. M. Forster's "Only connect . . ."

"Translation: it would be sort of dimly nice to maybe talk in some kind of indistinct fashion, probably." Ceri glared at the screen. "Right, I'm going to lecture now. To be that vague and at the same time stick to a theme, the taggers must *understand* English. Not just literal meaning but metaphors and nuances and stuff. Otherwise 'No man is an island' wouldn't be in there."

"So they could choose to communicate in clear?" suggested Joseph.

"That's it. They could spell out an absolutely unambiguous message, one word or one letter at a time. I can't imagine a good reason for doing it this way, but I have a suspicious enough mind to think of a bad one. The taggers know all about us but they don't want to let slip a single data point concerning themselves. So they feed our own phrases back to us. We aren't to be allowed the tiniest clue to their thinking from style or diction or word order. Does that seem sinister to you?"

Joseph sighed. "It was so much easier when aliens said 'Take me to your leader.'"

"Or 'Klaatu barada nikto.' Don't let me distract myself. Here's the 'instruments of darkness' cluster, with the *Tao Te Ching* quotes, Zen koans and that mystic cobblers from *Four Quartets* that would cost them a packet in permission fees if the Eliot estate got wind of it. The general flavor of all this seems to be that they're using an acausal comms route that bypasses the Usual Channels. 'The way that can be spoken of / Is not the constant way.' Which would be most interesting to know if it hadn't been the assumption we started with."

An intern came in with plastic cups of coffee, which made for a few seconds' natural break. Ceri burnt a finger and swore under her breath in Welsh.

"Gesundheit. What about those quarantine regulations?"

"I think that's the most interesting one," Ceri said cautiously. "C. S. Lewis and 'God's quarantine regulations'—the old boy was talking about interplanetary or interstellar distances saving pure races from contamination by horrible fallen us. Then there's a handful of guarded borders and dangerous frontiers from early Auden. 'The empyrean is a void abyss': that's *The City of Dreadful Night,* I actually read it once. Lucretius on breaking through 'the fiery walls of the world' to explore the boundless universe. There's a pun in there, I'm sure. Firewalls. Something blocks or prevents communication across deep space. Who? 'Masters of the universe.' Maybe for our own good, but who knows? In a nutshell: SETI was a waste of time. Don't let the coffee get cold."

Joseph sipped. "That seems something of a stretch."

"Well, right now I'm just talking, not publishing. And while I'm still just talking, I wonder whether we can try to talk back."

"Presumably you keep one of those acausal widgets in your handbag? Next to the black hole, no doubt."

"Of course not. Much simpler. The taggers are in tune with a particular medium—the Total Library—and they're messaging us by modulating it. We can modulate too, without any help from astounding super-science."

She hadn't seen Joseph wince before. For an instant his face was terrifying. "Ask a librarian to deface his own collection? You will be suggesting I ignore the SI-LENCE signs next."

"Just turn a blind eye and leave it to my criminal mind. When I was a girl in the valleys I worked out eight ways to nick books from the public library." And never did, and lay awake all night with a guilty conscience the one time she'd accidentally lost one, but let's not go there just now.

"While I am still in shock, whatever do you plan to say? That it is indeed vaguely nice to share a warm fuzzy lack of communication?"

"I rather thought of asking them for goodies. We haven't talked yet about the taggers' gift-exchange thread. *As You Like It:* gifts may henceforth be bestowed equally, and half a dozen more in that general ballpark. They can't be asking. They're already the Entities Who Have Everything—they've nicked all our books from the public library. Our architecture and our playing cards, our mythological terrors, our algebra and fire . . ." She waited half a beat.

"Borges. When you talk to a librarian about how he should turn a blind eye, Borges has to be in the offing."

"I never could resist a good digression, boyo. Sum-mary: all we can exchange with the taggers is information. They're waffling about gifts. There's no further information we can give them. So they must be offering something to us in exchange."

"Mmmm. A proof of Fermat's Last Theorem would be traditional, but that one is now far past its sell-by date. I suppose the mathematicians would like to know about the other thing, what is it? The Riemann hypothesis."

"Oh, *diawl*. Dry as dust. And how'd we express that horror as a set of artful quotations? What *I* thought of asking for was a global warming fix—some kind of clean power source with no greenhouse emissions. Cheap fusion. Zero-point energy. I don't believe what I've read about either, but maybe it's like that physicist's lucky horseshoe: it works even if you don't believe in it. And where's the harm in trying?"

"I admit to curiosity. Especially about how you plan to put across concepts like zero-point energy."

More coffee came, and then more still, while Ceri wrestled with search engines and the dictionary of quotations. "'Expecting something for nothing is the most popular form of hope.' Who's Arnold Glasgow? Anyway, he said it. And I must insist on having a line from the sainted sot of Swansea: 'Rage, rage against the dying of the light.' Then there's Blake, of course, with 'Energy is eternal delight!' "

The eventual result, they both agreed, was a monstrous hodgepodge and thus perfectly in keeping with the taggers' own approach. A pained but not quite protesting IT intern called Chaz rattled off a script that would spraygun the Total Library with Ceri's message. Joseph made a particular point of being absent in the director's toilet at the time of the fateful mouse-click. Despite all the TotLib apparatus of backups and recovery points, the instincts of a librarian died hard.

* * *

An hour passed. At the terminal, the now deeply bored Chaz ran his hundredth data scan. Anticlimax had settled on the white room like the leaden aftermath of a drinking binge. It had been a thinking binge, Ceri told herself blearily, but sometimes the hangover seemed much the same.

"You will be wishing to rest in your hotel," Joseph suggested.

"I suppose so. We don't even know whether the taggers operate on our timescale. They might live and think many times faster or slower. We don't know how long it takes them to prepare their tag payload. We don't know whether I did it right . . ." A general sense of running down. Sleep would be good.

"Sir," said Chaz, "something happened again. Mostly in the physics texts. Hundreds of new tags."

Ceri licked her lips. "Physics." Excitement seemed possible once more.

"Please, please do not expect miracles," Joseph said repressively. "Remember that their peculiar mode of conversation doesn't permit them to tell us anything we don't already know."

"But looking in the right order at chunks of what we know could so easily reveal something we don't. We may just need the hint. It's happened so many times in the history of science."

The internal numbering of the latest tags confirmed that their makers didn't count backwards and that the sequence containing "It is a truth universally acknowledged" was #1.

Just one quote-cluster from the new batch steered clear of the physics department. "That has to be the descriptor, the label on the tin. Let's see. From a Shakespeare sonnet, 'no such matter.' *They Do It with*

Mirrors—that's an Agatha Christie title. *Macbeth* and 'where men may read strange matters.' Another title: *Prometheus Unbound*. 'Turning and turning in the widening gyre.' " Ceri scanned onward. "Joseph, I have a bad feeling about this."

"Strange matter? All I know of it is the name."

"No, I think it's antimatter. Mirror matter. The perfect nuclear fuel with one hundred per cent conversion efficiency."

"In fact, something we already knew. We make the stuff, do we not, at CERN and places of that kind?"

Ceri shook her head. "That's tiny, tiny amounts. The production rate is, oh, billions of years per gram. What I'm terribly afraid we've been given, what a physicist will see when she puts those textbooks and papers together, is some space-rotation trick that flips matter into antimatter. Unlimited quantities." She called up figures. "Here. Total energy release of forty-something megatons when a single kilo meets normal matter and annihilates. No fiddly fission triggers, no critical mass to assemble: it just *does* it. You wouldn't need a huge amount to burn the whole biosphere clean."

"Ah. I don't suppose our friends' interesting cascade of phrases on the theme of gifts included any mention of Greeks?"

"Not even Danes," said Ceri at random. "Quote search, quote search, and here it is. *Timeo Danaos et dona ferentes*. I know it's Greeks really, but I always used to read it as 'beware of Danes bearing gifts.' "

"That," said Joseph solemnly, "was known as the Danelaw."

Ceri giggled, although it was a noise she didn't like making. She'd been talking too fast and nervously, maybe faster than the speed of logic. Good to have the brakes applied. "Thank you," she said.

"So. They like to gift others with dangerous toys. Perhaps out of malice—the afrit who smilingly grants your wish, knowing that it will destroy you. Perhaps only in a spirit of healthy experiment to see what we will do. By the way, what will we do?"

"I suppose we have a sort of duty . . ." Out of the corner of her eye Ceri saw her notes window change. She hadn't touched the keyboard or mouse. Just before the flatscreen went black and flickered into a reboot sequence, she saw the colored tags where no tags had been before. In her own notes. Surrounding the copied words "quarantine regulations."

Chaz wandered in and helpfully announced that the invulnerable TotLib systems were having their first ever unscheduled downtime.

When the Library came back up, it wasn't only Ceri's transcripts that had vanished in a puff of electrons. To Joseph's loudly expressed relief there had been a general clean-up, a thorough scrubbing of the library's defaced stacks from Jane Austen through to Zola. No tags anywhere.

"*Iesu Grist*. Call me a superstitious peasant if you like," Ceri murmured, "but I think the Masters of the Universe just stepped in."

Over a late supper in the Gasthof Schmidt, Ceri and Joseph managed to work themselves partway down from unnerving conceptual heights. A bottle of Riesling helped, and soon after the second arrived Joseph bashfully admitted that his wife and children were mythical. "The truth is that I often find myself curiously scared of attractive women." Communications were always a bugger, but sometimes contact could be made even across those fearful spaces. They celebrated with a brief though intense fling in the few days before duty called and Ceri boarded a Eurostar train for the first leg home to Oxford, the solitary flat, and her incommunicable researches at the Mathematical Institute.

Half a year later, in place of his regular reassurance that the Library stayed graffiti-free, Joseph sent an email whose header read: "What goes around, comes around." From the included links, Ceri gathered that the Human Genome Project was in a tizzy. What was thought to be an unidentified retrovirus had been tampering with the introns, the huge dead-code segments of our genome that seem to do nothing at all. The paired intrusions, suitably translated from the genetic alphabet, had an all too familiar structure. No one, as yet, had christened them "tags."

Ceri thought: *So they found another channel and something else to modulate. Too much to hope that it might be another and nicer Then. And does anyone get more than one deus-ex bailout?* Staring at her own thin hand again, this time with deep distaste: *tags. In there, tags.* She wondered what question the biochemists would want to ask, how they might contrive to encode it, and what the afrit's poisoned answer would be.

The Dark Man

Kristine Kathryn Rusch

Condi stepped out of the internet café, an ice-cold bottle of Coke in her hand. The street was dark except for the light spewing out of the café's door. Motorcycles were parked to her left, squeezed between smart cars that had slid bumper-first into slots too small for a regular car.

In America, this would be called an alley, if someone deigned to designate it at all. Crooked, covered with uneven cobblestones, winding uphill between darkened and graffiti-covered buildings, the street felt more like a path between main roads.

The internet café didn't help. It was the only business still open at 11 o'clock at night, still open and still doing business. The hotel across the way locked its doors promptly at nine, something she thought unfair in Rome, which like most Mediterranean cities remained awake and active long past midnight.

Fortunately, Condi was staying in a slightly more upscale place on the Via Purificazione, another alley-like side street in a slightly more desirable neighborhood near the Via Veneto. She wasn't there for the shopping;

she wanted to be as close to the American Embassy as possible without paying Westin Excelsior prices.

Not that money was an object. The Organization of Strange Phenomena Ancient and Modern was paying for everything, including the tiny, expensive bottle of Coke resting damply in her right hand. She had an unlimited expense account, and a salary fifty times higher than her going rate as one of the *Rocky Mountain News*'s best reporters— back when there had been a *Rocky Mountain News*.

Condi glanced over her shoulder. Inside the café, which wasn't really a café at all—just three narrow rooms of computers and two vending machines—the waif who ran the place was surreptitiously checking the information Condi had left on her computer screen.

The waif, with her big brown eyes, round cheeks, black-black hair, looked like a cute Italian kid straight out of *La Dolce Vita*, or at least she did until you factored in the piercings, the tattoos, and the leather bustier, which seemed just too hot to wear in this strange 100-degree Roman autumn. Condi had already clocked out, leaving the screen on a UFO social networking site filled with wackos.

The waif always captured that last screen, missing the important stuff—or so Condi hoped. She tried to check her e-mail several times per day on her iPhone, but the AT&T connection in Rome was spotty at best—hell, all wireless connections were spotty here—and she was afraid she lost a lot of information.

She waited until the waif stopped checking the screen capture. Then Condi sighed and stepped onto the cobblestone street, heading up hill to the Via Sistina. Ahead, she could hear music and laughter. Behind her, she heard the whisper of shoes against cobblestones.

She didn't have to turn around to know he was following her again.

*   *   *

She didn't know his name or even what he wanted, but she did know what he looked like. Black hair, high cheekbones, traditional Roman features, all assembled into a classically handsome face, one that could've been stamped on a coin a thousand years before, although he was taller than the average Roman and had broader shoulders.

He'd shown up on her first morning in Rome, sitting behind one of the flower vendors on the Spanish Steps, and he'd been around ever since. He had watched her with an avid interest that would have unnerved her anywhere else.

But this was Italy, and Italian men were famously forward. In her first week here, she'd had her butt pinched several times. She'd had her breasts brushed—*oh, scusi, signora*—and one man had caught her in a wild 1940s V-E Day-style kiss.

She had shoved him away, threatening in her excellent Italian to cut off his privates, cook them in olive oil, and serve them to the pigs. That had gotten her applause and a bit of distance. The vendors nearby, and there were dozens, called her the Untouchable American, and had even started to consider her as something other than a tourist.

She knew better than to expect to be treated like an Italian. It handicapped her, but she had accepted that when she accepted the assignment, silently cursing the location of the phenomenon.

Anywhere but Rome, famous for its hatred of tourists, with its centuries-old secrets and its thousand-year-long lies.

That she had picked up one tail didn't surprise her.

That she had picked up only one did.

*   *   *

Tavernas and (weirdly) gelato shops were open on the Via Sistina, sandwiched between shuttered clothing stores and restaurants. From the top of one of Rome's famed Seven Hills, light flowed down, bringing with it the music and laughter she had heard on the side street.

The walk up the hill was steep, the sidewalk narrow. The walk at night was best—fewer pedestrians, fewer limousines—but had its own treacheries. She had learned, in her six weeks in Rome, to beware large groups. Usually they included their fair share of pickpockets and thieves. Most locals looked the other way, figuring tourists got what they deserved.

The man behind her didn't want to attack her. If he did, he would have done so weeks ago. He wanted to observe her, for reasons she didn't want to think about.

She wished he wasn't here tonight. Tonight was crucial to help her plan for tomorrow morning, and she didn't want him to know what she was about.

The lights got brighter around the Intercontinental Hotel near the top of the hill. Two limousines were parked near the doorway, two doormen talking to the drivers as if they were all waiting for some VIPs to show up and show them around.

Just above them, on the Piazza Trinità dei Monti, sat the largest vendor cart Condi had seen in Rome. The cart was really a miniature market which sold everything from Gatorade to a cheap *panino* with the meat cooked right on the spot. The smell of grilled lamb filtered down to her now, and she wondered how the most expensive restaurant in the area—on the roof of the Hassler Hotel—liked the competition.

She stopped at the top of the hill, the city sprawled out before her. In the daylight, she could make out St. Paul's Cathedral and all the other landmarks. At night, they faded into a series of domed lights at the top of the other hills, with less-defined lights leading up to them.

The artists had folded up their carts and the professional beggars were gone. One of the nearby restaurants had illegally moved its tables onto the Piazza so that the patrons could enjoy the warm night. A string quartet played Vivaldi.

The Steps themselves were well lit, the flowers in the pots alongside looking festive in the bright lights.

Below, she could see the Barcaccia Fountain, and the crowd around it, drunk and partying. The restaurants on the Piazza di Spagna were open late, catering to the tourists.

She ignored them. They would be gone in a few days, replaced by other tourists, also bent on drinking their way through the hot Italian nights.

She was more interested in the Steps themselves.

Built between 1723 and 1725 by Francesco de Sanctis, the Steps took their name from the Spanish Embassy, which had moved there in the nineteenth century and had since moved on. Locals sneered on the area because it had long been home to the expatriate English community in Rome, a community that had once included John Keats and several other famous British literary figures.

Condi had learned all she could about the Steps—how long they had been there, how they were actually paid for by the French who once owned the church at the hill's top, the Church of Trinità dei Monti, which, so far as she could tell, was always closed.

She had walked up and down the travertine steps several times a day, always looking at one landing in particular, a place where none of the professional beggars ever set up shop, where tourists who normally sat down from exhaustion somehow never reclined despite a bit of shade.

She had several hundred photographs of that spot, some taken by tourists as far back as the 1920s, and some by professional photographers that were even older, going back to the invention of the box camera in the mid-nineteenth century.

Some photos were fascinating, some were not. Some were of the steps, glistening in the rain or gleaming in the sunshine, and some were of a dark form sprawled along them, looking like the black painted shadow of a body burned into the stone.

It had taken her months to figure out when the body appeared and when it disappeared. That had been part of her assignment—a crazy assignment that had come two days after the last paper she'd applied to reminded her that hundreds of reporters (even those with multiple investigative reporting awards) were out of work.

She had no idea how many of her unemployed colleagues had turned down work with the Organization of Strange Phenomena Ancient and Modern. Some days she liked to think she was the only reporter they had approached. Other days she wondered if she was the only reporter they had approached who had decided to check her integrity at the door.

Not that she had checked it entirely. She had told the Organization that she'd investigate any phenomenon they sent her to, but if she discovered a hoax—*and frankly,* she had said, *I think they're all going to be hoaxes*—she would let them know. She wouldn't sugar-coat anything, she wouldn't lie about anything, and she wouldn't spin facts just to support some conclusion they were paying her hundreds of thousands to confirm.

In her first six months with the Organization, she'd disproven a dozen so-called unexplainable occurrences. The one thing she'd learned as a reporter was that nothing was unexplainable. She just had to dig until she found the explanation, one that satisfied both her and her bosses.

Although standing at the edge of the Piazza Trinità dei Monti on the top of the Spanish Steps, she had a moment of doubt that she would ever find an explanation for the black form.

It was the first case that fascinated her. Reports of the form's appearance started in the months before John Keats died in the building right next to the Steps. Supposedly, Keats—ill with the consumption that would eventually kill him—looked out the house's window and saw the black figure appear.

It is an omen, he told his companion Joseph Severn. *I have seen Death. It awaits me, there, on those Steps.*

Severn saw the figure as well, and thought it a cruel hoax, a drawing made by someone who wanted to frighten the superstitious English. Hours later, he reported in his journal, the figure was gone, destroyed by one of the many wintry downpours that helped demolish what remained of Keats's health.

From that moment on, sightings of the black figure showed up in the literature and not always from English expatriates. Sometimes, the sightings showed up in the Italian press. Sometimes in travel journals of the very wealthy who had made Rome part of their continental tour.

Several artists—professionals as well as amateurs— added the figure into their paintings of the Steps. Sometimes the figure was part of a dark and sinister portrait, and sometimes it was the only black spot in the middle of a perfectly painted sunny day, complete with azaleas and beautiful women.

Even in the paintings, though, the figure was in the same position, sprawled along the steps, looking like nothing more than the shade of a dead man trapped for a moment in bright sunshine.

She had pored over all of the evidence—and thanks to the internet, there was a lot of it. She had found nearly two hundred years of paintings and photographs, amateur and professional, thousands of pages of diary and journal entries, plus every single mention in books about strange phenomenon published in every single language she could read.

She combined all of her data, and learned that the figure appeared with startling regularity. The average paranormal investigator never noticed because the appearances weren't to the minute. The paranormal investigators found that the figure appeared roughly every ten years within a particular time frame, but none of them had taken the time (or maybe had lacked the ability) to do the math.

The figure appeared ten years, fifteen days, and thirty hours from the previous appearance. It remained visible for thirty minutes. Nothing seemed to change this pattern. In previous sightings, people had grabbed it (*it felt like touching pitch,* one traveler had written), shaken it, tried to pick it up (*it didn't budge, as if it were attached to the very step itself,* wrote another traveler), and had poked it with various objects, including knives. Some had tried to light it on fire, and that hadn't worked either.

In 1971, the height of what Condi privately called "the crazies," paranormal investigators tried to slice bits off the figure. They had so-called psychics touch it, trying to get a reading, and they touched the figure with all kinds of things from thermometers to Geiger counters. They got nothing, no readings at all—and there should have been some kind of reading, even from a static state. The slices failed as well. The figure's black essence broke the knives. Someone left the scene to get a battery-operated meat cutter, but the figure had disappeared before that someone returned.

Ten years later, no one wanted to carve the figure up. Ten years after that, camera crews assembled to record the phenomenon, and they got as much information as the box cameras had a century before. Which was not much at all.

She had watched the footage of all of this, read all of the reports, and had decided that something did appear on the steps. Whether it was some kind of local/natural phenomenon, she didn't know. She really didn't have much of a plan herself, except that she would use some high-end analysis equipment that hadn't even existed twenty years before. (It had been twenty years since someone analyzed the figure, since the last appearance had occurred five days after 9/11. No one really cared about a spooky black figure in that week. The entire world had been fearfully focused on the United States.)

She had a hunch she wouldn't resolve anything this time either. She would gather enough material for a theory that someone else would have to prove ten years from now. Maybe she'd get a book out of it—one that featured a lot of lovely sketches, paintings, and photographs from the past 190 years. The Organization didn't care what she did with the information from her reports after she blogged about them and answered questions from commenters on the website.

Then the information belonged to her.

She was going to become known for the wacky and strange instead of the in-depth and insightful. That bothered her sometimes. At other times, she was realistic enough to remind herself that at least she would become known. So many of her colleagues had gone onto writing ad copy or teaching at community colleges.

She started down the Steps. They were slightly worn from nearly three centuries of constant use. She stopped just above the landing. The air felt chillier here. It always did, at least to her, and she knew that had nothing to do with the actual air itself, but her own frame of mind.

Just like the little shiver that ran through her the three times she had actually walked across the steps where the figure would eventually appear had nothing to do with the figure, and everything to do with her own irrational fear of what she might find.

"You know when it will appear."

He stopped behind her, too close like Italian men always were. She didn't move away. She didn't worry about him picking her pocket—she only had a few euros on her. Her credit card and identification were tucked into a money belt hidden beneath the waistband of her pants, practically invisible, or so her hotel mirror told her every morning.

She had to tilt her head to see his face. He stood one step above her. The light from below reflected off his skin. He was older than she had thought, with fine lines beneath his eyes and around his mouth. Laugh lines, her mother would have called them.

But he wasn't smiling now.

He was looking down on her like an avenging angel, the Church of Trinità dei Monti shadowing him from behind.

"Are you speaking to me?" she asked in her haughtiest Italian.

"You know that I am," he said. "Just like you know I have been watching you since you first came to the Steps."

She could have denied it, she supposed, although she saw no point. Just like she saw no point in backing away from him. That would only let him know he had power over her, power to startle her, power to unnerve her, power to make her worry for her own safety.

"You are waiting for it," he said, "just like I am."

She realized that anyone else listening to the conversation would hear that last comment as vaguely threatening, maybe even as something with sexual overtones.

But she knew there weren't any sexual overtones—at least, not intentional ones. She wondered briefly if he was one of those men who knew how handsome he was and used that knowledge subconsciously to control the people around him.

She had a hunch he did.

"Who do you work for?" she asked.

His eyes half closed, shielding their expression from her. She felt a surge of adrenaline. He didn't want her to know that piece of information.

"Are you one of those—what do you call it in English? Psychic investigators?" He used the English words for that last part, and he didn't try to hide his contempt.

"I'm not psychic," she said, "but I am hungry. Join me?"

She went around him, climbing back up the steps to the little restaurant on the Piazza. She didn't wait to see if he followed; she knew he would eventually.

She flagged down a waiter, let him seat her at a table near the flowers, and watched as the man crossed the Piazza.

He handed the waiter a credit card, then gestured toward the table. The waiter smiled as if they had shared some kind of secret, then he disappeared into the restaurant itself.

The man sat down across from her. "I have ordered wine and bread. The waiter shall bring menus in a moment."

She knew better than to refuse the wine, even though she really didn't want any. The figure was scheduled to reappear shortly after six AM, and she wanted to be clearheaded.

She had planned on only making a short visit to the Steps this night, hoping to return to her hotel room for a few hours of sleep so that she wouldn't be too drowsy come morning.

The bread arrived quickly, still warm from the oven, smelling divine. The waiter made a fuss of opening the wine, and spent nearly five minutes explaining to her its derivation, not that she cared.

The man studied her. When the waiter left, he leaned back in his chair. "You are not a typical American."

She shrugged. "I don't think there are typical Americans."

"You are not rude," he said.

"Thank you," she said. "I think."

He smiled. His teeth were even and very, very white. He had the look of a retired model, not of a thug. Which made him even more suspect in her opinion.

She sipped her wine. Red, rich, full-bodied, dark with a hint of pepper. She liked it more than she had expected.

"You said you were following me," she said.

"Do not play coy," he said. "You know that I was."

She shrugged again. "I thought you were too shy to say hello."

He laughed. "I am not shy."

"Clearly," she said.

"I was simply trying to be certain if you had a true interest or if you simply enjoyed the Steps themselves."

She hadn't thought of enjoyment. She knew that a lot of tourists did enjoy the Steps, spending hours here, chatting, eating, resting. But she had seen the entire area as something to be discovered, not as something to be enjoyed.

She wondered if her surprise at his comment showed on her face.

"True interest in what?" she asked.

"Now you are being coy," he said.

"I don't like elliptical conversations," she said. "Tell me what you're about."

The waiter chose that moment to bring the menus. She didn't even look at hers, ordering a cheese plate. Her companion didn't order at all, saying the bread would be enough.

After the waiter left, the man extended his hand. "I am Giuseppe."

"Condi," she said, taking his hand to shake it. Instead, he held tightly, then turned her hand upward, kissing the center of her palm.

It was an oddly intimate gesture and it sent an involuntary shiver through her.

"Condi," he said. "Like your secretary of state."

"Former secretary of state," Condi said, "and no, not like that at all. It's a nickname that stuck early that has no real relation to my given name."

Which she wasn't about to tell him. Condi was short for Constance D. Platte, which was, she always contended, a stupid name. Her family called her Connie D., which her friends mercifully shortened to Condi nearly three decades before anyone had heard of Condoleezza Rice.

Condi didn't take her hand back. She let him continue to hold it. She figured as long as he touched her, she had the right to ask him rude questions.

"So tell me, Giuseppe, what I should have a true interest in."

"Tomorrow morning," he said. "Six AM, you will be one of the few people on the Steps. We will all cluster around the same spot, waiting for him to return."

She suppressed a sigh. He suddenly sounded like a religious nutball. "Him?"

"We do not know his name. We call him the Dark Man."

The Dark Man—*L'uomo Scuro*. She liked how that sounded in Italian. It was a much better name than the figure, as she had been calling him.

"We?" she asked.

"Ah." Giuseppe let go of her hand, giving it a tender pat before setting it on the table as if her skin were made of glass. "Not until I know who you are working for."

"I'm a reporter." One of the few conditions she had was that she couldn't reveal the name of the Organization. Her boss told her the reason for that was simple: whenever anyone mentioned the Organization of Strange Phenomena Ancient and Modern, everyone assumed that it had bankrolled the specific result—which, her boss had reminded her, it had not.

"For whom do you report?" he asked.

"I got laid off from a Colorado paper, the *Rocky Mountain News*," she said. "Like so many of my colleagues, I am going to write a book. Unlike most of them, I am not going to write about politics or America or some environmental disaster."

"You're going to write about the Dark Man."

"Why not?" she said. "No one has published a definitive work in English."

"No one has published a definitive work," he said.

She slid her hand back as the waiter set the cheese plate down. It was large, on heavy bone china, with a dozen different cheeses. He set smaller plates in front of her and Giuseppe, then topped off their wine glasses, and flitted away, like a man who assumed people on a date needed privacy.

She took some cheese and some bread, making a small sandwich for herself. She never bothered to learn the names of the European cheeses, but she had come to recognize several, including some tart enough to go with the wine.

Giuseppe took some cheese as well.

"What's your interest?" she asked.

"I protect him," Giuseppe said simply.

"Against what?" she asked.

He smiled, only this time there was no warmth in his face. "Against people like you," he said.

She left shortly after that. Even though he said he would pay for the food, she left some euros on the table, ignoring his protests.

He made her uncomfortable; she didn't want to be beholden to him.

She took the long route back to her hotel, taking the Via Sistina to the Via Barberini because there would be more people and more light.

The wine she drank settled uneasily in her stomach, leaving a sharp aftertaste. When she reached the Piazza Barberini, she paused beneath an awning over a closed shop. The traffic—usually awful here—had virtually disappeared. The only sound was the water pouring through Bernini's famous fountain of Triton in the very center of the road.

Her heart was pounding. She waited ten minutes, stepping back into the shadows, but Giuseppe hadn't shown up.

Apparently he had stopped following her, now that he knew who she was and what she was about.

She hurried the long block to the Via Purificazione, then walked up the narrow street. Everything had shut down. She had to use her key to get into the hotel. The interior lights were on low. The night man had stepped away from the desk. She walked to the elevator, which seemed to take forever to reach the main floor.

As she rode upwards, she pulled her cell phone out of her pocket. She found the number for the Organization, but she didn't activate the call until she got inside her room and turned the tiny television to CNN International.

It was the middle of the afternoon in Colorado. Her boss answered, sounding surprised to hear from her.

"I had a strange experience," she said.

Then she told him all about Giuseppe, the way the man followed her, the way he had talked about the figure, and the fact that he had known exactly what time the "Dark Man" would appear.

"I need someone to look up the term *L'uomo Scuro*," she said. "And see if there are any notes about protectors. And I need it immediately."

Her boss didn't question her. He promised to have someone call her in fifteen minutes.

Unfortunately, fifteen minutes later, the person who called her was Ross.

She had never learned Ross's last name. She had worked with him before and he was, hands down, the best researcher on staff at the Organization. Unfortunately, he knew it, and made everyone else feel stupid.

"Haven't read your Dan Brown, huh?" Ross said by way of introduction.

Already irritation threatened to overwhelm her. "I read the source material long before Dan Brown ever thought of writing *The Da Vinci Code*." Listening to her own tone, she wondered who was trying to make whom feel stupid here. "I didn't meet a flagellant monk tonight."

"Not saying you did," Ross said, his tone dry and amused. "But you should have expected a secret society. You are in Rome, after all."

"Just tell me what you found," she said.

"The Dark Man has been part of Italian mythology about that spot since the Spanish Steps were built," he said. "I thought you knew Italian. You should've found this stuff on your own."

"I never heard it called the Dark Man before to-night," she said.

"Hmm," he said in a tone that completely condemned her for a lack of intellectual rigor. She tensed, then made herself breathe out slowly.

She was hot, she was tired, and she had to get up early.

"What else?" she asked.

"He has his own society," Ross said.

"What's the society called?"

"That's a question," he said. "Some kind of protector-ate, the Order of Something or Other. Very Dan Brown-like."

"It would help if I knew," she said.

"No one knows," he said. "It could be this order or that order. What everyone does know—"

And he emphasized "everyone," as if she were the only person on the planet lacking this knowledge.

"—is that if you try to hurt the Dark Man, someone will hurt you."

"Great," she said.

"You're not trying to damage it, are you?" he asked.

"No," she said. "I don't suppose this Order has put its vast knowledge about the Dark Man on the internet."

"It hasn't, but a bunch of conspiracy theorists have," he said. "They all have different theories."

"I'm sure I've found most of those," she said.

"Probably not," Ross said. "But I don't think it mat-ters. It's all the expected stuff anyway."

She wasn't sure what he meant by expected stuff,

but she was sure she could find out. "Which one do you believe?"

"It doesn't matter which one I believe," he said. "It's which one do they believe."

She suppressed a sigh, but she did roll her eyes, catching her reflection in the mirror across the room. She looked as exasperated as she felt.

"Which one do they believe?" she asked.

"Aliens," he said. "They think this is an alien invader, left behind."

"Just one?" she asked.

"Just one," he said.

"Who tries to attack all by his little lonesome every ten years?"

"I didn't make up the theory," Ross said, sounding defensive for the first time. "They're your nutcases."

"They're not mine either," she said, frowning. She hadn't expected that. This was Italy after all. Catholic, superstitious, filled with saints and relics and dark magic, not filled with little green men and misunderstood weather balloons like Roswell, New Mexico.

This time, she did sigh out loud.

"Will they hurt me?" she asked.

"Hurt you?" Ross repeated as if the sentence did not compute. "Maybe if you try to shoot the thing with your raygun. How the hell should I know?"

"You're the researcher," she snapped. "You should've found out if they're a threat."

"I'm good on short notice," he said. "I'm just not perfect."

"Oh, I never doubted that," she said, and hung up.

Aliens. UFOs. That fit into Strange Phenomena, Ancient and Modern. She almost wished it was a ghost, though, or a trick of the light, some kind of natural predictable *familiar* phenomenon.

She set the alarm on her phone. Five AM didn't seem that far from now.

She closed the curtains in her room, cranked up the air conditioning, and fell into a deep, exhausted sleep.

The alarm brought her out of it a moment later—or so it seemed. Five AM looked the same as midnight had, same darkness, same feel. She got up, turned on the lights, and took a quick shower.

Then she grabbed her equipment bag and headed back to the Spanish Steps.

The morning was cool, comparatively speaking. It had to be about 80 instead of the 100 that had stifled Rome for the past few days. She wondered whether fall would ever show up—and if it did, whether or not she would recognize it as a brand new season.

She trudged up to the Spanish Steps, noting as she went how many merchants were already up, cleaning the small sidewalks in front of their shops, and rearranging the wares in the window. She bought a pastry from a cart vendor she'd never seen before and ate as she walked, decided that the pastry was so good the vendor probably sold out long before she normally got up.

The carts at the top of the Spanish Steps were still shuttered. The professional beggars hadn't arrived yet. The restaurant tables, full and covered with food when she had left them, were stacked one on top of the other near the restaurant's doors.

A small group of people hovered near the top of the steps, staring at the city unfolding before them. The thin light of dawn seemed brighter than an average day in Colorado and made Condi feel like she was very, very far from home.

She walked past the group, not seeing anyone she recognized, and headed down the Steps until she was only a few yards from the spot where the figure would turn up.

She set up the video camera she brought, turning it on so that she would get the moment of appearance. She would also make a recording on her phone as a backup.

The rest of the equipment remained in the bag. She would only remove it if she needed it.

She sat on her perch, the travertine steps surprisingly cool through her khaki pants, and waited. She wanted the figure to appear. She needed it to appear. She didn't want to wait several more days for some kind of phenomenon that, until this point (at least for her), had only existed in artists' renderings.

Then Giuseppe sat down beside her, too close as usual. He wore a cologne as peppery as the wine had been the night before and just as strong. Clearly he had just gotten up as well.

"So," she said, irritated that he was sitting so close, irritated that he had frightened her the night before, irritated that he continued to bother her, "you guys think this is aliens, huh?"

He looked at her in surprise. She had a hunch that was the first unguarded expression she had ever seen on his face.

"You think I can't do research?" she asked. "I had simply thought you guys were a rumor until last night."

She didn't want to tell him she hadn't heard of his group until he had talked to her a few hours ago.

He didn't say anything. She pulled out her phone, cupping it in her right hand.

"What do you think this is," she asked, "some kind of portal and the aliens send one guy to it every ten years or so? Is this an invading army that hasn't quite got the concept down?"

She didn't try to cover the sarcasm in her voice.

"Not alien*s*," he said. "Alien."

"So you think it's alien. Tell me something I don't know."

He shook his head again. "An alien."

"That's what I said." She looked at the spot. "The one-by-one invading army. What keeps them out? Some kind of force field?"

"No," he said. "We think it's one single alien. The *same* alien. That it's always been the same alien."

He had her attention now. She moved her head so that she could watch him and the spot. "Over hundreds of years?"

"Yes," he said.

"I don't get it," she said. "Is this a projection?"

He shook his head. "He's out of phase."

"Out of phase with what?" she asked.

"Us," he said.

It took some explaining. Giuseppe had to switch from Italian to English and back again, because Condi didn't know the scientific terms. Twice he had to use some Latin cognates, and she had to guess.

It came down to this: the Dark Man, the figure, moved at a much slower rate through time. He had fallen or was injured or had done something that put him in this particular spot, and made him phase into human time perceptions only briefly.

In spite of herself, she got caught up in the theory. "How do you know it's time? Why can't it be something else, like an image or something?"

"Oh," Giuseppe said, "it could be a parallel universe that crosses into ours. But still there is some linkage, and time happens much slower in that other place."

"And you've decided that he's an alien and not a ghost because . . . ?"

"Because there were sightings of his ship," Giuseppe said.

"When?" she asked.

"As the Steps were being finished," he said. "I can show you the literature."

"I'd like to see it," she lied. She wished he weren't a crazy. She wished his theory was based in some kind of reality. But she should have known it wasn't when she first saw him trailing her with that protectiveness only the truly obsessed had toward the object of their obsession.

He continued to talk about it, and she asked the occasional question, surreptitiously glancing at the clock on her phone. She was experiencing time slowly, and she was convinced it was because of Giuseppe and the conversation.

"Don't you have an assignment? Aren't you supposed to be doing something?" she asked.

"I am doing it," he said.

She looked at him sideways. "Babysitting me?"

He gave an elegant shrug. "I must be able to report that you did not hurt him."

"Report to whom?" she asked.

He gave her a baleful look.

"I don't see why you're so secretive," she said. "Do you have aliens in your organization or are you afraid they'll find you out?"

"We do not know what they know," he said. "We do not know what they see."

She remembered her mother saying something very similar when Condi asked about God. *How can he watch billions of people?* Condi had asked. *Why would he care?*

The Bible says he does, her mother said.

But people wrote the Bible. What if it's wrong?

In exasperation, her mother had said, *We do not know what God knows. We do not know what he sees*.

"What do you mean, what they see?" Condi said to Giuseppe. They had five minutes until the figure appeared.

"Time and space," he said, "they are different."

"I know," she said, trying to keep the annoyance from her voice.

"The aliens experience time differently. So we do not know how they perceive the space around them."

She frowned at him. "So if the Steps were torn down tomorrow . . ."

"It would be, perhaps, like an earthquake to him. A sudden change. We do not know."

She looked at the spot on the Steps, which was still empty. "So you think the aliens are all around us, like the ultimate tourists. They walk the Spanish Steps like we do and we can't perceive them?"

"Something like that," he said, looking away from her.

"Then why do we see him?" she asked.

"Perhaps because he has not moved," he said. "Perhaps because he has crossed a little into our time."

Then he lowered his voice.

"Perhaps because he is dead."

She shuddered—and at that very moment, the figure appeared. Even though she had expected it, she jumped. He—and it was clearly a he—was sprawled along the steps like he had fallen there.

He was as big as she was, thicker than she imagined, and glossy black. The blackness looked shiny, like some kind of metal. She wanted to touch him, but didn't dare, not with Giuseppe next to her.

She checked to see if her cell phone was recording this. It was. Then she moved the phone to her other hand

and removed some of her equipment from her bag. She tried not to take her gaze off the figure.

He didn't move. He looked like he should move. He looked like he could easily get up. Two arms, two legs, a torso—very humanlike, except that she saw no features. No face, just a smooth surface.

She couldn't even tell if he had fallen (*if* he had fallen) face-down or face-up.

And the reports lied.

He had an odor. A faint one, dry and dusty but machine-like, almost like she had stepped inside an empty mechanic's bay.

She rubbed her nose, wondering if the scent was real or if she imagined it. Or if Giuseppe's cologne interfered with it.

"May I touch him?" she said. "I promise not to hurt him."

"We do not know what hurts him," Giuseppe said.

She glanced at him. "If you're right and he's experiencing time slowly, he won't even know that I brush against him."

Giuseppe didn't argue. So she leaned forward and swiped her finger along the figure's arm.

She shuddered. Pitch wasn't quite right, but close. Like tar that hadn't completely set—rubbery, but soft, almost like partially baked cookie dough. But that wasn't right either.

Something in the feel of him was wrong, so wrong she wanted to step away. She resisted the urge to rub her fingers against her pants. Instead she touched them to one of the handheld analyzers the Organization had supplied her with.

Other people had gathered. Many had cameras and cell phones, others had handheld pieces of equipment. They were taking readings. One man, using the light meter for his camera, said the light was different in the area around the figure than it was just a few meters away.

She didn't know what to make of that, just like she didn't know what to make of all the information she was gathering. Most of it made no sense to her. She was there to run the equipment, not analyze the data.

She did as she was told, collecting everything, watching and working, and listening to what everyone else said.

Somewhere in the confusion, Giuseppe moved away from her. The figure was all that existed for her—for her and the dozen people around her, people trying to figure out the phenomenon just like she was.

Then, just as suddenly as he appeared, the figure vanished.

And, it seemed, the morning got a little brighter. Had the man with the light meter been correct? Had the figure changed the light? Or had he brought a bit of his slower-moving universe with him?

She backed up the readings on the USBs the Organization had provided her. Then she gathered the camera she had placed a few feet away.

She was shaking, her breath coming in ragged gasps. She was in some kind of shock, some kind of near-denial. She wanted to tell herself that the thirty minutes hadn't happened, and yet it had.

And that was the surprise. She never expected the figure—*L'uomo Scuro*—to appear. Only the name Dark Man wasn't right either. He was something else. She would have thought him a robot or a sculpted bit of art if she hadn't touched him.

If his strange skin (should she call it skin?) hadn't been warm.

She shuddered.

Giuseppe made his way toward her. She stepped away from him. The experience had been too weird to dissect. She didn't want his perspective to contaminate hers.

She gathered her belongings, took one last shot of the empty place on the Steps, then climbed up them. At the top of the hill, she tried to send the data from her phone. She couldn't tell if it went through.

She would have to send it all through the internet café, and she really didn't want to.

But she had no other choice.

The waif was not there as the café opened at seven, which had to be some kind of record, a business opening that early in Rome. Another young woman, this one without piercings, wearing a tasteful sundress, didn't seem interested in Condi at all.

Condi sent the information as well as a brief blog, promising to send backups by FedEx later in the day. Somehow the Organization would get the information.

She didn't know what they would do with it.

She didn't know what she would do with it either.

But it made her feel odd.

As she watched the little blue bar that told her the information was going across the internet, traveling as bits of information across a space impossible to traverse instantly when the first appearance of the figure was first recorded, she tried to calm herself down.

She had felt like this when she had discovered corruption in Denver's city council elections. She had felt like this when she had found the smoking gun in a military airplane crash not far from Fort Collins. She had felt like this during all the major discoveries of her career.

Only she had known what those meant.

She wasn't sure what this one meant.

Except that it had shaken her assumptions.

Frankly, she had said during her job interview, *I think they're all going to be hoaxes.*

Only this one was not. She had investigated the area for weeks, knew there was nothing beneath it, no way for the figure to suddenly appear without some obvious help.

Unless someone was using technology she didn't understand—and had used that technology for centuries.

She gathered her equipment, put it away, used the remaining computer time to surf the news sites, seeing if anyone covered the reappearance of the Dark Man.

Not yet. But she suspected he would appear on You-Tube quite soon now—and she felt tempted to put him up herself.

But that would mean editing her phone video, taking out the conversation with Giuseppe, which she had deliberately sent back to the Organization.

She didn't know what they would think about his theories. Had she heard them without seeing the figure, she would have dismissed them out of hand.

But she couldn't now, no matter how much she thought of Ross making fun of her.

The theories made an odd sort of sense. The same kind of sense that most of Rome's legends made. That it was founded by Romulus, that Peter the Apostle had founded a church in this place, so far away from Jerusalem that he had actually been buried here.

Yet the past lived in Rome, more than in any other place she had ever been. If someone—something—were to phase in and out of time, this would be the place, because time was strange here. Old and new and forward and backward all at once.

It was, she privately believed, the reason her phone did not work well here, although it worked well in Paris and London and Berlin. Those cities had history, yes, but they were modern. They had a twenty-first-century feeling, clearly built on the foundations of the past, not dwelling within the past.

She shook her head, gathered her stuff, and stopped long enough to buy herself a Coke. A cold, sweet example of the modern era.

She carried it outside, stopping at the door like she had the night before, watching the girl inside shut down her computer. No screen capture this time. Maybe it hadn't mattered. Maybe just the waif was trying to steal information.

Maybe Condi had imagined all of it.

All of it except the Dark Man.

And Giuseppe, who waited for her in his usual spot, looking a bit shaken himself, somewhat vulnerable.

Now was the time to dissect the experience, to share perspectives.

She needed to talk to someone. And Giuseppe, at least, would listen.

Even if he was one of the crazies.

Even if she was too.

One Big Monkey

Ray Vukcevich

RayVuk tweets, "Hey @MarsMom how are you guys doing in the habitat today?"

To which MarsMom tweets, "We are starting a game! Shiro calls it The Fermi Game! Stay tuned!"

All six people in the Mars simulator tweet. We also get limited news from more conventional sources, but all we ever see on TV is the outside of the habitat in Russia and maybe some boring interviews with people who should probably be doing more science and less talking. Statistics. It's like they are trying to put us to sleep.

The direct links of social media have all the good stuff. It's so exciting!

Three men and three women locked up in the habitat for more than five hundred days! We can't help making couples of them. Aside from MarsMom (Carol from London) and Ookami (Shiro from Japan), there is VictorOnMars (the Russian), DaveToMars (the American), Trella (Estrella from Mexico), and FarOutMars (Farida from Iran). We arrange and rearrange them. We like to tease Victor and Dave by turning them into a gay couple, and they sometimes protest too much.

Because Shiro mostly looks like what you expect a young Japanese scientist to look like (slender, neat, half the time wears a necktie and neutral facial expressions), he takes great pains to violate this stereotype. He has a bolt of lavender lightning in his hair. He claims to be a member of a sect of Christians who handle poisonous snakes, but when pinned down, he can answer no questions about Christianity or snakes.

"Each of us," he says, "will construct a solution to the Fermi Paradox."

You know the one: if the universe is full of intelligent beings, how come we don't see them or hear from them? You say that sounds more like a salon than a game? Well, it is sort of a salon, but with a twist! Once you construct your solution, you must make up CHARACTERS who have POWERS! Then we'll all get together, and the theories will slug it out!

But Shiro, what does all of this have to do with snakes?

Nothing! It has absolutely nothing to do with snakes!

Ookami tweets, "Come on you guys! It'll be fun!"

I am Ookami, the big bad wolf, but I have a surprise for you. Open me up and out jumps Alice! When you sink into the mind of a modern Alice master such as myself, you should be prepared for an illuminating ride as it is my turn to entertain these snooty bastards. Maybe I won't come out about being Alice; it's not like they would understand it, anyway. They would call me a cliché, oh, Shiro, you silly otaku, if they knew about my Alice manga. They would lift eyebrows and then look away, muttering about comic books and worrying about me becoming a little blond girl in the heat of battle. That is so opposite to the real situation! My Alice steals up on you in the night and engulfs you like a manta ray, you little fishes. I will not be defeated! Besides, Farida is the real cliché in the group. The most beautiful women in the world are from Iran, and here she is so startlingly gorgeous she stops clocks as she passes, bananas peel themselves and ejaculate at her touch, walls pulse with heavy breathing, overflying birds drop dead with erotic squawks and splatter on the outer skin of the habitat. I will surprise them. Alice to the left of us, Alice to the right. It's not my birthday! Most likely iThink, ha ha, that when a society can make reality be anything they want, they all turn around in their heads and look inward—iPut the clouds in the sky and the birds in the trees; why look out at things you cannot change when inside reality can be whatever you want it to be? There might be holdouts, hardliners, Luddites, but in the end, the temptation will be too great, thinking creatures will shape their realities, and if everyone has gone inward, it's not so surprising they are not knocking themselves out to talk. Why bother? If they want us, they can just make us up. But the strange thing is, why have we not done it already ourselves? If you consider that once we go in, we might stay in for thousands and thousands of years, making "in" the most common state, and "out" very rare, and why would we think this time right now is one of those rare times? Isn't it statistically more likely that we live in ordinary times? And if we live in ordinary times, shouldn't we be in already? So, maybe we have already gone in, and that is why we hear no one out there. Even if there are one or two civilizations shouting into the cosmic wilderness, we don't hear them because we are not really listening. We are only pretending to listen. We are also only pretending to go to Mars, doubly pretending in that we are pretending that this time in the habitat is a real Mars mission, and when that real mission happens, it will only be simulated, so why are we bothering? Isn't that a flaw in your theory, Ookami-san, as Carol might say? Thinking this was being very

clever and making sense, which it might I suppose from
a motherly perspective, and she might have a point. If
we are already "in" why are we not living lives of wild
excitement? Why can't we fly just by flapping our arms?
Why do we have to pretend to go to Mars instead of just
getting in a rocket ship and zip zoom fire the landing jets
and watch out you buggy Martians, we've come! There
is an obvious answer to that. Maybe this was all you
could afford, Shiro. Okay, but not so bad, me, educated,
picked to be in the Mars habitat, of all my countrymen
who might have been picked, it was me! And it will be
me who is Alice. None of the others will be Alice. They
all want to be Alice, of course, but I won't lose! In the
end, I will be the ultimate Alice. I will be the one to really go to Mars! The rabbit hole is mine! I will get tall, I
will get small. We'll have tea!

Ookami tweets, "There is a constant low rumble or
hum right at the edge of perception in the habitat."

FarOutMars tweets, "Hooray! A game! Yay, Shiro!"

Just because you like snakes and have some psy-
chodelic purple in your hair doesn't mean you are edgy
and cool, Shiro, who thinks he is so clever. Don't you
mean psychedelic, Farida? I do not! Don't tell me what
I mean, people are all the time telling me what I mean.
It makes me so angry! I'll bury you all up to your necks
in the sand, and rabbits will hop by and fart in your
faces! Tee hee, Farida, bunnies, you are so cute, cud-
dly, we want to squeeze you! Will you squeak when we
squeeze you? I'll bet you do squeak. Get away from me,
you smelly donkeys! And what's with the Alice references? Has he gone crazy? Will Google Alice. Probably
not the English book, probably not the AI program, but
it could be, I guess. Not this, not that. OMG! Manga! Of
course! What else? I must IM Trella about Shiro and his
Alice manga—maybe leak it wider somehow. Take that!

What kind of CHARACTERS can I come up with to counter Alice? Okay, bunnies, white rabbits with magic powers and big eyes, or Persian bunnies with huge, horrible swords! Not that the swords will matter much since you'll all be smothered in your beds with rabbits sitting on your faces by that time anyway! You think you know me. You don't know me! No matter what I come up with, the others won't get it, they'll be all oh how nice, Farida, you're so creative. Oh, don't look so serious, cutie pie, everyone is kidding! Maybe it's the wind. Maybe there is a kind of radio wind that blows communications from other worlds away from us. Maybe the universe is full of communication but when it drifts toward us, the wind blows it away. Maybe we just happen to be in a particularly windy spot so nothing that comes our way ever really gets here. Will they like that? Will they think that might be worth thinking about? Space wind? That's so darling! And those cute bunny CHARACTERS! The "hum" is driving me crazy! How is this even a game? I don't see how anyone can win, but I do see how we can all lose. We will look so foolish, and we will feel bad about looking foolish. Rats! I hate this.

FarOutMars tweets, "I will spend all of my free time today playing my clavichord!"

RayVuk tweets, "Out here there is too much noise for a clavichord. Even when everything is turned off at night, there is a low buzz."

Several twibes of Twitter people interested in #MarsHab have arisen. Members of the twibes all have much to say about The Fermi Game. Hundreds of solutions to the paradox have been suggested.

DaveToMars tweets, "Thanks for all the suggestions, tweeple, but I must come up with something on my own!"

Of course, they wouldn't let her bring a real clavichord, but has that stopped her? It has not. She rolls out a printed keyboard and plays and plays and sometimes if you listen very very carefully, you can hear the notes! I swear. We all pretend to hear them anyway just so we can be close and watch her, she is so pretty, until she shoos us all away. There is a simulated delay in network communications, not that it really matters. They pretend not to know about our phones. We pretend not to know about them, too. That is, I pretend the others have not also smuggled their phones into the habitat, and they pretend not to know about mine. It's a ridiculous charade since some of us call each other. Whoever is out there watching us has probably decided they can learn things by observing the way we communicate with each other clandestinely. Or maybe they are just getting sloppy on this late mission. I wonder if Victor would pick up? I would like Victor more if he had boobs, he could keep his dick. Jesus, I will now put my red face under my wing like an embarrassed bird, which is to say a bird without pants, which would be them all, wouldn't it, bare-assed birds of the world unite! If I had been making up this game, I would not have asked where is everyone. Instead I would have asked why do we care? We are like children. Look at us! See what we can do! Do you love us the best for being so smart? To hell with all the ingenious suggestions. It really just boils down to loneliness. We look out at the universe and feel deep down there is no one there. Maybe we are the first. Someone has to be the first. Maybe we will fill the universe with ourselves and then someday someone will be wondering who is out there and they will look and find creatures just like themselves! Maybe they will even speak English, like in the movies where everyone in the universe speaks English. Everyone speaks English here. Everyone speaks Russian, too, but that is just a side effect of how we were chosen to be in this Russian experiment. How many times are they going to do this? Will they learn anything new from us? Will any of us still be young enough to actually go on a real Mars mission? My CHARACTERS are rugged pioneers. Their strange POWER is that they can use any tool without even reading the instructions. We are the guys who seek out and settle new worlds using tools! I am so lonely. That's it, really. We care because we dread the thought of being alone in the dark. All of us are locked up alone in our own heads. But lately, it's not so quiet. My ears are ringing, or maybe something has come loose in the structure of the place. I don't know.

DaveToMars tweets, "Hum or no hum, I'm off to the gym. I will use every piece of equipment in there, you lazy comrades!"

RayVuk tweets, "The hum is out here, too, Dave! I thought it was my computer, but it's not just that. RT @ DaveToMars Hum or no hum . . ."

MarsMom tweets, "My babies are all up and busy! I am so proud of the way we are all working together!"

The center cannot hold or something like that. I wish I could just go lie on the beach and a beautiful boy would bring me a drink with a little umbrella in it and when he handed it to me our fingers would brush and one thing would lead to another and he would scoop me up so easily and he'd be running with me in his arms running like a dark stallion across the sand and the waves would be lapping at his feet and my hair would be flowing back in the wind we'd be making as he ran. Well, we wouldn't really be making wind, hee hee, but there would be music and the sun would warm me everywhere, where did my suit go, I don't care, little huts ahead and palm trees. I hate them, the hulking, stinking American, and Farida, the Persian doll, is she even real?

I want to pull her arms and head off and look down her throat to see if there are mechanical parts down there. I'm going to slap Shiro, I know it, one of these days, I'm going to snap and slap him, first one way on the left cheek, whap! And then the other way on the right cheek. Whap whap! That will make his monotone rise up a little, I bet. Oh, no, Estrella is making chocolate chicken. I can smell it. Is it her turn to cook again? Time flies! My stomach has only just got over the last chili assault, you don't own the world, Victor, I don't care if it is Russia outside, in here it is not Russia! Go eat a cucumber! I want what you all want, I want to hit someone. Quiet, children. Shush. We don't really want to be noticed. We need to be cautious. If we must go out into space, we must be prepared. Just look at everyone else. So quiet, so discreet. Why do you think that is? Surely everyone is not just being polite. Isn't it possible they are all hunkered down so the Bad Thing doesn't notice them? My CHARACTERS are children, and their POWER is silence. I don't want to play games, we never play nice when we play games, can't we all be more supportive? Go to your rooms! I vant to be alone! You ungrateful dummies. Off with your heads!

MarsMom tweets, "I'm going to take a nap, everyone. Call me if you need me!"

The twibes are all abuzz wondering if Mom seems a little peeved. What in the world did we do? Farida's twibe wonders. Dave, Victor, and Shiro are clueless. We'll cheer her up, Trella's twibe cries. Mom's twibe is mum on the whole subject.

Trella tweets, "Two words! Chicken molé!"

I wonder if I can get away with poisoning them all. I could twitter for them. I could file their reports. Make phone calls with voice-changing software. I could fake a massive camera failure, and when the outside world

finally caught on, I could be sick in my bed, cross-eyed,
sweating, is that you, Mama? (MarsMom tweets, "What is
it @Trella?—not you Dead Carol! I want my Mommy!)"
Wait a minute! Why am I not thinking in Spanish? You
are thinking in Spanish, Estrella, it is just that when your
thoughts go out into the universe they pass through the
Universal Translator and come out the other end in the
language of whoever is reading your mind. And who
would be reading my mind? Hey, maybe everyone in the
universe is reading my mind! Oh, I hope not. They will
know I want to poison everyone! This is so spicy, Trella!
Yeah, right, you macho bozo, I know you'll keep choking it down, sweat running down your red face, because
it would be just too embarrassing to let the other boys
think it is too hot for you, and they will be just the same,
men are so easy to poison, it won't be so easy with Farida
and Carol who will be nibbling cautiously. Chocolate!
Women love chocolate. I love chocolate. Maybe everyone else in the universe can hear our every thought, and
we are some kind of handicapped creatures who cannot
hear one another but who cannot also shut up. Shut up!
The universe wants us to just shut up! We are driving
them crazy with our unrestrained thoughts. They have
isolated us because it is just too painful to be around us,
or maybe we are just too pathetic. We all have Tourette's
syndrome! Maybe my CHARACTERS are savage de-
tectives like in my favorite book, and their POWER is
poetry! Maybe the game gimmick will be to see who can
read my mind just in the nick of time and put their fork
down and escape their fate!

Trella tweets, "Soup's on!"

RayVuk tweets, "Something is approaching. Can't
you feel it?"

VictorOnMars tweets, "I am as ready as the next guy
to play games!"

I do understand that my political anger isn't really even political. It's just anger. We are angry creatures. Angry and loud, and we never shut up about it, which is why no one likes us. Silly Shiro, Ookami, the wolf, he is a lamb, I am the real wolf, the thing that goes bump in the night. I don't actually get to do much bumping in the night. You dogs! I will let the beast out and paint the walls with blood! I will make a 3, 2, 1 pyramid of skulls! Wait, that would mean the top skull would have to be mine. Maybe I'll use a cantaloupe as the top skull, maybe I'll paint my face on the melon. Why do we not hear from other creatures in the universe? Why do they never visit? Assuming they don't, of course. Assuming it's nonsense that they just like to play games in our fields and probe the anuses of peasants. Maybe we are being punished for something. Maybe humanity is in solitary confinement. Maybe we are just one creature who has been locked away so long its mind has fragmented into all of us. Maybe we are really God, but God who has committed some inconceivable sin and has been condemned to spend all of His days alone. This is a meditation of the unnamable. Of course, that just kicks the can down the road. We are God and we neither see nor hear aliens because we have not yet made them up. I am so gloomy when I am not angry. My CHARACTERS will be political prisoners, and their POWER will be anger. They will revolt and take hostages and kill the hostages by throwing them out of second-story windows! I can hardly hear myself think. The hum is like a crowd just outside the door, muttering, grumbling, talking about me, I wonder if they have torches and pitchforks. It's nearly time to gather in the dining room for Shiro's Fermi Game; I wonder if the others will wear costumes. Should I wear a costume? And if so, who should I be? The runaway Russian Ayn Rand maybe. I would need some ugly shoes for that one. Or maybe I should be Gandhi with only a piece of cloth. I could go either way.

VictorOnMars tweets, "Showtime, Comrades!"

Doors everywhere bang open and Alice and Alice and Alice run into every space some growing huge and others squeaking down small like mice or hotfooting cockroaches swarming over the farting rabbits with swords who fence with John Wayne clones wielding axes and screwdrivers while silent children stand by unsmiling but shooting creepy eyebeams at all the gauchos shouting poems at the chain gangs. Something stirs the battle like a long finger in paint, and the hum crowds out everything. It's not our phones, it's not our computers, forget about the refrigerator, it's more than the sounds of animals and waves and cities and machines.

RayVuk tweets, "The noise has pressed me flat, but suddenly I can see you! I don't know how, but there you are!"

All six of you, billions and billions of us looking at you, looking at us, I'm on the phone with my mother and Facebook chatting with my anime buddies, Skype this, WOW that, SL avatars gather to consider The Fermi Game, and it's like big hands have grabbed us, the whole world, and squeezed. It's all happening at once and to everyone, and we are all together, until we are really just one big thing, and once we are one big thing, that big thing can suddenly talk to all the other big things out there and they are all like, hello hello it's so good to see you finally get it together, we thought you might never do it, yours is such a unique situation. It hardly ever happens like this, in fact, no one can remember it ever happening like this, but now that we know it can happen like this, surely it has happened before and we have just forgotten about it, some of us will be looking into it, it will be fascinating to find out if anyone else has ever done it like this. Yes, yes, those six parts of you who are so much the focus of this merging were mostly right, and you will soon be going to Mars. All of you! No one will be left behind. The tech for that trip is such that pieces like RayVuk, who will be a lot older when this happens, might as well be sitting right there in the captain's chair, might as well turn to his left and ask Alice, "How are you doing this morning, pumpkin?" He can call the mind of all humanity "pumpkin" because he is one of the billions of grandfathers, and you have certain privileges as a grandfather. Grandmothers will call Alice something quite different—maybe "sweetie."

Did Trella poison them all? No. Humanity became one big thing just before anyone could taste the molé, before Carol could give the order for Dave to use his axe, before Farida could loose her farting bunnies, before Victor could depress everyone into jumping out a window and off a bridge, but not before Shiro and everyone, absolutely everyone, became Alice.

The Space Caterpillar blows smoke rings, and then says, yes, we did use "wind" to hide evidence of our existence from you and keep you in the dark all these years, and yes, we are not so common in the first place, and yes, the speed of light really does seem to be the ultimate limit which means many creatures go in and never come out, and yes, there is a Very Bad Thing, but it won't get to you for a long long time, and if you decide to go in, after all, you won't feel a thing when It gets there, but you were wrong about being God who has done something to get tossed into solitary confinement (unless we are all God—oh, no, let's not think about that!). Instead you were isolated because of an unfortunate biological condition in which you broadcast your unrestrained, hurtful, lovely but loud, awful, truly shameful, how could you think such things, thought babble all the time without pause, and we blew that away, too, away from most of the rest of us, the ironic part being that you could not even hear yourselves, so chances were small you would ever become Alice and join us, but then you overcame your handicap with mechanical prosthesis!

Who would have thought?

And soon you will all be on your way to Mars!

You are now, at long last, really one big monkey. Yes, you had to wind yourself up, but your cymbal playing is very nice. We like it. Hello, hello, dear Alice.

The Taste of Night

Pat Cadigan

The taste of night rather than the falling temperature woke her. Nell curled up a little more and continued to doze. It would be a while before the damp chill coming up from the ground could get through the layers of heavy cardboard to penetrate the sleeping bag and blanket cocooning her. She was fully dressed and her spare clothes were in the sleeping bag, too—not much but enough to make good insulation. Sometime in the next twenty-four hours, though, she would have to visit a laundromat because *phew*.

Phew was one of those things that didn't change; well, not so far, anyway. She hoped it would stay that way. By contrast, the taste of night was one of her secret great pleasures although she still had no idea what it was supposed to mean. Now and then something *almost* came to her, *almost*. But when she reached for it either in her mind or by actually touching something, there was nothing at all.

Sight. Hearing. Smell. Taste. Touch. _____.

Memory sprang up in her mind with the feel of pale blue stretched long and tight between her hands.

The blind discover that their other senses, particularly hearing, intensify to compensate for the lack. The deaf can be sharp-eyed but also extra sensitive to vibration, which is what sound is to the rest of us.

However, those who lose their sense of smell find they have lost their sense of taste as well because the two are so close. To lose feeling is usually a symptom of a greater problem. A small number of people feel no pain but this puts them at risk for serious injury and life-threatening illnesses.

That doctor had been such a patient woman. Better yet, she had had no deep well of stored-up suspicion like every other doctor Marcus had taken her to. Nell had been able to examine what the doctor was telling her, touching it all over, feeling the texture. Even with Marcus's impatience splashing her like an incoming tide, she had been able to ask a question.

A sixth sense? Like telepathy or clairvoyance?

The doctor's question had been as honest as her own and Nell did her best to make herself clear.

If there were some kind of extra sense, even a person who had it would have a hard time explaining it. Like you or me trying to explain sight to someone born blind.

Nell had agreed and asked the doctor to consider how the other five senses might try to compensate for the lack.

That was where the memory ended, leaving an aftertaste similar to night, only colder and with a bit of sour.

Nell sighed, feeling comfortable and irrationally safe. Feeling safe was irrational if you slept rough. Go around feeling safe and you wouldn't last too long. It was just that the indented area she had found at the back of this building—cinema? auditorium?—turned out to be as cozy as it had looked. It seemed to have no purpose except as a place where someone could sleep unnoticed for a night or two. More than two would have been pushing it, but that meant nothing to some rough sleepers. They'd camp in a place like this till they wore off all the hidden. Then they'd get seen and kicked out. Next thing you knew, the spot would be fenced off or filled in so no one could ever use it again. One fewer place to go when there was nowhere to stay.

Nell hated loss, hated the taste: dried-out bitter crossed with salty that could hang on for days, weeks, even longer. Worse, it could come back without warning and for no reason except that, perhaps like rough sleepers, it had nowhere else to go. There were other things that tasted just as bad to her but nothing worse, and nothing that lingered for anywhere nearly as long, not even the moldy-metal tang of disappointment.

After a bit, she realized the pools of color she'd been watching behind her closed eyes weren't the remnants of a slow-to-fade dream but real voices of real humans, not too far away, made out of the same stuff she was; either they hadn't noticed her or they didn't care.

Nell uncurled slowly—never make any sudden moves was another good rule for rough sleepers—and opened her eyes. An intense blue-white light blinded her with the sound of a cool voice in her right ear:

Blue-white stars don't last long enough for any planets orbiting them to develop intelligent life. Maybe not any life, even the most rudimentary. Unless there is a civilization advanced enough to seed those worlds with organisms modified to evolve at a faster rate. That might beg the question of why an advanced civilization would do that. But the motives of a civilization that advanced would/ could/might seem illogical if not incomprehensible to any not equally developed.

Blue-white memory stretched farther this time: a serious-faced young woman in a coffee shop, watching a film clip on a notebook screen. Nell had sneaked a look at it on her way to wash up in the women's restroom. It took her a little while to realize that she had had a glimpse of something to do with what had been happening to her, or more precisely, *why* it was happening, what it was supposed to mean. On the heels of that realization had come a new one, probably the most important: *they* were communicating with her.

Understanding always came to her at oblique angles. The concept of that missing sixth sense, for instance— when she finally became aware of it, she realized that it had been lurking somewhere in the back of her mind for a very, very long time, years and years, a passing notion or a ragged fragment of a mostly forgotten dream. It had developed so slowly that she might have lived her whole life without noticing it, instead burying it under more mundane concerns and worries and fears.

Somehow it had snagged her attention—a mental pop-up window. Marcus had said everyone had an occasional stray thought about something odd. Unless she was going to write a weird story or draw a weird picture, there was no point in obsessing about it.

Was it the next doctor who had suggested she do exactly that—write a weird story or draw a weird picture, or both? Even if she had really wanted to, she couldn't. She knew for certain by then that she was short a sense, just as if she were blind or deaf.

Marcus had said he didn't understand why that meant she had to leave home and sleep on the street. She didn't either, at the time. But even if she had understood enough to tell him that *the motives of a civilization that advanced would/could/might seem illogical if not incomprehensible to any not equally developed,* all it would have meant to him was that she was, indeed, crazy as a bedbug, unquote.

The social worker he had sent after her hadn't tried to talk her into a hospital or a shelter right away but the intent was deafening. Every time she found Nell it drowned everything else out. Nell finally had to make her say it just to get some peace. For a few days after that, everything was extra scrambled. She was too disoriented to understand anything. All she knew was that *they* were bombarding her with their communication and her senses were working overtime, trying to make up for her inadequacy.

The blinding blue-white light dissolved and her vision cleared. Twenty feet away was an opening in the back of the building the size of a double-garage door. Seven or eight men were hanging around just outside, some of them sitting on wooden crates, smoking cigarettes, drinking from bottles or large soft-drink cups. The pools of color from their voices changed to widening circular ripples, like those spreading out from raindrops falling into still water. The colors crossed each other to make new colors, some she had never seen anywhere but in her mind.

The ripples kept expanding until they reached the backs of her eyes and swept through them with a sensation of a wind ruffling feathery flowers. She saw twinkling lights and then a red-hot spike went through her right temple. There was just enough time for her to inhale before an ice-pick went through her eye to cross the spike at right angles.

Something can be a million light years away and in your eye at the same time.

"Are you all right?"

The man bent over her, hands just above his knees.

Most of his long hair was tied back except for a few long strands that hung forward in a way that suggested punctuation to Nell. Round face, round eyes with hard lines under them.

See. Hear. Smell. Taste. Touch. _____.

Hand over her right eye, she blinked up at him. He repeated the question and the words were little green balls falling from his mouth to bounce away into the night. Nell caught her lower lip between her teeth to keep herself from laughing. He reached down and pulled the hand over her eye to one side. Then he straightened up and pulled a cell phone out of his pocket. "I need an ambulance," he said to it.

She opened her mouth to protest but her voice wouldn't work. Another man was coming over, saying something in thin, tight silver wires.

And then it was all thin, tight silver wires everywhere. Some of the wires turned to needles and they seemed to fight each other for dominance. The pain in her eye flared more intensely and a voice from somewhere far in the past tried to ask a question without morphing into something else but it just wasn't loud enough for her to hear.

Nell rolled over onto her back. Something that was equal parts anxiety and anticipation shuddered through her. Music, she realized; very loud, played live, blaring out of the opening where the men were hanging around. Chords rattled her blood, pulled at her arms and legs. The pain flared again but so did the taste of night. She let herself fall into it. The sense of falling became the desire to sleep but just as she was about to give in, she would slip back to wakefulness, back and forth like a pendulum. Or like she was swooping from the peak of one giant wave, down into the trough and up to the peak of another.

Her right eye was forced open with a sound like a

gunshot and bright light filled her mouth with the taste of icicles.

"Welcome back. Don't take this the wrong way but I'm very sorry to see you here."

Nell discovered only her left eye would open but one eye was enough. Ms. Dunwoody, Call-Me-Anne, the social worker. Not the original social worker Marcus had sent after her. That had been Ms. Petersen, Call-Me-Joan, who had been replaced after a while by Mr. Carney, Call-Me-Dwayne. Nell had seen him only twice and the second time he had been one big white knuckle, as if he were holding something back—tears? hysteria? Whatever it was leaked from him in twisted shapes of shifting colors that left bad tastes in her mouth. Looking away from him didn't help—the tastes were there whether she saw the colors or not.

It was the best they could do for her, lacking as she was in that sense. At the time, she hadn't understood. All she had known was that the tastes turned her stomach and the colors gave her headaches. Eventually, she had thrown up on the social worker's shoes and he had fled without apology or even so much as a surprised curse, let alone a good-bye. Nell hadn't minded.

Ms. Dunwoody, Call-Me-Anne, was his replacement and she had managed to find Nell more quickly than she had expected. Ms. Dunwoody, Call-Me-Anne, had none of the same kind of tension in her but once in a while she exuded a musty, stale odor of resignation that was very close to total surrender.

Surrender. It took root in Nell's mind but she was slow to understand because she only associated it with Ms. Dunwoody, Call-Me-Anne's unspoken (even to herself) desire to give up. If she'd just had that missing sense, it would have been so obvious right away.

Of course, if she'd had that extra sense, she'd have understood the whole thing right away and everything would be different. Maybe not a whole lot easier, since she would still have had a hard time explaining sight to all the blind people, so to speak, but at least she wouldn't have been floundering around in confusion.

"Nell?" Ms. Dunwoody, Call-Me-Anne, was leaning forward, peering anxiously into her face. "I *said,* do you know why you're here?"

Nell hesitated. "Here, as in . . ." Her voice failed in her dry throat. The social worker poured her a glass of water from a pitcher on the bedside table and held it up, slipping the straw between her dry lips so she could drink. Nell finished three glasses and Ms. Dunwoody, Call-Me-Anne, made a business of adjusting her pillows before she lay back against the raised mattress.

"Better?" she asked Nell brightly.

Nell made a slight, noncommittal dip with her head. "What was the question?" she asked, her voice still faint.

"Do you know where you are?" Ms. Dunwoody, Call-Me-Anne, said.

Nell smiled inwardly at the change and resisted the temptation to say, *Same place you are—here.* There were deep lines under the social worker's eyes, her clothes were wrinkled, and lots of little hairs had escaped from her tied-back hair. No doubt she'd had less rest in the last twenty-four hours than Nell. She looked around with her one good eye at the curtains surrounding them and at the bed. "Hospital. Tri-County General."

She could see that her specifying which hospital had reassured the social worker. That was hardly a major feat of cognition, though; Tri-County General was where all the homeless as well as the uninsured ended up.

"You had a convulsion," Call-Me-Anne told her,

speaking slowly and carefully now as if to a child. "A man found you behind the concert hall and called an ambulance."

Nell lifted her right hand and pointed at her face.

Call-Me-Anne hesitated, looking uncertain. "You seem to have hurt your eye."

She remembered the sensation of the spike and the needle so vividly that she winced.

"Does it hurt?" Call-Me-Anne asked, full of concern. "Should I see if they can give you something for the pain?"

Nell shook her head no; a twinge from somewhere deep in her right eye socket warned her not to do that again or to make any sudden movements, period.

"Is there anyone you'd like me to call for you?" the social worker asked.

Frowning a little, Nell crossed her hands and uncrossed them in an absolutely-not gesture. Call-Me-Anne pressed her lips together but it didn't stop a long pink ribbon from floating weightless out from her mouth. Too late—she had already called Marcus, believing that by the time he got here, Nell actually would want to see him. And if not, she would claim that Marcus had insisted on seeing *her,* regardless of Nell's wishes, because he was her husband and loyalty and blah-blah-blah-social-worker-blather.

All at once there was a picture in her mind of a younger and not-so-tired Ms. Dunwoody, Call-Me-Anne, and just as suddenly, it came to life.

I feel that if we can reunite families, then we've done the best job we can. Sometimes that isn't possible, of course, so the next best thing we can do is provide families for those who need them.

Call-Me-Anne's employment interview, she realized. What *they* were trying to tell her with that wasn't at all clear. That missing sense. Or maybe because *they* had the sense, they were misinterpreting the situation.

"Nell? *Nell?*"

She tried to pull her arm out of the social worker's grip and couldn't. The pressure was a mouthful of walnut shells, tasteless and sharp. "What do you want?"

"I *said,* are you *sure?*"

Nell sighed. "There's a story that the first people in the New World to see Columbus's ships couldn't actually *see* them because such things were too far outside their experience. You think that's true?"

Call-Me-Anne, her expression a mix of confusion and anxiety. Nell knew what that look meant—she was afraid the situation was starting to get away from her. "Are you groggy? Or just tired?"

"I don't," she went on, a bit wistful. "I think they didn't know what they were seeing and maybe had a hard time with the perspective but I'm sure they saw them. After all, they *were* made by other humans. But something coming from another world, all bets are off."

Call-Me-Anne's face was very sad now.

"I sound crazy to you?" Nell gave a short laugh. *"Scientists* talk about this stuff."

"You're not a scientist, Nell. You were a librarian. With proper treatment and medication, you could—"

Nell laughed again. "If a librarian starts thinking about the possibility of life somewhere else in the universe, it's a sign she's going crazy?" She turned her head away and closed her eyes. Correction, eye. She couldn't feel very much behind the bandage, just enough to know that her right eyelid wasn't opening or closing. When she heard the social worker walk away, she opened her eye to see the silver wires had come back. They bloomed like flowers, opening and then flying apart where they met others and connected, making new blooms that flew apart and found new connections. The world in front of Nell began to look like a cage, although she had no idea which side she was on.

Abruptly, she felt one of the wires go through her temple with that same white-hot pain. A moment later, a second one went through the bandage over her right eye as easily as if it wasn't there, going all the way through her head and out, pinning her to the pillow.

Her left eye was watering badly but she could see Call-Me-Anne rushing back with a nurse. Their mouths opened and closed as they called her name. She saw them reaching for her but she was much too far away.

And that was how it would be. No, that was how it was always, but the five senses worked so hard to compensate for the one missing that people took the illusion of contact for the real thing. The power of suggestion—where would the human race be without it?

Sight. Hearing. Smell. Taste. Touch. _____.

Contact.

The word was a poor approximation but the concept was becoming clearer in her mind now. Clearer than the sight in her left eye, which was dimming. But still good enough to let her see Call-Me-Anne was on the verge of panic.

A man in a white uniform pushed her aside and she became vaguely aware of him touching her. But there was still no *contact*.

Nell labored toward wakefulness as if she were climbing a rock wall with half a dozen sandbags dangling on long ropes tied around her waist. Her mouth was full of steel wool and sand. She knew that taste—medication. It would probably take most of a day to spit that out.

She had tried medication in the beginning because Marcus had begged her to. Antidepressants, antianxiety capsules, and finally antipsychotics—they had all tasted the same because she hadn't been depressed, anxious, or psychotic. Meanwhile, Marcus had gotten farther and farther away, which, unlike the dry mouth, the weight gain, or the tremors in her hands, was not reversible.

Call-Me-Anne had no idea about that. She kept trying to get Nell to see Marcus, unaware they could barely perceive each other anymore. Marcus didn't realize it either, not the way she did. Marcus thought that was reversible, too.

Pools of color began to appear behind her heavy eyelids, strange colors that shifted and changed, green to gold, purple to red, blue to aqua, and somewhere between one color and another was a hue she had never found anywhere else and never would.

Sight. Hearing. Smell. Taste. Touch. _____.

C-c-c-contact . . .

The word was a boulder trying to fit a space made for a pebble smoothed over the course of eons and a distance of lightyears into a precise and elegant thing.

Something can be a million light years away and in your eye at the same time.

Sight. Hearing. Smell. Taste. Touch. _____.

C-c-c-con . . . nect.

C-c-c-commmmune.

C-c-c-c-c-communnnnnnnnicate.

She had a sudden image of herself running around the base of a pyramid, searching for a way to get to the top. While she watched, it was replaced by a new image, of herself running around an elephant and several blind men; she was still looking for a way to get to the top of the pyramid.

The image dissolved and she became aware of how heavy the overhead lights were on her closed eyes. Eye. She sighed; even if she did finally reach understanding—

or it reached her—how would she ever be able to explain what blind men, an elephant, and a pyramid combined with Columbus's ships meant?

The musty smell of surrender broke in on her thoughts. It was very strong; Call-Me-Anne was still there. After a bit, she heard the sound of a wooden spoon banging on the bottom of a pot. Frustration, but not just any frustration: Marcus's.

She had never felt him so clearly without actually seeing him. Perhaps Call-Me-Anne's surrender worked as an amplifier.

The shifting colors resolved themselves into a new female voice. " ... much do either of you know about the brain?"

"Not much," Call-Me-Anne said. Marcus grunted, a stone rolling along a dirt path.

"Generally, synesthesia can be a side effect of medication or a symptom."

"What about mental illness?" Marcus asked sharply, the spoon banging louder on the pot.

"Sometimes mentally ill people experience it but it's not a specific symptom of mental illness. In your wife's case, it was a symptom of the tumors."

"Tumors?" Call-Me-Anne was genuinely upset. Guilt was a soft scratching noise, little mouse claws on a hard surface.

"Two, although there could be three. We're not sure about the larger one. The smaller one is an acoustic neuroma, which—"

"Is that why she hears things?" Marcus interrupted.

The doctor hesitated. "Probably not, although some people complain of tinnitus. It's non-cancerous, doesn't spread, and normally very slow-growing. Your wife's seems to be growing faster than normal. But then there's the other one." Pause. "I've only been a neurosurgeon for ten years so I can't say I've seen everything but this really is quite, uh . . . unusual. She must have complained of headaches."

A silence, then Call-Me-Anne cleared her throat. "They seemed to be cluster headaches. Painful but not exactly rare. I have them myself. I gave her some of my medication but I don't know if she took it."

Another small pause. "Sometimes she said she had a headache but that's all," Marcus said finally. "We've been legally separated for a little over two years, so I'm not exactly up-to-date. She sleeps on the street."

"Well, there's no telling when it started until we can do some detailed scans."

"How much do those cost?" Marcus asked. Then after a long moment: "Hey, *she* left *me* to sleep on the *street* after I'd already spent a fortune on shrinks and prescriptions and hospitalizations. Then they tell me you can't force a person to get treated for anything unless they're a danger to the community, blah, blah, blah. Now she's got brain tumors and I'm gonna get hit for the bill. Dammit, I shoulda divorced her but it felt too—" The spoon scraped against the iron pot. "Cruel."

"You were hoping she'd snap out of it?" said the doctor. "Plenty of people feel that way. It's normal to hope for a miracle." Call-Me-Anne added some comforting noises, and said something about benefits and being in the system.

"Yeah, okay," Marcus said. "But you still didn't answer my question. How much do these scans cost?"

"Sorry, I couldn't tell you, I don't have anything to do with billing," the doctor said smoothly. "But we can't do any surgery without them."

"I thought you already did some," Marcus said.

"We were going to. Until I saw what was behind her eye."

"It's that big?" asked Marcus.

"It's not just that. It's—not your average tumor."

Marcus gave a humorless laugh. "Tumors are standardized, are they?"

"To a certain extent, just like the human body. This one, however, isn't behaving quite the way tumors usually do." Pause. "There seems to be some gray matter incorporated into it."

"What do you mean, like it's tangled up in her brain? Isn't that what a tumor does, get all tangled up in a person's brain? That's why it's hard to take out, right?"

"This is different," the doctor said. "Look, I've been debating with myself whether I should tell you about this—"

"If you're gonna bill me, you goddam better tell me," Marcus growled. "What's going on with her?"

"Just from what I could see, the tumor has either co-opted part of your wife's brain—stolen it, complete with blood supply—or there's a second brain growing in your wife's skull."

There was a long pause. Then Marcus said, "You know how crazy that sounds? You got any pictures of this?"

"No. Even if I did, you're not a neurosurgeon, you wouldn't know what you were looking at."

"No? I can't help thinking I'd know if I were looking at two brains in one head or not."

"The most likely explanation for this would be a parasitic twin," the doctor went on. "It happens more often than you'd think. The only thing is, parasitic twins don't suddenly take to growing. And if it had always been so large, you'd have seen signs of it long before now.

"Unfortunately, I couldn't even take a sample to biopsy. Your wife's vitals took a nosedive and we had to withdraw immediately. She's fine now—under the circumstances. But we need to do those scans as soon as possible. Her right eye was so damaged by this tumor that we couldn't save it. If we don't move quickly enough, it's going to cause additional damage to her face."

Nell took a deep breath, and let it out slowly. She hadn't thought they would hear her but they had; all three stopped talking and Call-Me-Anne and Marcus scurried over to the side of her bed, saying her name in soft, careful whispers, as if they thought it might break. She kept her eyes closed and her body limp, even when Call-Me-Anne took her hand in both of hers and squeezed it tight. After a while, she heard them go.

How had they done that, she marveled. How had they done it from so far away?

Something can be a million light years away and in your eye at the same time.

Her mind's eye showed her a picture of two vines entangled with each other. Columbus's ships, just coming into view. The sense she had been missing was not yet fully developed, not enough to reconcile the vine and the ships. But judging from what the doctor said, it wouldn't be long now.

Timmy, Come Home

Matthew Hughes

At first, they were just shadows and whispers in Brodie's dreams, voices he could not quite hear, movement he could not quite bring into focus. Then the shadows and whispers began to filter into his waking hours, and he sought help.

"Neurologically, there is nothing wrong with you," said the neurologist. "Your brain is anatomically and functionally normal. We found no lesions, tumors or chemical anomalies."

"What does that leave?" said Brodie.

The neurologist spread his hands. "Psychiatric causes?"

The psychiatrist said, "You're not schizophrenic. I find no dissociative tendencies."

"So I'm normal? But I hear voices."

"You hear voices but you don't know what they're saying. Most people who hear voices know exactly what they're saying. The voices tell them to do things. Often they are things they shouldn't do. Sometimes they are things no one should do."

"So I should feel good about that?"

The psychiatrist interlaced his fingers and said, "How *do* you feel about it?"

The psychologist said, "You fall in the middle of the bell curve on every measure I've taken of you, except two." The man looked through the sheaf of papers before him, found one and scanned it. "In intelligence, you're in the top percentile." He looked at another. "In terms of affect, you seem to be sad."

Brodie sat in the patient's chair, a comfortable armchair upholstered in brown leather. "They told me I was bright in high school," he said. "I don't know if I'm sad. I'm just me, the way I've always been."

"I'm a little concerned that you live such a solitary life—"

"*I'm* not concerned," Brodie said.

The psychologist made a gesture of acquiescence. "It's not uncommon in cases of exceptional intelligence. And you don't seem to be actually depressed."

Brodie ignored the motion that he saw indistinctly from the corner of his right eye and the barely audible susurration that seemed to come from just behind his right ear. "If there's nothing wrong with me," he said, "then what's wrong with me?"

The psychologist stroked his chin. "How does it affect your life?"

Brodie thought for a moment. "Minimally," he said. "It comes and goes and I can usually ignore it. But, steadily, it comes more often and lasts longer."

"What is it that bothers you most? The inability to control it?"

"At first, yes. Now I'd just like to know what they're trying to tell me."

The psychologist zeroed in. "'They'?" he said.

"There's more than one voice," Brodie said.

"How do you know?"

"I just do."

"And what makes you think 'they' are trying to tell you something?"

Now it was Brodie's turn to spread his hands. "Why else would they be trying so hard to get my attention?"

The parapsychologist said, "Have you experienced any instances of precognition, lengthy periods of déjà vu, astral projection?"

"No."

"Would you like to?"

"No."

The exorcist closed the book, rang the bell and snuffed out the candle and said, "Are they still there?"

"Yes."

"Dammit. Now we'll have to start over."

The medium said, "I hear the name Walter. Does that have any meaning to you?"

"I don't think so."

"Not your father's name?"

"No."

"A childhood friend?"

"Nuh-uh."

"Maybe an uncle? A pet?"

"Goodbye."

"Close your eyes and imagine you're sitting in a darkened movie theater. The screen is bright white and in the middle of it is a small black dot."

"All right."

The hypnotist's voice was warm and calmly assured.

It reminded Brodie of his mother's voice when he was young. "Concentrate on the dot."

"Yes."

"The more you concentrate, the more relaxed you feel."

"Yes."

"All you can see now is the dot."

"Yes."

"It's growing larger. Now it fills the screen."

Brodie made an involuntary sound.

"What's wrong?"

"I don't like it."

"What don't you like?"

"The big dot. It's too big. Too dark. Too . . . deep."

"All right. It's not a dot. It's an *x*. Is that better?"

It was. Brodie felt his anxiety fade.

"You're becoming more and more relaxed," the woman said. "Your feet are relaxed."

Brodie's feet were very relaxed.

"Your legs are relaxed."

He felt the muscles of his calves and thighs slacken pleasantly.

"Now your abdomen and your lower back are relaxed."

"Yes." The word came on a sigh.

"Your shoulders and your upper back are relaxed."

"Mmmm."

"And your neck."

"Ungh."

"You're relaxed from the top of your head to the tip of your toes. You've never felt better."

It was true. He'd never felt better. "Mmm," he said.

"Wonderful. Now turn your attention to the whisper in your right ear."

"Yes."

"As you listen, it gets louder."

Brodie listened. The whisper grew louder.

"As it gets louder, it becomes clearer."

"No," he said. "It doesn't."

"Concentrate. Your hearing is becoming much sharper. You could hear a pin drop in the next room."

Brodie's hearing became sharper. The hypnotist's voice sounded more crisp. But the whispering remained an undifferentiated sequence of sounds.

"I can't make it out," he said.

"You're still relaxed, more relaxed than you've even been before."

"Yes."

"Let the sound come to you. Let it become clear."

Brodie did as he was told. But the whispering did not become clear.

The hypnotist was a plump, grandmotherly woman. The room where she practiced her profession was as congenial as she was. "I want to try something else," she said.

"It didn't work," Brodie said. "Nothing I've tried has worked."

"We got somewhere," she said.

"True."

"So it's worth trying a different approach." She leaned back in the comfortable chair that faced and matched Brodie's. "You get a feel for these things. I've got a feeling that there's something buried in you."

"I don't think so," he said. "I had a completely untroubled childhood. My parents didn't beat me or cast me as a supporting player in their own psychological dramas. I was not ritually abused or locked in a dark closet."

"Even so," she said, "you're throwing up a lot of dust right now."

Brodie thought about it. "I am, aren't I?" He agreed to come back for another session.

"Completely relaxed."

Brodie made a contented, compliant sound. The chair held him like the palm of a warm hand.

"Now you're standing on a high place. You can see very far in every direction."

"Yes."

"In one direction, you can see your childhood."

"Yes."

"What does it look like?"

"Sunny. Bright colors. I see my dog, Willy."

"What happened to Willy?"

"He got old. The vet put him to sleep. It didn't hurt him."

"It made you sad?"

"Yes. I cried. Mom and Dad cried, too."

"Think about Willy."

"Okay."

"Now think about the dot in the middle of the screen. Think about it getting larger."

Brodie shifted in the chair, as if preparing to stand.

"You're still very relaxed, as relaxed as you've ever been. You're completely safe."

He settled back.

"The dot cannot harm you. It cannot harm Willy. You can think about it without being troubled."

"I don't like it."

"What don't you like about the dot?"

"It's a hole, a dark hole."

"Why does the hole bother you?"

Brodie shifted nervously. The chair wasn't supportive now. It was confining. "Because you can't get out."

"The hole is going away now. It's far away where you don't have to worry about it."

Brodie relaxed, settled back into the chair. "Good."

"Now you're back on the high place, looking over your whole childhood."

"Mmm."

"You've got a telescope that lets you focus on any time in your childhood, any event. You can see yourself and other people, see what you were doing. And Willy, too."

"Yes."

"Look through the telescope now and see a time when you were frightened by a hole."

Brodie grunted.

"You're still far away from that time, just seeing it through a telescope."

"Okay."

"The you that was frightened then doesn't have to be frightened now."

"Okay."

"You're safe and relaxed. Nothing can hurt you."

"Yes."

"Now look through the telescope. What do you see?"

Brodie looked.

"We're getting somewhere," the hypnotist said.

"I suppose," Brodie said. "But where?"

He could remember what he had seen, because the hypnotist had told him he would. At first, the scene had been contained within a circle, just as if he had viewed it through a telescope. Then, as she had told him to zoom in on it, the image had filled the inner screen of his mind.

He saw himself—his much younger self; he could not

have been older than five—sitting on the old couch in the living room. Willy, still just a pup, was lying on the carpeted floor, licking his paws, paying no attention to the television.

Now the image shifted its point of view, so that Brodie was looking over his earlier self's shoulder. The television was showing an old movie about a boy who had a dog—a bigger dog than Willy, a collie. Now the dog on the TV was barking. Willy looked up at the sound, then went back to his grooming.

A woman wearing an apron over a long dress was asking the collie what was wrong. The dog's boy was nowhere in sight. The animal ran off a short distance, stopped, turned back to the woman, barked.

"Is it Timmy?" she said. "Find Timmy!" The dog ran off, barking, and she followed it out of the shot. As the scene changed, Brodie had felt a chilling shock pass through him. The hypnotist had had to tell him to freeze the scene in his memory so that she could spend a few minutes calming him and distancing him from the events. Finally, he was ready to go on.

And then, when the moment of revelation came, all that he recalled was a shot of the dog barking at the edge of a hole in the ground—a hole partly covered by splintered boards. Then came a shot of a little boy, his blond hair seeming to glow against a surrounding darkness, looking up toward a dim light far above, with the sound of the dog barking off-screen, and the woman's voice calling, "Timmy! We're going to get you out of there!"

"Can you remember now what was so frightening about that television show?" the hypnotist asked.

But Brodie couldn't remember. Seeing it now, in his mind's eye, and stretching to recall what emotions his little-boy self had felt, all those years ago, he came up blank. "No," he told the grandmotherly woman, "fact is, I don't even recall being scared. I just felt ..." He searched inside himself and after a moment it came to him, "So sad. I was so sad for the little boy. He'd fallen in the hole."

"Why was that so sad?"

"I don't know," Brodie said. "I just knew that it was the absolute worst, the absolutely saddest thing in the world. I couldn't bear to think of it."

Brodie's response to the memory of watching the TV show about the kid who fell in the hole had been so strong that the hypnotist wanted to let the emotions settle before she asked the crucial question: What did this have to do with the shadows and whispers that still plagued his dreams and, more and more, his waking moments? She let that wait until his next visit.

Before she put him under, the woman said, "We're going to go back to the memory of the boy in the hole. It won't be so difficult now that you've confronted the emotion, and we'll try and see how that memory connects to what's happening to you now."

Brodie wasn't averse to using the telescope to go back to his long-ago self again, sitting on the couch watching TV. In the few days since they had uncovered that memory, he had thought quite often about what had happened. The whole business puzzled him. He accepted that some part of him hadn't wanted to remember feeling so sad, had buried the memory and had had to be led gently back to it.

So it was with more curiosity than apprehension that he relaxed in the comfort of the chair and allowed the hypnotist's soothing voice to take him back to the high place, then through the telescope to the boy on the couch. And from that came ... nothing.

"Put yourself back in the boy's body," the woman said. "Look around the room. Are there shadows in the corners, perhaps a curtain blowing in a window that you see from the corner of your eye?"

"No."

"What do you hear in the background? Is anyone talking in another room, talking softly?"

"No."

"Your hearing is getting much stronger. You can hear every sound around you. What do you hear?"

Brodie listened with the boy's ears. He heard a distant radio playing rock and roll, the sound of water running. "Wes Fordham," he said, "the teenager who lives next door. He's washing his car. He loves that car."

"Anything else? Your hearing is even sharper now."

"No, nothing."

"Where is your father right now?"

"At work."

"Where is your mother?"

"In the kitchen, reading *Reader's Digest*. It came in the mail today. She likes to read it. Sometimes she reads me funny bits. They make me laugh."

The hypnotist took him back to the high place. "Was there another time when you were frightened about a hole? Before the time you saw the TV show?"

"I don't remember."

"Look back across your childhood, even to the earliest times you remember. Was there a time when you were frightened by a hole?"

"I don't remember."

"You can use the telescope to examine the farthest-away parts of your childhood. Look closely."

"There's nothing."

"You need fear nothing. You are perfectly safe."

"I'm not afraid. I just can't see anything."

The hypnotist told him to put down the telescope. She relaxed him further, took him deeper into the trance. Then she said, "You are on the high place again. Before you stretches your childhood."

"Yes."

"Now look down at your feet. You are standing on a flying carpet."

"Okay."

"You sit down cross-legged on the carpet and tell it to fly over your childhood."

"Yes."

"You are perfectly relaxed and safe. You are flying over your childhood, toward the earliest years."

"Yes."

"You fly past the day you saw the TV show about the boy who fell in the hole."

"Yes."

"Now you are flying over the years when you were a toddler."

"Yes."

"Now you are flying over the time when you were an infant."

"Yes."

"Now you are flying over the moment you were born."

"Yes."

"The carpet keeps flying, carrying you further back."

"Yes."

"Back to when you were growing in your mother's womb."

"Yes."

"You are very relaxed, very safe."

"I am safe."

"Now the carpet takes you back before you were in your mother's womb."

"Yes."

"Where are you?"

Brodie was silent.

"What can you see?"

"The ..."

"Your eyesight is very sharp. You can see very clearly."

"Yes."

"What do you see?"

"The tatuksha."

"What was that? What do you see?"

"The tatuksha."

"What is the tatuksha?"

Brodie's face collapsed in sadness. His mouth fell open, the corners turned down in a grimace of despair. Tears flowed down his cheeks. "I've fallen into it," he said. "It's dark. I can't get out."

It took her a long time to bring him back. At first, he refused to recognize the existence of the flying carpet. He wept and made odd sounds that might have been words or might have been wordless cries of anguish. She spoke soothingly, telling him he was safe, that the darkness could not hurt him. Finally, she got him to focus.

"You see a white dot in the darkness."

"A white dot."

"It's above you. Look up and see it."

"Yes. I see it."

"It's the way out of the tatuksha."

"Too far."

"Look down at your feet."

"No feet."

"You have feet. Wriggle your toes." He had taken off his shoes for the session. She saw his toes move in his socks.

"I have feet."

"You are standing on the flying carpet. Look down and see it."

"I don't . . ."

"It's underneath your feet. It brought you here and it will take you back."

"I see it."

"It is a strong carpet."

"Yes."

"A magic, flying carpet."

"Yes."

"Now it lifts you up, toward the white dot."

"Yes."

"The dot grows larger. You focus on it. You see only the white dot."

"I see it."

"It is the way out of the darkness. The way out of the tatuksha."

"Yes."

"Now the carpet is lifting you back into the light. You are free."

"Yes." Brodie began to weep again, but not from despair.

"You see ahead of you your life, all the moments that led up to this moment."

"I see it."

"The carpet is flying you back to this room, this chair, where you are safe and relaxed and nothing can harm you."

"Yes."

"In a few moments, you will wake. You will be calm and rested. You will remember what happened. You will remember the tatuksha, but it will not frighten you. Because you escaped from it. And now you are here and safe."

*   *   *

She played him the tape recording of their session. Brodie listened. He winced when he heard the agony in his voice.

"Does it mean anything to you?" she said. "That word, tatuksha, does it call up any memory?"

He shook his head. "In a way," he said. "It's like something I've heard before and forgotten. Or maybe something I've heard in a dream."

That week, whenever Brodie lay down to sleep, the whispers were in his ears and the shadows flickered at the corners of his vision, even when his eyes were closed. It seemed to him that they were more insistent, and when he dreamed, the whispers were louder, clearer. He heard "tatuksha," and it seemed that he heard other words, too; the shadows became faces, strange faces, not human. And yet familiar. But when he awoke he could remember none of it.

"I have to tell you," said the hypnotist, when he came to her again, "I had never done a past-life regression before. To be honest, I'd never quite believed in it. Now I'm not sure what to do."

"I want to try again," Brodie said.

"First, let me tell you this: a friend of my sister's is married to a philologist."

"I don't know what that is."

"He studies the development of languages through time. I asked him what language the word 'tatuksha' might have come from. He checked his references and found nothing."

"What does that mean?"

She leaned across the space between their chairs and touched his hand. "It may mean it's just a word your mind made up."

"Not from a past life?"

"Under hypnosis, the mind wants to cooperate. Ask it for something that isn't there, and sometimes it manufactures an answer. It's called confabulation."

"No," said Brodie.

"No?"

"No. Something happened. I'm hearing other words in dreams now."

"Tell me about them."

"I can't remember them when I wake up. I want to try under hypnosis."

She frowned. "I'm worried that I might be leading you up a false trail."

"Don't be," he said. "I'm not."

She didn't take him back to the tatuksha. She took him into his dreams. The shadows came and the whispers. He tried to make them clearer, struggled to hold the images in his mind's eye, the sounds in his mind's ear.

"Relax," she said, "let yourself float, as if you were on a warm river, drifting slowly."

He relaxed.

"You let the images come to you. You make no effort to focus. They just pass before your eyes. The sounds wash over you."

"Yes."

"What do you hear?"

"Tatuksha."

"What else?"

"Kekkethet. Estittit."

"What else?"

He made other sounds. She wrote them down on a pad.

"What do you see?"

"The sort-of faces. But they won't stay still. They keep changing, flickering, dissolving."

"In your hand is a remote control, like for a DVD player. When you click it the images pause. You can examine them."

"Yes."

"Do you recognize anyone?"

"Some of them are movie stars. Jimmy Carter. The Dalai Lama."

"What do you think of Jimmy Carter?"

"A good man, kind."

"What about the Dalai Lama?"

"The same."

"How do you feel about the faces in your dream?"

"Good. They're kind people. They want to help me."

She brought him out of the trance. "I don't know if this is helping you," she said.

"I think it is. I feel . . . better."

The woman looked worried. "For me, this has gone way off the map. I'm thinking I should refer you to another practitioner. Someone who does past-life regression."

"But you don't really believe in that," Brodie said.

"I didn't. Now I'm starting to."

"Tatuksha," the hypnotist said. "Kekkethet. Estittit." She spoke three more words that Brodie had heard in dreams, words that they had recovered together when she had led him to revisit those dreams under hypnosis. "What do they mean to you?"

"Nothing."

She put him under again, took him to the high place and the carpet, then flew him back beyond his mother's womb. It was a smooth and easy ride.

"Where are you?" she said.

"I . . . I can't describe it. A familiar place. But I can't make it hold still. It all flows. In different directions, all at once."

"What are you doing?"

"Looking at something."

"What are you looking at?"

"Tatuksha."

"What is tatuksha?"

"The place you don't go."

"Why don't you go there?"

"Can't get out."

"Kekkethet," she said. "Estittit." She said the other words.

He nodded as she said them, like a man remembering.

"What do they mean?" she said.

His face brightened. "I have to die."

She didn't want to see him again, recommended another hypnotist. He refused to go away. He found out where she lived and came there.

"I'm frightened," she said. She would only open the door a little and spoke through the crack.

"Of me?"

"For you."

"It's all right," he said. "You have helped me. I need you to help me just a little more."

"Help you how?"

"To get out of the hole."

Her living room was messy but the chair was comfortable. He closed his eyes and her voice came to him through the darkness. He knew she was worried, frightened even, but she strove to keep her tone calm and assured. "You look up and see the white dot."

"Yes." It hung above him, very far, unreachable, but he was confident now, the sadness fading.

"It's the way out of tatuksha."

"Yes."

"Look down at your feet, see the flying carpet."

"I see it."

"It is a good carpet, a strong carpet. You have faith in it."

He felt it, soft beneath his stocking feet. It was worn in places, yet strong. "Yes."

"Now it lifts you up, toward the white dot."

"Yes." It pressed against his soles. He began to ascend.

"The dot grows larger."

It grew to the size of a winter's full moon, then became gibbous as in autumn. "Yes."

"It is the way out of tatuksha."

"Yes." The light from the glowing circle grew brighter and now it was warm on his head and shoulders. He raised his hand and felt its gentle heat on his upturned palms. It was nearer now, wider than he was.

Her voice dwindled in his hearing. "Almost free now. Then the carpet will fly you back to this room, back to where you are safe."

"No," Brodie said. "Not here. Here is tatuksha."

"Safety," she said. He heard her trying to keep her voice calm, trying to bring him back. "Here is safety."

"No," he said. His eyes opened. He was looking at her, across the small space between their chairs, a space that was now growing immense; at the same time he was looking up into the warm glow. The woman, the chairs, the room were all trapped now in a dwindling circle of fading light, falling into the surrounding shadows, becoming shadows. He saw her tiny shadow-head jerk back, and he supposed she must have been startled by what she was seeing in his eyes, seeing the reflected glow of his destination. Perhaps she even felt its warmth, radiating from him, spilling into lonely, cold tatuksha.

"What is happening?" He heard the alarm in her

voice, though now it came to him as barely more than a whisper.

"It is all right," he said, closing his eyes again. He felt sad for her, left behind in the shadows. But it could not be helped. "I must go now."

"Where? Where are you going?"

"To Estittit," he said. The light bathed him, warm as cream. It flowed over him, through him. The voices that had been whispers in his dreams were clearer now, stronger, full of surprise and joy, familiar. The shadow motions were forming into fluid patterns, flowing in ways he now remembered.

"Where is Estittit?" came the hypnotist's fading whisper from below.

"Home," he breathed.

There was a coroner's inquest. The past-life regression aspect of the story caused a brief sensation in the media and a longer one in the blogosphere. But the verdict of death by natural causes eventually tamped down the tumult.

The tabloids and cable news services spread the hypnotist's name widely. Notoriety was no longer fame's ugly stepsister; now they were twins. Celebrities consulted her. Her practice grew. She learned to live with it.

The entity that had been Brodie became itself again. It was a long process, shedding the gray ash of tatuksha, but there was infinite time to rediscover the subtleties of the eight thousand effulgences, each with its five thousand tints and tones. One by one, or in clusters, it regained its one hundred and eight senses, until it could be invited once more into the great sympathic dance.

The entity roiled and insinuated itself among the

multiforms, now cohering to the richness of the center, now arabesquing out to the filigreed edges. It embraced and was embraced by the Host, penetrating even as it was penetrated, swallowing that which swallowed it. It sang the endless song, the grand harmony ever dissolving, ever reforming, only to dissolve and reform again.

It reposed in bliss. But always it kept, in a pocket that was not really a pocket, a small fragment of the poor, tiny thing it had been when it had become Brodie. And sometimes, when it passed by—or through, or around, or overunder—a newly forming node, it would reveal the cold, sad cinder and then it would make the terrified new entity promise never, ever, to go near tatuksha.

A Waterfall of Lights

Ian Watson

Two summers earlier, of a Friday evening, Roderick and Nancy and Nick and I had a beer-fueled discussion in one of the snug rooms in the Eagle and Child, where Tolkien used to meet up with his Oxford author chums. A chinwag about the possible existence of alien civilizations.

The Bird and Baby, as it's known to the locals, was serving a *green* guest ale, something I'd never encountered before. By "green" I don't mean that it was an ecologically worthy beer produced not too far distantly from organic ingredients, but that it was almost grass-green in hue. This brew turned out to be made from young *un*roasted hops, hence the color. Surprisingly tasty and refreshing it was too. Green beer led to the notion of little green men visiting Earth to sup it, although of course our ale might make them sick due to their alien biology.

Nick dearly wished that fellow astronomers would stop wasting time on the search for extraterrestrial life.

"*Microbial* life's fairly likely elsewhere in our galaxy, but as for anything more complex: forget it!"

Because, you see, complex intelligent life on planet Earth was the result of a long series of lucky accidents ...

"If the sun were in a more crowded part of the sky, supernovas or gamma bursts would have sterilized the world repeatedly—"

If there'd been "bad Jupiters" orbiting nearer to the sun or more eccentrically, forget any planet Earth at all. Early random collisions gave us our spin axis and our length of day—yet without a moon the hefty size of our Earth's tilt angle would wander, hopelessly destabilizing climate.

"What's more, our sun's a quarter richer in heavy metals than other nearby stars, hence Earth's iron core—"

—which caused our vital strong magnetic field.

Earth could so easily have become a hell of heat like Venus, or alternatively a permanent iceball—although *without* massive glaciations, higher plants and animals might never have evolved.

If there hadn't been the right proportion of land to water! If there hadn't been continental drift! If *this* had not happened *thus*. If *that* had not chanced to occur. A list as long as your arm. Every single condition needed to be fulfilled.

"Including a mighty impact wiping out the dinosaurs?" prompted my Nancy.

Nick shook his half-bald head. "No, some dinos might have evolved intelligence, so we could have had Saurus sapiens instead of Homo sapiens."

"But not speaking Latin," she teased. "I suppose Saurus sapiens would have drunk green beer. Them being mainly green in pictures."

"Nobody knows what color—" He broke off, well aware of her sense of mischief. "I'll grant you," he resumed, "that the same long lucky streak might have happened in some other galaxy far away. But as for our own there's unlikely to be anything as complicated as a crab out there." Nick was partial to eating soft-shelled crabs for starters at the Vietnamese restaurant. "The *real* question isn't where are the aliens, because they simply aren't—but *where are the A.I.s?* Where are the artificial intelligences, eh?"

"But we haven't made any yet," said Roderick, whose own field was ophthalmology. "Surely we haven't? Ah, are you meaning A.I.s created by actual aliens many galaxies away from us? Yet a few billion years *ago,* so that by now they've had ample time to replicate over vast distances?"

Roderick liked to keep up with a whole range of popular science beyond his specialty, practiced at the Nuffield lab within the John Radcliffe Hospital up in Headington where he was a consultant. We *all* did so. My Nancy wasn't just a pretty face gracing admin at the Botanic Garden; she had her degree in plant sciences. And I directed the School of Geography and the Environment, though never let it be said that geographers play second fiddle in the science orchestra! We'd all been close since we were undergraduates a couple of decades earlier, obviously Nancy and I the more so. Maybe Nick was the *purest* scientist, in a sense.

"What I mean," said Nick, "is where are the A.I.s from the *parent* cosmos of ours—presuming that we budded off from a previous cosmos."

And Nick treated us to the explanation that an artificial intelligence would by definition be immortal—as well as able to redesign and enhance itself in due course into something godlike; and the A.I. would have one goal for sure, namely *survival,* which must include surviving the death of the universe it arose in . . .

"*Consequently* A.I.s from previous cycles of existence must have passed through into our own universe, and after fourteen billions years they've had plenty of time to spread everywhere and manipulate on a grand scale if they care to."

"Maybe they don't care to?" said Nancy. "If intelligent life's so rare, maybe our galaxy's a nature reserve set aside for us?"

Nick snorted. "Along with *all* of observable space? True, there seems to be something very big indeed that's tugging from beyond the observable boundary—"

"A.I. HQ?" I quipped.

"Tom, how would they know anything about us unless they already visited? In which case they'd surely leave at least one clone A.I. hereabouts to observe developments. Anyway, *nothing* can have visited us from beyond the observable boundary. That's the whole point of a boundary—even light hasn't time to visit."

"Maybe they use short cuts, Nick," said Roderick slyly.

"It's ridiculous to imagine an entire universe being cordoned off for the sake of one inhabited world, which might be snuffed out any old time by a big asteroid hitting us! Or whatever disaster. Why bother to do so, in any case? Your trouble, Rod, is that you always extend things to absurdity. Or reduce them."

"An extending rod or a reducing rod," Roderick mused.

"I believe there are *rods* in the eyes," I said.

"Rods gobble up light, thus we see at night," Roderick rhymed. "We can spot a single candle seventeen miles away."

"Surely not," I said. "I don't believe that."

"We could carry out an experiment," Roderick said merrily. "How about if we all take a holiday somewhere without any light pollution, say in tents in the middle of the Sahara desert?"

"Why would anyone want to see a candle seventeen miles away?" asked Nancy. "And how about all the Saharan starlight? Isn't that brighter than candles?"

"And where," said Nick, "are the A.I.s from the *grandparent* of our present universe, and from *its* grandparent? Given an infinite succession of universes, A.I.s that tunneled through from one universe to a successor universe *ought* to be here."

I wondered what Tolkien would have made of this discussion in his snug. Maybe he'd have begun trying to invent an alien language ... And would he have approved of green beer for Hobbits?

"Maybe the tunneling bit is too difficult?" suggested Nancy, twirling a golden lock.

"For biological life, yeah. But for immortal *information*—?"

Nick's mobile rang, tootling a theme from Holst's *Jupiter*.

"There's been a gamma ray burst in—well, the galaxy only has a catalogue number," he apologized, draining his glass speedily.

"When would that have been?" asked Nancy. "A billion years ago?"

"More like four. Um, billion."

"Ah, the urgencies of astrophysics."

His mobile tootled again, and now he was apologizing to his wife Lucy. He would just take a quick squint at the data, then be home for dinner. No, he hadn't forgotten that Lucy's mother was visiting. Shrugging, Nick departed into the leafy avenue of plane trees that was St. Giles.

Roderick sighed. "I ought to marry a woman called Lucy. Or maybe Lucia. Named for light."

"Maybe," said Nancy in a kindly way, "you should simply marry a *woman*."

At forty-six, Roderick was perhaps unlikely to. He was affably shambly looking in his person, although obviously there must be a high degree of delicacy to his touch, given the corresponding delicacy of eyes, or vice versa. Maybe the right word was gentleness. But we all knew that he had desired Nancy, in vain. Paradoxically this was one of the strings that united us four. Also, Nancy and I hadn't had kids. By now Nancy was on the age-cusp of never being able to. My fault: low sperm count—just my bad luck, one of those things. We'd talked about having my sperm mixed with a donor's in case one of mine, swept along with the crowd, proved to be lucky. But we hadn't done so. Nancy filled our house with orchids.

Whereas Nick had married his Lucy almost inadvertently, so it seemed. A secretary, originally, at the Department of Astrophysics, she'd become starry-eyed about him. Now they had two teenagers, Philip and Philippa, names that had struck me as a failure of imagination in the domestic department or some peculiar economy measure. Or maybe something dynastic: Nick's strong-willed barrister father was a Philip.

"Did you know," said Roderick, "that St. Lucy had beautiful eyes, so she was deoculated as a martyrdom? Her symbol is a pair of eyes on a saucer."

"That's *squirmy,*" protested Nancy. "Doesn't make it any better by saying deoculated."

"She's the patron saint of the blind, but I don't have her picture in my office. Could be off-putting, hmm?"

"A Lucia *mightn't* be well-advised to marry you."

I noticed that Nancy didn't say "a Lucy" since Lucy was Nick's wife, just as Nancy was mine. Probably Roderick had mentioned St. Lucy in the past—the story did ring a bell, though not a loud one; he'd been a *lapsed* Roman Catholic even in our college days.

Fairly soon it was time for us to go our separate ways, Nancy and I by bus to Summertown, Roderick on foot to his bachelor home in Jericho. And thus it was time for his traditional non-crushing bear-hug of Nancy, and for her to peck him on the cheek.

Out of vague curiosity I looked up St. Lucy. Apart from her beautiful eyes, she was a Christian virgin heiress with a big dowry, ordered to marry a pagan. Her refusal led to her martyrdom. And it occurred to me that in Roderick Butler's eyes my Nancy might bizarrely classify as some sort of virgin in the sense that I'd never made her pregnant. Consequently he could venerate her? Not exactly ... more like regard her as a still nubile Venus who happened to be tied to the wrong chap. Or a bit of both.

I recalled a holiday we'd all been on together five years earlier, including Mrs. Nick, although not the kids who opted to stay with her parents for a week; two weeks stuck on a canal in a narrowboat had little appeal for young Philip and Philippa. We could understand why when we arrived at Somerton Deep Lock, which resembled, especially in the rain, a wet version of Doré's Hell. However, we managed to have a fairly good time, especially at canalside pubs, in one of which I remember a folksinger chap causing Roderick, after several pints, to burst tipsily into a rendition of "Billy Boy," which goes thus:

> *Where have you been all the day,*
> *Me Billy Boy?*
> *I've been out with Nancy Gray,*
> *And she's stolen me heart away,*
> *She's me Nancy, tickled me fancy,*
> *Oh me charmin' Billy Boy.*

> *Is she fit to be a wife?*
> *me Billy Boy.*
> *She's as fit to be a wife,*
> *As a fork fits to a knife.*
> *She's me Nancy, tickled me fancy,*
> *Oh me charmin' Billy Boy.*

Hmm, yes exactly. Nancy tickled me fancy. Is she fit to be a wife?

Afterwards, Roderick's snores rumbled in the confines of the narrowboat, and in the morning he denied all knowledge. Amnesia due to beer. Nick and Lucy teased him a bit, but Nancy didn't, nor did I. During that fortnight no love-making occurred due to the limited privacy of our boat, so to Roderick's subconscious Nancy may have seemed chaste.

When Roderick offered Nancy a state-of-the-art examination at his lab, which would involve him staring deep into her eyes, she diplomatically claimed to have visited Vision Express in town just recently. Roderick included me in this invitation, though more as an afterthought. He didn't raise the matter again.

What Roderick did raise, when we all met up for another convivial drink, accompanied by a meal, this time in the King's Arms at the end of Broad Street, was Nick's assertion that the absence of A.I.s was a big puzzle.

"Didn't we cover all that last time?" Nancy said. "By the way, what did the gamma ray burst have to say?"

"What it basically said was: tough luck for any life in that galaxy. Well now, I think I said you can forget about the absence of intelligent aliens being a mystery, due to a suitable planet like ours being a one in a zillion chance."

"Although there still might be brainy aliens far far

away?" I chipped in. "On the principle that someone has to win a lottery now and then, given billions of galaxies?"

"Too far away *ever* to be known to us. Or too distant in time. Or both."

"Yet immortal A.I.s ought to be everywhere," said Roderick doggedly.

"Or at least some sign of them. In my view."

"In . . . your . . . *view,*" Roderick repeated, sounding rather as if he was a skeptical tutor addressing a bumptious student. "In your *view.*"

"Are you taking the piss, by any chance?"

"Absolutely not. A notion came to me . . . I fancy the fish and chips."

Nick glanced at the chalked menu board. "Good notion!"

It was a year later that Nancy and I received, by the very same post, invitations to a private viewing at the Museum of Modern Art in Pembroke Street, *RSVP* to email address. The artist: Jon Bell. Title of exhibition: *Eye Watch You.* Scientific Advisor: Roderick Butler (plus his eminent qualifications). Neatly penned on the printed cards: *Hope to see you! RB.*

Why send two separate invitations? An error on the part of some secretary at MOMA? It seemed more as if Roderick hoped to ensure that Nancy would pay full attention. And what was Roderick doing mixing with modern art? He hadn't mentioned any such thing in the meanwhile. Jon Bell was blurbed on the back of the card as a leading techno-conceptual artist with a background in electronics as well as being a graduate of Goldsmiths' College in London.

I phoned Nick. Yes, he and Lucy had also received an invitation, although Lucy probably wouldn't be going.

An invitation. *An*. No, Roderick hadn't let on about this new string to his bow.

I tried to phone Roderick several times to give a verbal RSVP, but in vain. His mobile went to voicemail, and his shared secretary at the Nuffield lab said he wasn't available.

We'd have to wait and see.

Jon Bell looked the epitome of cool, dressed all in black, which made him seem even more slim and wiry, slim oblong black sunglasses, a ring in his ear and a minimalist black beard, Vandyke-lite. Numerous acolytes or colleagues were present, several with tiny wifi computers on which they tapped, or internet phones with which they shot video clips, so that what was happening was enhancedly *happening*.

Trays of wine. Some blow-ups around the walls of dissected eyeballs. A beaming Roderick, wearing his professional suit, although with a rakish yellow cravat at his neck.

"What's going on?" I asked him.

"Wait for the show," he told Nancy, and yes, me too. "I hope you'll be impressed."

Occupying the large downstairs gallery, to which we duly trooped, was a huge transparent perspex globe, seated upon a square steel framework, in front of which stood a short flight of steps. A whirr of motors, and the—what was that called again?—yes, the *cornea* descended to give access to a circular doorway into this enormous eyeball. What was now the upper surface of this access, of blue-green plastic—slim bands of blue and green radiating out from a round transparent center—must be the iris, right? Whirring too, a crystalline disk of plastic rose upward within hydraulically: the lens of the eye undoubtedly. As that final obstacle rose, a multi-stranded cable that looked fiber-optic, connecting the midpoint of the lens to the rear of the, oh yes retina, rose up, sagging somewhat. A disc of thick see-through plastic provided a flat floor within to stand upon, for say half a dozen people without crowding . . .

"You'll notice the resemblance of the eye to an old-style diving bell," declared Jon Bell. "The *humor* of Bell's bell is that it should really be full of liquid! Unlike a true diving bell, which keeps liquid out. You'll have to imagine that the air inside is liquid. We could of course pump liquid in after it closes up, but then participants would need bathing costumes and oxygen masks. So I omitted that aspect."

Wineglasses in hand, people laughed appreciatively.

From the back of the eye, corresponding I supposed to the optic nerve, a multitude of optic fibers protruded, many looping around to attach themselves to the rear half of the sphere all over the outer surface, others leading to electronic gear and a computer tower.

The gallery lights dimmed somewhat.

Fish-eye images of us guests upstairs a few minutes earlier—there must have been tiny concealed cameras—and now downstairs (hidden cameras here likewise!) flashed around the interior of the giant eye while we gazed in a sort of childish wonder, and projected out onto the gallery walls distortedly enlarged, bouncing in and out, coalescing, separating, inverting randomly. Faces zoomed in and out, and bits of body, and hands holding wineglasses, quite a few looking like night-vision and also infrared images. What a dizzying dance of visions of ourselves.

Of a sudden Jon Bell clapped his hands.

"Pay ATTENTION, Eye!"

All the images promptly rushed to the back of the eye, forming a mosaic, which quickly became a single curved image of all of us gathered in front. What I'd taken for Lucite must be something smarter, maybe bonded in layers.

I whispered to Nancy, "Do you suppose Roderick put up any of his own money for this?"

"Well, that could be a good investment if Charles Saatchi or some Russian billionaire buys it ... sort of like Damien Hirst's Diamond Skull? But, like, *why?*"

Just at the moment Roderick surged, seized Nancy by the hand with a hasty *excuse-me,* as if cutting in on a dance floor, and tugged her towards and up the steps on to the cornea hatch, where he paused to call out: "Room for four more inside!" Jon Bell beckoned at three of the prettiest young ladies present and an austere chap who might be an art critic.

As soon as the chosen few were inside the big chamber, the iris descended and the cornea rose.

What my eyes saw from outside was how I imagined a psychedelic trip, not that I'd ever taken LSD or mushrooms or whatnot. The doors of perception opening up, and all that, though for me the hatch was shut; Nancy later confirmed my impression, and she *had* taken a few naturally occurring substances in the past, which seemed quite allowable for a botanist. To what extent had Roderick arranged all this in order to dazzle and impress her?

But never mind about the dazzling head-trip—or more correctly eye-trip—in company with Roderick. The astonishing thing came after Nancy was back beside me, when Roderick occupied the cornea hatch, lowered once more, and, standing beside Jon Bell who hopped up to join him, made a little speech, filmed to be streamed by the artist's online cyberchums.

"How do we pay attention to what we see?" Roderick asked. "There's an almost psychedelic jumble of different lights inside the eye. Blue's always out of focus, for instance, so how do blue things appear to have sharp edges? It's because our retina is an extremely sophisticated computer. Hidden away behind a carpet of blood vessels and nerves, as though the system is back-to-front, and almost invisibly transparent, our retina's as thin as paper, yet it has at least ten different layers of neurons to process and edit and compress information. Some cells can compress to a thousandfold! Our retina is the brain that intervenes between the world and our brain. And because of that, our sight is extraordinarily acute—"

I remembered about seeing a single candle flame at a distance of seventeen miles . . .

"—which of course is how we first made tools, and therefore all of technology subsequently. We talk about hypothetical intelligent aliens *out there* and we listen with our radio telescopes for decades in vain—no evidence of any, nor that we've ever been visited in the past. Yet in our universe there ought to exist one kind of immortal intelligence—and emphatically I'm *not referring to a God*."

By now the guests were regarding Roderick in a puzzled, though indulgent, way.

"I mean artificial intelligences brought into existence by intelligent aliens in *previous* universes and which survive forever from universe to universe, unlike their makers. They ought to be here, even observing us, since intelligent biological life must be very rare. *So where are they?*

"I declare that I know where they are! They are in the amazing computers of our eyes, the retinas. Not one in each retina, no no, for individual people die or are blinded. The A-Eyes, as I call them," and he spelled out the word, "are each distributed among millions of individuals, connected by photonic entanglement—"

"But that's bananas!" Nick exclaimed at me. "Information can't be conveyed at a distance by entanglement—"

"Shshshsh," said Nancy.

"They see what we see in mosaic form, time-sharing on our retinal computers while busy with their own computations. This will become evident as we gain more sophisticated insight, yes, you might well say *in*-sight, into the retinal computer, which I for my part intend to pursue from now on. Ladies and gentlemen, let me introduce you to the aliens in our midst, the super-intelligent evolved immortal creations of aliens from another cosmos which preceded ours! They are in your very own eyes! We don't see the aliens in our universe because it is *through* those alien intelligences that we perceive!"

Jon Bell and his electronic-art cronies burst into applause, grinning. So did almost all of the audience because this seemed to be yet more of the art event, an authentic happening for dessert. Nancy and I clapped our hands too, so as not to spoil Roderick's moment of glory, though Nick refrained: "Either he's lost it totally, or else he's having us on . . ." And guests queued up to experience a trip in the eye-globe, winking or gazing meaningfully into one another's eyes.

Afterwards, Roderick accompanied us ebulliently to the Miter in the High Street, at one point linking arms with Nancy who still seemed dazed by the psychedelic visions.

"So how did you team up with this bright new star of Brit Art?" I asked as soon as I'd downed my initial gulp of ale.

"Well now, I needed an art event as a showcase for my revelations in case my medical colleagues thought I'd gone loopy. I wouldn't have been able to publish this in any orthodox form. Really, we need nanotechnology to validate this, although I've applied for a research sabbatical to see what progress I might make." Roderick chuckled. "Obviously the Nobel Prize is a good way off yet."

Nick hesitated. "You *believe* what you said?"

"Dear chap, it's the answer to your conundrum. *But,*" he added significantly.

"But?" Nancy obliged by asking.

"Can any of you guess the other reason for an art event that's quite likely to make a few waves, even more so when it transfers to London?"

Nick made a show of scratching his head. "Um, to get in the news and attract funding from an eccentric billionaire?"

"The news, yes, that's part of it. Jon says he's fairly sure *Eye Watch You* will go viral on YouTube and people's phones and whatnot. The point is that this is out in the open now, unstoppably. I didn't want the A.I.s to notice prematurely in case they took exception to being revealed."

Paranoia . . . ?

"They'd already have *seen* what you were up to," I said. "I mean, if they exist."

"Tom," patiently, "a distributed intelligence can only *sample* what it sees, say for a few seconds or even microseconds. It wouldn't exactly read my mind! Yet there's a point where something can be detected and *appropriate measures taken* before it's too late, to suppress information—"

I wondered what measures he had in mind? Blindness? An induced stroke?

"—and beyond that point simply too many people know the idea."

For a moment I thought Nancy was about to reach

out to pat his hand, which Roderick might have misinterpreted. She said gently, "Isn't this idea of yours a bit like a conspiracy theory? You can present some evidence—as with the fall of the Twin Towers being a controlled demolition—but it can't be proved, even if it's plausible. And so the theory soon gets linked up with other far-out ideas that are definitely potty, such as that humanoid lizards secretly rule the Earth. Which devalues the original theory."

My Nancy had recently read a book about conspiracy theories. According to some energetic chap American presidents and the British royal family were lizard-human hybrids in disguise.

"But I didn't say anything at all about retinal A.I.s *controlling or influencing* human behavior."

"Conspiracists might do so—leading to silliness. I don't want you to expose yourself to ridicule." Evidently the rush of excitement caused by her trip in the Eye was giving way to wiser counsels. Yet then she went on, perhaps unadvisedly, "Or ... are you actually hoping to *provoke* a proof, on the part of your A.I.s? Rather than protecting yourself, instead: some detectable response?"

At which, a gleam came into Roderick's eye, as it were!

"The Eye serves several purposes," he said contentedly. Or did he say "the eye"?

"What about the eyes of chimps, for instance?" Nick chipped in. "Are they parts of A.I. as well? What about cats?—they see pretty well."

Roderick waved away such irrelevancies.

The private viewing of Jon Bell's *Eye Watch You* did indeed go viral over the next few days. The artist must have been rubbing his hands in glee, anticipating the transfer to a London gallery, or even a preemptive purchase by a collector for a large sum in Oxford itself.

A week later, sevenish of an evening, came a ring-ring.

"Tom Cooper here," I said. I like to identify myself fully on the telephone since the way most people merely say *hullo* strikes me as silly. *Is that you, yes it's me.* And what if you don't immediately recognize which "John" someone is out of half a dozen possible candidates?

"Thank goodness, I managed it!" Roderick's voice sounded at once anxious and exalted; and what did he mean?

"Can you and Nancy possibly come round right now? It's fairly urgent."

"Well . . . yes, I suppose—I'll need to check with Nancy."

"Do tell her it's *important*. Would you mind ringing Nick to ask him as well?"

"Can't you ring him yourself?"

"I mightn't succeed! I'll explain when you come."

Jericho is the part of Oxford between Walton Street, former location of the Nuffield Ophthalmology Lab, and the canal; hence Roderick buying a house within what had previously been easy walking distance of his workplace. The building of the canal in the later eighteenth century, to bring coal quickly and cheaply to the city, caused a veritable ghetto of laborers and craftspeople, which became a crammed slumland of terrace houses, prey to cholera and other degradations. Nowadays the area is highly gentrified and expensive. Naturally the terrace houses remain small, but they're very bijou, much desired by young professionals; and Roderick of course remained a bachelor.

Nancy and I had taken a taxi to his door, its pointed

archway of bricks painted in red and yellow just like those arches in the Great Mosque of Córdoba in a minor key. In contrast his New Age neighbors on one side had gone for all the colours of the rainbow, up one side of the arch and down the other.

The door opened and Roderick blinked at us.

"Nancy? Nick?"

"Can't you see properly?" she asked.

"Come, come." He blundered ahead of us to his living room, where he located a comfy armchair into which he subsided with a sigh of relief. A framed print of Seurat's pixelated *Bathers* hung over the fireplace, and an impressionist Monet lily pond by the window.

"What's wrong?" asked Nancy.

Roderick held up his palms as though determined to count how many fingers he had.

"I'm seeing text scrolling down all the time. Beautiful text! You're just like a vague mirage behind this golden curtain or waterfall. But I'm buggered if I can read any of it. The symbols aren't any alphabet I've ever seen or ideograms or math or music . . ."

"When did this start?" I asked.

"About an hour ago. I just watched for a while, bewitched, trying to make sense of a single squiggle, but they never stay; they scroll down as I say." His descending hand indicated the rate of descent, about a foot every couple of seconds. Personally I'd be able to read a document in English at that speed, but the task would become cumulatively exhausting.

Of course his grey eyes looked exactly the same as ever, although just to be sure I stepped closer.

"It's retinal, damn it, Tom. *You* can't see anything."

"And you, er, reckon it's the A.I.s communicating with you?"

"What else can it be? I haven't been drugged by some

security service and had super cyber contact lenses stuck over my iris. Precious data is passing away every moment, just supposing that I *could* understand it . . ."

"Maybe," said Nancy to calm him, "after a while the message repeats and carries on repeating."

Just then the doorbell rang and I went to let in, predictably, Nick, whom I quickly briefed in the hallway. Nick promptly took out his phone to find Google News, then other sites in swift succession.

He announced as he entered the living room, "No reports yet on the web of the same thing happening to other people. Hullo there, Roderick. So how did they zero in on you?"

"Maybe it's a bit early for reports," said Mary. "This only started an hour ago."

"If it's happening to many people there'd be reports already, believe me."

"Maybe the victims, I mean, the contacted people can't see clearly enough to send reports. Maybe they're too distracted."

"Oh well, of course that's a possibility." Nick stooped and peered at Roderick's face just as I had done.

"I told you it's retinal!" Roderick protested at whatever blur he was seeing. "You can't see what I see! And they found me because my identity's all over cyberspace at the moment, so they carried out an Oxford-specific eye-search."

"For your eye-dentity," I said.

Nick had spied a large notepad upon a bookshelf. Seizing and flipping the notepad open to bare pages, he produced a pen and thrust both at Roderick.

"Can you copy anything? Stick with a first line and follow it down."

Roderick tried, bless him, but his bit of scribble was such a squiggly mess.

"Lost it already . . ."

"Can you write *the quick brown fox?*"

That Roderick could manage readably, but I could have done so blindfolded.

"Just testing," said Nick. He blinked rapidly, as though trying to induce the same phenomenon in himself, to no avail. "Roderick, have you phoned Jon Bell?"

"It was hard enough calling Tom!"

"Conceivably your Mr. Bell might see this as another publicity opportunity, if he isn't affected himself—ah, but does he have a blog?"

"The link's in my laptop upstairs," said Roderick. "Oh, this cascade of golden lost opportunities!"

"Never mind, I'll just search the Web." Which Nick proceeded to do on his phone.

And before long he announced, "Excellent, Bell's latest posting, some blather about artichokes, is only fifteen minutes ago. So he's unaffected. I believe we shouldn't tip him off till we've slept on this. Besides, Rod's problem might simply stop if it's psychological or neurological. Him getting overexcited. Like people having visions of angels."

"This is *real*. Look, I do *know* about peculiar neurological visual effects."

"But you aren't a psychiatrist. Psychiatrists usually deal with visions."

"Softly," said Nancy.

"Why should you want to dismiss this," demanded Roderick, "when it's such a breakthrough I'm beholding? First contact with the retinal A.I.!"

"If they're so artfully intelligent, they should have slowed the pace and made what you're seeing comprehensible."

"Give a chimp Shakespeare to read when it can't even read," muttered Roderick.

"Humans aren't *that* dimwitted," said Nick. "We can

read starlight and understand it. The way you describe this seems more like trying to read something of huge significance in a dream—the words go out of focus because there isn't actually any text, just a sensation of a text, a wish that there *could* be a text that reveals stuff. I've had dreams like that."

"If only there was some way of showing you what I'm seeing!" roared Roderick in frustration. "Some way of displaying this! Of linking the back side of a retina to a monitor screen!"

I said, "I hope you aren't thinking along Biblical lines: *if thine eye offends thee . . .*"

"Of course not! Is that what the A.I.s might be hoping? That I'll psychotically pluck out my eyes? I doubt it!"

"Oh Roderick," said Nancy, "what shall we do with you? Would you prefer to go to hospital for observation . . . or should we stay with you overnight and see what's what in the morning?"

"Observation? By my own peers, who will see nothing! I can't inconvenience all of you. Only one of you needs stay. I shan't do anything foolish."

We exchanged glances. *One of us.* Was Roderick hoping that Nancy would volunteer? Woman's nursing touch and all that . . .

"If we get you to bed," I said, "since I know it's a double bed, I can share it just in case." I contrived some humor. "No monkey business, mind you! Acceptable?"

"I might keep you awake. I don't know if I can go to sleep with what I'm seeing. It doesn't stop when I shut my eyes. It's permanent."

"Till it stops," said Nick. "Hospital might be better, for sedatives."

"So you can sleep on the sofa here," said Roderick quickly. "Thank you, Tom. True friend, and so forth."

I said, "We can argue about bed or sofa later, but frankly I'm quite hungry. Should one of us pop out for a takeaway? Could you eat Indian, Rod?"

"Saffron rice and golden message ... might be confusing."

"Okay, fish and chips. Eat by feel. And I prescribe some strong *beer* to relax you."

I'd packed Nancy off back home and Nick too. In loosened clothes I dozed on the sofa, living room and bedroom doors open. In the wee hours Roderick's bellow of *Tom!* broke a dream.

Up I rushed. Switching on the bedroom light caused Roderick, upright in bed in his purple paisley pajamas, to throw his hands over his eyes, then peek cautiously through his fingers.

"It's gone, it stopped, I thought I'd gone blind—"

"But you aren't, are you?"

"Everything seemed so black after the golden dazzle. They've stopped downloading, Tom. Maybe those were instructions for building a device to display what the brain perceives ..."

"Pretty stupid instructions if you can't read them until *after* you've carried them out."

"Maybe they're all stored in my brain now."

I thought. "Did you manage to fall asleep?"

"I don't know. I'm not sure ... Why?"

"Put another way, did your conscious awareness switch off?"

"Oh, I see what you mean. Like a computer crashing, interrupting the message. No, I think I must have received everything. At least for the moment. What a relief." He rubbed his scalp. "Is it all up here ... or lost?"

Or *never was,* I thought. To what extent had the hallucination been for Nancy's benefit, even though Roderick mightn't be aware of this? I went downstairs to heat mugs of milk mixed with a lot of dark rum.

In the morning on the sofa—a clock showed six—the phone woke me, so I answered it, precise as ever: "Roderick Butler's house. Tom Cooper speaking."

"Who?" The voice sounded vaguely familiar, and hectic. "Never mind. Is he there? Please get him! Tell him it's Jon Bell and something crazy scary is happening to me. It's like a waterfall of lights—"

Rare Earth

Felicity Shoulders and Leslie What

Callum and his friend Juarez pushed in between com-
muters on the MAX train. A guy in a pirate hat
frowned at Callum's saxophone case, but most people's
eyes skipped over them—Juarez was made up in green-
face for a zombie flashmob, and Portlanders tried to be
too cool to react. There was enough weirdness to keep
them busy not reacting: it was the day before Rose Festival started, an excuse for people to act crazy, if they
needed an excuse. They'd even seen a guy wearing a turtle shell, which Juarez swore had something to do with
the slow food movement. Juarez wore a camo jacket
with his dad's name, "Juarez," stitched across the pocket.
Callum's coat was from his dad too, black motorcycle
leather, inherited.

They had been downtown where Callum had been
playing his sax for spare change. The light rail train
started moving east toward the Burnside Bridge and
home.

"How much did you make?" Juarez said. "Enough
for a latte?"

"You know I'm saving my money." Callum examined

the coins he'd scooped out of his sax case. "Here, you take half."

"All I did was meditate."

"Zombie Zen is performance art."

"Well, here." Juarez shoved a big bag of venison jerky at his friend. "From my dad."

Callum dug into the jerky. His grandma had slipped a snack bag into his coat like he was a toddler, but he wasn't about to eat it. Peanuts and raisins older than he was, and a rock. She'd collected a shitload of these McNugget-sized things over the years, old and weird with translucent skins and blue veins inside. Like Grandma. He called them her crazy moon agates. They sure weren't edible.

Juarez pointed out the window at the carnival rides on the waterfront. "You going to the Rose Festival this time?"

"Always. Gotta take Grandma Vera."

"*Pobrecito.*" Juarez pouted exaggeratedly. "You want to come over for dinner? Homemade tamales."

"Thursday's pizza night. Besides, the Mommandant thinks I'm at home babysitting Grandma."

"Or the other way around." Juarez grinned, a bit ghoulish with his smeared makeup and dangling fake eyeball. He ducked off the MAX at his stop, and Callum scribbled in his spiral notepad for the last few minutes of the ride. *Parasitic,* he wrote. *Copacetic.*

Grandma Vera's front door was blown open. The living room curtains were closed and the room dark except for Fox News on the TV. Callum left his sax in the foyer and rushed inside. "Grandma?" he called. "You here?" He imagined her wandering around barefoot, in her old night-gown. "Grandma!" he called, and didn't breathe until he saw her toddle out of the kitchen and switch on a light.

"You're just in time for snack." The side of her lip was caught under her false teeth, giving her a goofy smile. She had trouble accessing the part of her brain that told her what to do next. *RAM,* he wrote on his spiral pad. *Ramnesia.* She was holding a Pyrex bowl of peanuts and raisins. He led her to the cleared spot at the dining room table.

"You shouldn't walk around in the dark. You could trip," Callum said. Grandma's house was choked with clutter, stuff Vera called "ephemera" and his mom, Lily, called "fire hazard." Rolled maps, cardboard boxes of old ration coupons and death certificates, stocks from companies even Wikipedia had never heard of. Civil War uniform buttons she called "undug." Only the up- stairs, where Lily and Callum had lived since his dad died, was clear. Vera had owned an antique shop in the Pearl District before it got fancy, but now she sold her stuff online. Except lately, she mostly bought things and forgot to sell. Her eBay feedback hovered around 34 percent positive. "Bid on *Life* magazine, got toaster," one bidder had posted.

"I know where everything is," she scoffed. She picked at the raisins, offered him some from her hand. He pre- tended to eat and hid them in his pocket with the others. She was wearing a butt-ugly velveteen choker with one of her crazy moon agates glued in the center. *"That's* different," Callum said.

"Charles gave it to me," she said, and looked off into the distance.

Lily shouldered the door open and yelled, "How many times have I told you not to leave your instrument on the floor?" but she was carrying a pizza box and it smelled like garlic and pepperoni, so Callum got up to give her a hand.

"Would you set the table?" Lily said, waving him

away. Her face was puffy, her voice tight. "What's that thing around your neck, Mom?" She flopped open the pizza, her half Veggie Nirvana and theirs Omnivore Bliss. Thank God she'd gotten over veganism, because a pizza without cheese was just wrong. Lily didn't say another word until they had finished the pizza and thrown away the paper plates. Of course the word was "homework."

Grandma picked up the remote to change channels. Not the usual news-bots. Yellow balls of light bobbing across a meadow. More exciting than static, but not by much. "Turn up the sound," she said. "I can't hear what they're saying."

Lily took the remote and switched off the TV. "Homework," she repeated, and Callum retreated upstairs.

He woke up to the Dandy Warhols on his old CD-alarm and Mom retching in their shared bathroom. She still hadn't admitted she was knocked up. She was delusional to think she could hide it. This was middle school biology, not rocket science.

He hesitated outside the bathroom door, imagining Lily coming up with some lie to explain her morning barf ritual, maybe slandering last night's pizza. Why did she need another kid anyway? Not like she was doing such a great job with him.

He decided to skip showering and get out while he could. After a kitchen raid, he walked to Hawthorne, inhaling the last quantum particles of Pop-Tart as the bus pulled up. He flashed his pass to the driver. The bus was almost empty, except for a Bible-bot finger-reading psalms in the front seat and a girl named Abby Reeves from AP English near the back. Abby wrote sestinas and dyed her hair the shade of a blue jay's wing. Callum sloped toward the seat across from her.

He gave her a sideways nod, and balanced his notebook on the end of his sax case. *Incognito. Inamorata,* he scribbled.

The bus trundled off into light traffic. The sidewalks were all ghost town. Too quiet for a Friday morning.

Abby hooted, and he saw she was grinning. She shook her phone. "School's canceled!" She walked across the aisle, and fell into the seat next to him. Her bag slumped over his sax case. "Callum, right? I'm Abby."

The bus stopped on a red, long enough to read a newspaper box headline: "STRANGE GLOBAL PHENOMENA."

Thanks, *Oregonian,* he thought. That explains things. "What's up with school?"

"Canceled because of Martians,'" she said.

Usually she ignored him, so why was she playing him now? "Are you serious?"

"Sometimes," she said. She pulled a netbook from her bag. Her camisole flashed enough boob to observe with peripheral vision. Abby tapped in CNN.com and turned the screen toward him. Her arm bumped his. Balls of light like on the TV, only red and swarming along some street in Idaho, overlapping, rising and falling like a stream. "OFFICIALS CALL FOR CALM," scrolled below the image. "4 DEAD IN POCATELLO."

"Wow," he said. An alien invasion called for something more intelligent than "wow," but all the good words were on his spiral pad and not in his head. "How'd the people die in Pocatello?"

"They were fried to death. Apparently the aliens shoot lightning if you try to touch them."

"I always thought there'd be flying saucers and ray guns," he said. "Take me to your leader stuff."

"Nope, no *War of the Worlds.* They just popped up in

Europe, Asia, everywhere. Different colors, but no one knows why, or where they're going."

"What do they want?"

"Maybe they don't want anything," she said. She reached across him for the stop cord. "Maybe floating around is all they do. Anyway, what do you wanna do today?"

"Good question," Callum said, worried she'd suggest something that cost money.

"Let's hang out," she said, and stood. He followed her from the bus, walrus-graceful lugging his saxophone and backpack. He tried to fall into step, though his stride was a foot longer.

"I go to this rehearsal space to chill," Abby said. She threw him a look. "Write poetry. Vocalize, sometimes."

He knew this street. They'd be passing Sid's Music. "Okay if we check something out first?"

"Onward," she said.

He walked ahead and felt dumb for forgetting to hold open the door. Sid looked up from behind his desk, where he was watching green balls of light dance across his portable TV. He wore a Mariners hat, a jersey with "Ichiro" across the back, and a sour expression. "Game's supposed to be on," he said.

Callum pointed to the tenor sax hanging on the wall.

Sid carefully handed it down. "No change: no rent, no layaway, no pity discount," he said.

"It's gorgeous," Abby said, touching the mother-of-pearl keys and the feather tracery on the bell.

The lacquer was stripped in places but that didn't matter. "It's two thousand dollars," Callum said. "All the great jazz saxophonists played tenor."

"I'll take your word for it," she said, not in a mean way.

Callum fingered a few bars, listening to the hollow thudding and clacking of the voiceless sax. In a while he said, "Let's go," and laid the shining instrument on the countertop. "Thanks, Sid."

"Come back when you have money."

The rehearsal space was around the corner, in a run-down building papered with gig announcements and offers for lessons. Abby pulled open the door, held it until he was inside. It smelled of old carpet glue, pot smoke, maybe a little cork grease. Candles and the glow of laptop screens instead of overhead fluorescents. A couple of figures lounged on the beat-up old furniture. Callum got out his phone to text Juarez, ignored two missed calls from his mom.

" . . . blowing it out of proportion. Obviously there are bound to be other species in the universe. Don't be humanocentric." Some guy, hunched over his laptop in the corner—Lex, king of the stoners.

"Anthropocentric," Meg from band said. She was one of those obnoxious kids who owned and played four different instruments.

"Hey," Abby said, taking off her coat. "Meet Callum. I rescued him from the 14 bus." She squeezed two chairs together, and motioned for him to sit.

"Boing Boing calls them lightning attacks. Says they only happen around high-tension power lines. The aliens probably don't even mean to do it," Lex said.

"That's bogus. They know exactly what they're doing. They've been consuming rare earth minerals, like the ones China's been stockpiling," Meg said.

"Cerium, used in fluorescents," said Lex, proving only that he was a fast Googler. "Dysprosium, used in reactors. Neodymium for lasers. We need this shit or there's no technology. They eat all our rare earth, we'll revert to cavemen."

Callum scribbled, *Rare Earth*. In the dark room it was hard to focus. Abby leaned her shoe onto his boot.

"You guys worried?" Abby asked.

"No," Meg said. "I can live without my computer." She lit a bong, passed it around.

Abby shook her head and said, "Not right now," so Callum passed, too. She pointed to the sax case, said, "Wanna play something?"

"Yeah, go for it," Lex said.

The horn always took a couple of minutes to warm. Callum held the neck and tried not to think of Abby and the way her slender arms crossed under her B-cups as she leaned in to watch. The space was small and he played as softly as he possibly could so he wouldn't blast her away, his version of Billie Holiday's "Don't Explain."

When he finished, Lex said, "That's dope."

Meg stifled a yawn, and said, "I'm more of a rocker chick," and he thought, yeah, I bet you are, you stuck-up little shit.

Abby rested her hand on Callum's arm. "That helped," she said. "It's crazy to think about an alien invasion. I mean, we're still in high school."

"Crazy," he said. Grandma Vera coped by ignoring the obvious while Mom couldn't stop worrying about everything. Grandma Vera's way had its merits. "Don't think about it," he said, which must have been a good thing to say, because she oonched closer.

Meg stood, and set the bong against the wall behind a chair. "Rose Festival?" she said.

"Maybe later," Abby said.

"See you there," Lex said, and walked out with Meg, letting the door bang shut.

Abby's hand was still on his arm. Callum found himself looking into her left eye, then her right, unable to meet both at once. Better than staring at her boobs, but still psycho. "It's going to be okay," he said, but then it wasn't.

The door swooshed open and it was his mother, glistening with rage and raindrops. "When school is over, you come home," she said. "That's doubly true when school is canceled because of a *national emergency*."

"Oh God, Mom," was all Callum could say.

"I knew you'd go to Sid's and moon over that stupid instrument, and he knew you kids would be up to no good and hanging around here," she said. She was dressed for collecting insect samples in the field, galoshes and mud-streaked overalls under the poncho.

"Mom," he said. "Be cool."

"Cool?" she said, waving her plastic-tented arms in prophetic frenzy. "There are aliens over Coeur d'Alene. There are aliens over Ashland and Olympia and Bend. There are aliens coming *here*." As if she hadn't embarrassed him enough, she switched to her sarcastic tone and said, "I don't think I've met your friend, Callum."

"My mom does this, too," Abby whispered, and they traded understanding glances.

"Abby Reeves," he said, "meet my mom, Lily Fitzpatrick. Mom, meet Abby. Abby edits our school literary magazine," he said, because his mom couldn't always look at a person and know she was about more than her hair.

"Nice to meet you, Mrs. F."

Lily's eyes swept with practiced suspicion over the broken-down chairs, the amp, the magazines on the coffee table, and stopped on the centimeter of bong peeking out from behind a chair.

"There were other people here," Callum said. "We weren't smoking."

"*This* time," Lily said, but at least she believed him.

"Can I give you a ride anywhere, Ms. Reeves? I'm sure you have parents who care enough to worry."

"No thanks, Mrs. F. I'm good."

They stood, faced each other.

Abby slipped a folded slip of paper into Callum's palm and said, "Later." She waved goodbye and flowed around his mom into the rain.

He was left alone with his kick-drum heart and his motionless mother.

"Car, Callum. Now."

She drove faster than usual. Callum adjusted his sax case so it didn't squinch his boot against the door.

"They're really coming, Callum. I heard it on the news."

"I thought they were in Idaho," he said.

"They're all over, not that you'd know. You see a pretty girl, who cares about aliens?"

Callum actually thought he saw her pull a smile. He unfolded Abby's paper and read the ten digits and the cursive scrawl, "Text me." He switched the stereo on, found it tuned to NPR.

"Leave the dial alone," Lily said. She didn't usually protest when he tuned her out with music.

" . . . time it does seem clear that the phenomena, widely considered extraterrestrial creatures, will converge over Northwest Oregon. Area residents are encouraged to evacuate calmly, and to lessen traffic congestion through use of carpools," said Kristian Foden-Vencil, OPB News. "FEMA recommends keeping a safe distance from the aliens. Should they approach you, abandon any smartphones, computers or other electronic appliances, which may attract the beings. Severe burns and electrical shock may result from physical contact."

Lily shut off the radio. "Jeez," she said. "I can't take this. It really would take the end of the world to separate you from your phone."

Callum programmed in Abby's number and gave her a ringtone he'd pay attention to.

"We need to focus," Lily said. "Pick up Grandma Vera. Plan what to pack and where to go." She chirped the horn at a Suburban stalled at the green light.

"Focus," he said. "On what to pack." Like Lily was any good at that. Her closet was full of boxes of Dad's clothes. Dad's books. Dad's tools. You could bring the past with you but it didn't make it any less past.

The sky was dark with clouds. "Finally," Lily muttered as she turned onto their gravel driveway. "Now let's get Grandma and get out. Go pack. Hurry."

He moved the sax case to the trunk and dragged the backpack up the steps behind Lily.

"Grandma!" she bellowed. "Time to go."

Callum trudged up to his room, and replaced his Spanish and biology texts with the *Tao Te Ching,* found his dad's Kershaw blade, bottled water to wash down Juarez's dry venison. He wadded up underwear and socks, tee shirts, jeans. He opened the plastic file box where he kept his notebooks, dropped photos and sheet music onto the shifting heap of spiral-bounds, shut the box and wedged it under his arm. He gathered up batteries and ballpoints.

His mom had been slamming cupboards in the kitchen, but now it was quiet. Then a flash. Thunder. A cloudburst and an ocean of rain.

Callum stooped to look out the window at the sodden backyard and Lily running across the grass, toward the old garage where Grandma Vera stored a particularly rich deposit of clutter. Green light seeped from the open door. He was downstairs and out the back with his backpack before he could think about it. His shoes deepened the muddy dents Lily had left in the crabgrass lawn. "Mom," he called, and heard her yell the same.

Lily was standing just outside the garage, like she couldn't make herself step in. And there was Vera, enthroned in an old caned rocker, surrounded by six green spheres as big as volleyballs. They had steadily glowing cores the size of ping pong balls, surrounded by swirling color. Points glinted and faded on their borders.

Their light played on shelves piled with old boxes and broken trophies. Everywhere boxes overflowed with seashells, playbills, photographs ruined by mold. Grandma was holding a pickle jar full of her moon agates. She was all smiles, dressed in her Sunday clothes, hair *Beetlejuice*-frizzy.

Callum grabbed Lily's clammy hand. "We have to do something," he said.

The spheres rotated like electrons around Grandma Vera's head. "Beautiful . . ." she murmured. She pursed her lips and made a humming noise that was not a melody or a background track or an *Om*. More the crackling, electric buzz of a cheap-ass amp.

Lily dropped his hand and started forward.

"Mom, what are you going to do?"

She stared at him, but didn't answer.

"The radio said something about them liking technology. I'll get my laptop. Maybe we can lure them off," he said.

"Yes, go get something," Lily said, and he turned back to the house, grateful to be doing something. Then his mom's expression registered, the way she'd totally agreed with one of his suggestions without even looking for a way to shoot it down. He headed back.

Lily was in the garage now, blocking his view of Grandma. "Leave her alone," she said, shrill above Vera's gargling buzz. Callum saw her hand raised against the alien glow, then there was an explosive bang and Lily was thrown back onto the gravel.

"Mom," he whispered. He knelt beside her, and bowed his head over her open, still mouth, straining to hear a word or a breath. He shouted, "Help!" but his grandmother didn't even notice they were there.

It was Callum's second ride in an ambulance. All that way with Dad on the gurney just to hear a doctor explain how sudden death was often the first sign of coronary artery disease. Callum remembered the beaten look on Lily's face when she'd told him they were moving in with her mom. He felt guilty for hoping he didn't live with *his* mother when he was forty. If he got to forty. Sometimes it didn't seem like that would happen. He was holding Lily's balled-up poncho. His dad had died in February, so he'd told the paramedics his mother was in her second trimester. There were two guys in EMT suits, one driving and the other EMT-ing. They crossed the Hawthorne Bridge into downtown.

The paramedic sitting beside his mom said, "She's back," and he saw his mom's eyes flutter open, bloodshot. They were yellow-brown, which had never struck him as creepy before. Predator yellow. His hazel eyes, part hers and part Dad's—were they scary, feral too? A line of raptor eyes stretching back along the generations. *Dawn. Spawn,* he wrote. Things your ancestors left behind that didn't fit in boxes.

"You okay, Mom?" he asked, which was sort of stupid. She'd spent an hour unconscious.

Lily nodded. Her hair had gone frizzy, like Grandma Vera's. They'd bandaged her right hand, burned where she'd touched the alien or it had zapped her, whatever you wanted to call it. Intravenous raindrops dripped into her other arm, accompanied by a steady, flashing light. The light froze, an alarm sounded and the paramedic fiddled with the IV pump. Lily's hands and face were swollen, her skin stretched and pale. Even lying down, her belly was pretty obvious.

A motley mob spilled from the park blocks, stopping traffic. People carried signs: "The End Is Near," always a classic; "Free beer in Valhalla." A turtle guy brandished posterboard that said "TURTLES ALL THE WAY DOWN." The windshield wipers threw gouts of rain off the glass. Callum heard a car horn nearby, brakes and metal crunching. The ambulance driver glanced back and said, "Just a fender-bender," and kept driving. His uniform was dark under the arms.

"What's happening?" Callum asked, and the driver gave him a *better not to know* kind of look.

"How's she doing?" the driver asked. He was sweating.

The paramedic tending Lily said, "BP's down. She's alert and stable."

The driver said, "Hospitals are closed to anyone who isn't critical." It was unclear if he was telling his partner or apologizing to Callum and Lily. He pulled into the downtown Fred Meyer lot. "We can't take you home. We've got a hundred more emergencies all over town." He slowed and whooped the siren, and the ambulance stopped beside an empty shopping cart corral. They pulled the IV, shrugged Lily into a wheelchair and lowered her to the asphalt.

"She's going to be okay. You'd better take her home," the driver said.

Lily said, "I want to lie down."

Callum said, "It's okay, Mom. We'll go back to Grandma's." He slid the poncho over her head, hooked his backpack over the wheelchair handles and took hold of the grips. Lao Tzu had said, "To lead people, walk behind them," so he led his mother through the lot. The door of a metallic green Beemer was open, displaying the asscrack of a tweeker tangled in wires from the dash. The tweeker noticed them, glared, managed to start the engine and weave his way toward Burnside. A couple of blocks down, there were pirates on the loose, a turtle guy and regulation street crazies. No buses went by. They passed an impromptu prayer circle. One of the prayer-circlers broke off and hurried over to them, waving a plastic palm frond at Lily's belly. "Look at you, at your age! Like Sarah and Hannah, blessed by God. Will you pray with us?"

"Take me home," Lily said, her skin the color of non-fat milk. "Please."

"You okay?" Callum asked. She wasn't acting like the mom. And usually she'd be mad about the "at your age" thing.

She nodded, held up one finger and said, "Hold that thought." She doubled over and threw up. The palm frond woman backed away.

"Good timing, Mom." Callum said, and steered her east. They were still a long way from their side of the river.

"I feel better," Lily said.

"Want something to drink?" Callum asked. He dug through his pack, located water.

"Got any food?" Lily said.

He hesitated. "Maybe a granola bar."

"Something salty?" Lily said. "I want savory."

"Savory," he said. He hesitated. There was Juarez's venison jerky, but maybe this wasn't a day for vegetarianism. He offered her a thick strip from the bag. She mouthed it like a cigar to suck out the salt.

They passed by the 76 Station, and saw the gas monkeys had abandoned their posts. Customers were pumping their own gas, just like it was some other state, not Oregon. Two chicks ran by carrying Nordstrom bags overflowing with shoeboxes. One smiled at Callum and he couldn't *not* notice how her boobs jiggled under her shirt.

A zombie flashmob had gathered at the corner of Third and Burnside. A dozen or so, dressed in a variety of tatters and crudely smeared green makeup. Lipstick painted on like blood drops. They did their zombie-mayhem thing and menaced some wasted pirates. One pirate ripped the stuffed parrot from his shoulder and pretended to eat it. Switching sides.

He wanted to write, *Embrace the rot,* but he kept pushing. The zombies limped their Frankenstein-monster walk toward the river.

Callum texted Abby. *Where are you?* He couldn't tell if it went through. A tall zombie in a green coat staggered toward them, chomping his teeth. He broke character to clap Callum on the back. Juarez.

"Z'up, Callum?" Juarez said, "Mrs. Fitzpatrick."

"Hey," Callum said. "Don't eat me." He offered him the jerky and Juarez gnawed off a chunk of venison.

"Dude. I met your girlfriend. She's tasty." Juarez waved over a too pretty, blue-haired zombie, who staggered a bit, then dropped the act.

"Mrs. F. What happened to you?" Abby asked.

Lily said, "Struck by lightning."

"Oh my god! Really?"

"Sort of," Callum said, but she didn't press, and he was glad, because he didn't want to explain.

"The aliens are inside the city limits." Abby said, wide-eyed.

"We know," Callum said.

"We saw some at the Festival Village."

"Kristian Foden-Vencil just interviewed some science-tard on the radio," Juarez cut in. "About how the aliens are zapping our asses. They eat rare earth and create magnetic energy fields." Juarez smirked. "Magnetricity. They eat dirt, man, and they shit magnets. They are, like, totally alien."

Abby said, "Rare earths are minerals—not dirt—and they're using the rare earths to make magnetic mono-poles. Magnets with only one pole. Not north *and* south. Just north. Yin with no yang."

"Or Yang with no yin," Callum said. He liked how she wasn't afraid to be smart.

"Dudes. This is cutting-edge crap," Juarez said. "It's not even in our physics text."

"Our physics texts are thirty years old." Callum said.

"This just doesn't seem real," Abby said.

"Yeah, I know what you mean," Callum said, watching a girl walk by on her hands.

"Any more jerky?" Lily said.

"I thought your mom didn't eat meat," Juarez whispered.

Callum shrugged and handed the bag to his mother. "We gotta get home and rescue Grandma Vera."

"Oh," said Juarez. He looked guilty. "I forgot to tell you something important."

"What?"

"We saw your grandma down at the Village, play-ing Our Lady of the Alien Spheres. She looks like she's wearing an electric Lady GaGa bubble dress. The aliens are all over her. But here's the weird thing—she remem-bered me. She never remembers me. Wacktacular."

Callum heard his voice getting high and tight, like Lily's voice when she chewed him out. *"That's* what's weird? My grandmother is swimming in lightning-spitting aliens, and you're all, 'Oh, I forgot to tell you'?"

Abby looked pale under her hastily applied green. "That old lady was Callum's *grandma?*"

"You saw her, too?"

"I didn't know you were related," Abby said. "Sorry."

"At least you don't have to walk across the bridge," Juarez said.

This is your brain on drugs, Callum thought, but he craved a smoke himself.

A guy at the back of the zombie flashmob chanted "Braaaaains" and on cue the zombies surged toward the river.

"Let's find Grandma," Callum said, swept up in the march of the undead.

Everything and everyone converged on the waterfront. A constellation of blue spheres spilled out from Stark Street. More unearthly glow, deep orange, on the Morrison Bridge. If you weren't drunk or stoned you were scared. People were drinking and dancing out onto Naito Parkway. Most of the Rose Festival Village tents were knocked down, vendor stalls abandoned. The city was lit up with blue and red and gold.

Abby put her hand on Callum's elbow. "How often does your grandma run away?"

"Not usually," he said, distracted by her touch.

A male police officer stood guard while his lady partner cuffed a skeezy guy wearing only a glow-in-the-dark orange life jacket and unlaced Doc Martens boots. It was gross. Not something you wanted your mother or your girlfriend to see. Girlfriend. Hardly. Good thing she couldn't read his thoughts.

"Callum," Abby said. "Look." She pointed to a bunch of men marching toward the main stage. They hoisted a woman on their shoulders with green spheres orbiting around her head.

Grandma Vera. She did look like Lady GaGa. Well, Lady GaGa's grandma. Her legs were crossed demurely at the ankles and she was fingering her moon agate choker.

"Whoa," Juarez said. "It's like some mosh Aztec ritual. Like the Mother Goddess Coatlicue with her necklace made from human hearts."

Grandma Vera's handlers deposited her on a bed of plywood. One of the men presented her with a pickle jar before backing away. She rose slowly to her feet.

"Callum," Lily said, her voice heavy somehow. "Help Mom."

He didn't want to let go of the wheelchair handles.

"I'll stay," Abby said.

Lily nodded her approval.

Juarez said, "Dude, I'm coming with you," and the two boys pushed through the crowd, body-chucking anyone who looked too drunk to shove back. Sirens blared in the distance. You could smell beer and popcorn and dread. Usually the Festival night sky blazed with carnival rides and the streaking circle of the Ferris wheel, but tonight the sky bloomed with alien light. The rain had faded to a drizzle. Faces tipped from shadow to a warm green light.

Juarez aimed his phone to snap a picture. Onstage Grandma Vera pulled a moon agate from her pickle jar and held it up to the crowd. Her greenies surged upward, mimicking the motion of her hand. They wanted that moon agate.

The pickle jar was full of moon agates.

Callum did the math. Holy shit. Grandma Vera was screwed.

Juarez saw it, too. "Rare earth, dude. Maybe you can distract the aliens with my cell," Juarez said, and slipped his phone into Callum's pocket.

He had two cell phones. No way to know how many aliens that would feed. "Help me up," Callum said, and Juarez laced his fingers together so Callum could climb to the stage. "Hey, Grandma," he called. "It's me."

Grandma Vera ignored him.

Callum offered up the phones, but Grandma's green spheres showed no interest. Maybe the aliens were finished with feeding and had moved on to another phase. Grandma Vera leaned over like she wanted to throw her moon agate into the audience. Seemed like a really bad idea. Callum reached out by instinct and stopped her by closing his hand over hers. The alien spheres widened their orbit until they were circling them both. Welcome to Grandma's world, Callum thought. Great.

"Grandma," he said. "It's Callum. I need you to give me that moon agate thingy."

"Oh, honey," she said. "These look like agates but they're much more special." She relaxed her veiny hand in his, and his fingers closed around the not-agate. "Your grandfather and I bought out every rock hound in the Gorge. We didn't know what they were, but I liked them." She dipped her free hand into the jar and came out with four more not-agates, five.

Blue aliens streamed across the broken tents and the sparse police line, into the crowd. They floated over the outstretched hands of zombies, steampunks and children, drunks, hipsters and fools. More poured out of the streets of downtown, a patchwork of red spheres and white and violet, all floating toward Vera. The aliens looked the same, just different colors. Like cousins coming together for a family reunion.

Blue aliens joined the green in their widening circuit around Vera, and now there were twelve orbs whizzing around her. More heading her way.

Callum closed his fingers around the wide glass mouth

of the jar. This wasn't in the manual. "You have to give me all the special rocks, Grandma." He bent to kiss her on the forehead, and she let go of the heavy jar with a sigh. She was still so strong, carrying this all the way from the Hawthorne district. Or maybe magnetricity had fueled her strength. "Gimme your necklace, too."

Vera made a sweeping gesture that brought her hand dangerously close to one of the spheres, and he tensed up and felt like puking at the thought of her getting fried. But the circle she made with her arm stopped inches short of the closest alien. "Okay, dear. We're family. Whatever I have is yours." She unfastened the hook, and Callum let her drop it into the pickle jar. He held the jar close to his chest. The aliens' focus changed and their orbit closed around him. They were his aliens now. His shoulder blades tried to touch across his back. This was what he'd wanted, right?

"Stay here, Grandma. Stay here," he said. He scrambled off the stage with the pickle jar. Magnetricity lined up his red blood cells like a stack of coins. His eyebrows and lashes popped up and his scalp tingled. "Get away," he said to a wide-eyed woman trying to bow down to him in the mud. He stepped over a passed-out hippie and crammed his hand in the top of the jar to keep any rocks from falling out, the way you'd cram your hand into a French horn bell to bend the pitch.

He stumbled onto the bike path, his boots falling loud against the cement. Few people ventured near the water, afraid, maybe, of falling into the darkness. The river smelled muddy, wild after the day's rains. The aliens were dazzling and bright, beautiful, just as Grandma Vera had said. But who had asked them to come here and mess up his life? Oh, yeah. Probably Grandma.

Blue and green aliens followed him. This was like that game of hot potato. You did not want to be left holding the pickle jar. Grandma Vera had found the McNugget rocks in the river basin years ago. He didn't know why the aliens had come back to this river now. He didn't want to know. He just wanted them to go back into hiding.

Good music worked because it created a melody that dissolved into unbearable tension as patterns were repeated, unexpected dissonances introduced. You threw in harmony that pulled you toward a resolution. The air felt like those tense moments before the music became pleasurable again. He held the jar by the lip and spun around once, twice, three times, like an Olympic hammer thrower. He let go and the jar soared over the Willamette. Green and blue aliens swooped along the parabola of the jar's path until it dropped into the river. The aliens hovered just above the surface. Water splashed up and crackled like breaking ice as it met the flame-bright edges of the spheres.

"Callum! Callum!" Abby called. She and Juarez battled the mud to move the wheelchair forward. Vera stomped along behind them. When they reached Callum, Lily held out her good hand to hold his.

They watched the spheres form a circle over the water. White, red, gold, joined blue and green. The perimeter expanded as more arrived. Maybe a hundred aliens in all. A psychedelic light show reflected up from the water. He forgot to remember to be afraid.

The circle divided like a class breaking into small groups, with formations of three aliens here, five aliens there. A red with a green and a yellow and a purple, a blue with orange and dirty gold. In the small groups the aliens lost their spherishness. The colors ran and the shapes rushed together. A sound rose, a feverish, buzzing, deafening cosmic amp.

"Dude," Juarez said. "They're like, doing it."

Once he spoke it was obvious Juarez was right. Each mating group thrummed like a drum roll. Light strobed. Sparks flew. Callum felt embarrassed watching something so private.

"Not in front of the children," Abby said with a laugh.

They came with sonic-boom blasts so loud even Grandma Vera covered her ears. After the thunder-crack climax each mating cluster smoorged into one big ovoid about three feet wide. Instead of angsty and colormashed, the alien's glow was serene and white. Another thundercrack. Another ovoid formed. And on and on. They were witnessing the fucking miracle of life, like seeing a blimp coming out of a chrysalis. One alien blimpoid curveted in mid-river and one drifted to the Hawthorne Bridge to slowly spiral up a support.

One blimpoid floated toward the bank, toward Callum. He was too tired or enchanted to be scared. The alien stopped a yard away, shadowing him. The axes of the thing rhythmically swelled and contracted like it couldn't decide whether to be wide or tall.

"Can you see me?" he asked.

He strained to hear an answer. This alien was definitely digging him, aware of him in the same way he was conscious of it. Its frequency slowed to match his heart rate. He remembered the *snack* in his pocket, let go of Lily's hand and plucked Grandma's moon rock out of the bag of old peanuts and raisins. He offered it to the alien. Is this what you want? he asked. Or maybe he only thought he said it.

The alien kept doing its alien-oscillation thing. It didn't want the McNugget any more than Callum did.

"Where did you come from?" he asked.

"That's pretty obvious," said Juarez. "Somewhere with rare earths."

"That could be, like, anywhere in the universe," Abby said.

Across the river, a white ovoid rose above the crowd like a lost balloon. Thirty yards up, it burst into shards. Light spewed out like cinders seeding the clouds. Callum watched the creature near him to see if it would do something. Friends don't let friends explode. No response. The cycle of dimming and flashing remained unchanged. Another blimpoid rose to the level of the low-hanging clouds and exploded closer. This time he heard something plunk into the water.

This couldn't be good. "Uh, maybe we should move," Callum said. But they stood, transfixed.

"Bon voyage," said Grandma Vera, as their blimpoid floated up, like the others. Its light flashed brighter, then dimmed.

Poof. Crack.

No more alien.

Alien dust glittered in the clouds. Something hard struck the ground next to Callum's boot. Another McNugget. He let it cool for a moment and picked it up from the mud.

"Dude. You're touching alien jism." Juarez was all right, but there were things he didn't understand. He didn't know how lucky he was his dad was still alive.

"Respect, man," Callum said. The rocks weren't jism. They weren't even rocks. "They came back to bury their corpses," he said. "Along the river."

"Like salmon spawning," Lily said. Her voice broke. She opened her hand and Callum set a rock corpse in her palm and they were all quiet for a moment. He was thinking about the funeral, about the finality of first rocks hitting the casket. The funeral was sad because it marked an end to one time, but the end made a new beginning possible. How Lao Tzu.

"I don't get it. Why didn't we know about them?" Abby said.

"I think they were buried, and people dug them up, and thought they were something normal like thunder eggs."

"I dunno, I'm starting to wonder about thunder eggs." She had the cutest smirk.

"So they ate rare earths and then it took thousands of years to digest their dinner?" Juarez said. "Gross."

"Something like that," Callum said. "They woke up when it was time to reproduce."

"I'd wake up if it was time to reproduce," Juarez said.

Most of the aliens had gone up now, the next generation carried away on the winds to gather strength and await their time.

Lily handed her rock corpse back to Callum. "Let them rest with the others," she said, but she was asking him, not telling him what to do.

Callum carried both rock corpses to the bank and skipped them past the shallows and into deep water. He stared across the river, toward East Portland and a soft glow at the base of the clouds.

"Well, I'll have something to tell my grandchildren someday," Grandma Vera said.

Lily looked ready to argue. "One of your grandchildren already knows," she said. "Sometimes he knows more than the rest of us." She rested her hand on her belly. "But you should definitely tell this little one about it. He'll want to know."

"He?" said Callum.

"He," said Lily, and Callum opened his notebook to start writing down names.

(Special thanks to Loren Bruns.)

The Vampires of Paradox

James Morrow

Imagine a walled city rising against a cerulean sky in a faraway desert. Before the massive gates stands a guard who possesses an infallible ability to know when a person is lying. The guard's duty is to ask everyone who seeks admittance to state his business. If the petitioner replies with a true account, the guard will permit him to enter freely and leave in peace. If the petitioner states his business falsely, the guard will take him to the gallows and hand him over to the executioner. One day a traveler comes out of the desert, approaches the city, and, offering the guard a sardonic smile, says, "I have come to be hanged."

Although I have no hard data on the matter, I believe I know more about paradoxes than any assistant professor north of Battery Park and south of Herald Square. For the past twenty years I've sought the holy grail of absurdity in every nook and cranny of Western civilization. Thus far no dragons have crossed my path, no ogres, trolls, or griffins, and yet my quest has often proved perilous. Over the past decade three initially auspicious marriages have crumbled before my

eyes, largely because the corresponding wives couldn't
be bothered to understand my burning passion to de-
finitively deconstruct Zeno's disproof of common sense
before some upstart Columbia grad student beat me to
it. My department head, the reprehensible Dr. Virginia
Sayles, has likewise regarded my specialty with scorn.
From the instant I got on the tenure track she began
playing political games with my pet project, the Bertrand Russell Institute of Paradox Studies, first moving
it out of the philosophy building and then off the NYU
campus entirely, so that today I pursue my research in a
subterranean office in NoHo.

A paradox may be resolved in one of three ways.
First, we can embrace the seemingly unacceptable conclusion. In the case of our suicidal traveler, we might
argue that he is simultaneously hanged and sent away
unharmed, but such a solution is beneath the dignity of
rational minds. Second, we may find fault with the reasoning that led to the contradiction. Concerning our lie-
detecting guard, we might insist that his quandary—do
I deliver the traveler to the executioner or not?—only
appears to be genuine, and an obvious course of action
lies before him, but such a demonstration would be beyond my powers. Third, we may attack the paradox's underlying premises. That is, we might attempt to establish
that the notion of stating one's business truly or falsely
is incoherent on first principles, though I cannot imagine
a sane person taking such a position.

On the day the desperate abbot entered my office in
need of an unassailable absurdity, it took me a while to
realize that he'd slipped past Mrs. Graham and padded
softly up to my desk, so intently were my thoughts fixed
on that desert traveler and his equivocal death wish.
Peering through my grimy basement window at the cav-
alcade of feet and paws marching down Bleecker Street,

I decided that the guard's dilemma owed its structure to the classic Liar Paradox, to wit, "What I am saying now is false." I tell my students that anyone who desires a more concrete version of the Liar Paradox should take an index card and write on the front, "What's on the other side is true," then turn the card over and write, "What's on the other side is false." So venerable is this contradiction that, when Bertrand Russell devised his notorious antinomy concerning the set of all sets that are not members of themselves, he was happy to frame it as a version of the Liar Paradox—though the problem he identified is rather more profound than that.

"Dr. Kreigar, I presume?"

I rotated my beloved swivel chair. My visitor, a towering figure in a black cassock, introduced himself as Abbot Articulis, the head of "a small and dwindling monastic community that traces its origins to that magnificent heretic, Quintus Septimius Florens Tertullianus, also known as Tertullian."

"How dwindling are you?"

The abbot heaved a sigh. He was a handsome man with anthracite eyes and a lantern jaw. "There are only six of us left—me, three monks, and two nuns, maintaining our Adirondack monastery with the help of a small staff."

"If Tertullian was a heretic, why do you follow him?"

"Because we are heretics, too. So you see, our Order is free of contradiction. Well, not entirely free, for it was Tertullian himself who famously asserted, concerning the Resurrection, *'Credo quia absurdum,'* 'I believe because it is absurd,' though what he actually said was, *'Certum est, quia impossibile'*—'it is certain, because impossible.' Forgive me for interrupting your meditations, Dr. Kreigar. I shall state my business quickly, after which you may return to staring out the window."

"Call me Donald."

"Bartholomew."

"Are you sure you came to the right university?" I asked. "Drop by Fordham, and you'll be up to your eyebrows in fellow Catholics. Me, I'm a lapsed logical positivist who now believes in the rarefied God of Paul Tillich, which I suspect won't do you much good."

"For all I care, you could be a raging atheist," Articulis said, "as long as you can supply our monastery with what it needs: a robust paradox. Having read your book—"

"Which one?" My personal favorite is *The Title of This Book Contains Threee Erors,* but I'm better known for *Adventures in Self-Reference* and *A Taxonomy of Nonsense.*

"Adventures in Self-Reference. It convinced me you're the man of the hour. Five potent paradoxes are already in our possession, but unless we acquire a sixth—I know this sounds ridiculous—without the sixth, the world will be laid waste by a voracious metaphysical menace."

"I see." Thus far my visitor's résumé failed to match the profile of the typical East Village lunatic, but that didn't mean he was a harmless Hudson Valley monk. "Metaphysical menace—fascinating. If it's a *theological* conundrum you seek, I'm afraid most of them aren't particularly confounding. Can God make a stone too heavy for Him to lift? If you think about it, the Omnipotence Paradox—"

"It has an answer," Articulis interrupted, studying the Escher print beside my bookcase, *Ascending and Descending*: thirteen hooded figures climbing a rectangular stairway clockwise and getting nowhere, even as another thirteen descended counterclockwise with the same result. "No, God *can't* do that, and by the way it doesn't matter, for He nevertheless remains all-powerful with respect to making and lifting stones. Specify any coherent weight—a hundred trillion tons, a thousand trillion tons—and He will easily fashion the expected object and drop-kick it across the universe. No, Donald, we are not interested in trivial riddles involving God's presumed limitations."

Evidently I'd misjudged the man. Articulis knew something about paradoxes, and perhaps about voracious metaphysical menaces as well. "I immediately think of Bertrand Russell's great and bewildering insight concerning categories," I noted. "Might that one turn the trick for you?"

"Alas, we're already running Russell's Antinomy at full capacity. The fact is, you won't grasp the nature of our plight without visiting our monastery and observing the Order in person. Might you come on Sunday afternoon? You could stay for dinner, spend the night, and leave the next morning. I believe you'll get a journal article out of it, perhaps a whole book."

I gazed inwardly, scanning the dreary parameters of my insipid life. My four-week summer school class, Philosophy 412: Varieties of Infinity, met every afternoon at 3:00 PM, which meant I could take my sweet time returning from Rhinebeck on Monday morning. "Fine. How long is the drive?"

Articulis shrugged and pulled a slip of paper from his cassock. "By train the journey takes slightly more than an hour. I've presumed to write out the directions"—he set the paper on my desk, anchoring it with my pewter sculpture of Escher's *Band van Möbius*—"and we're prepared to advance you fifty dollars toward gasoline."

I waved away his offer. "Keep your money. Academia pays better than Jesus."

"True, Donald, though our winery does make a small profit. Château Pelagius, have you heard of it?"

I was astonished to learn that Articulis' heretics were responsible for the best bargain red to be found in any Greenwich Village bodega. "Not only have I heard of it, I've got six bottles on my shelf."

"Driving toward Rhinebeck on Route 9, you may find yourself revisiting Achilles' fruitless attempt to outrun the tortoise—or do you agree with Charles Peirce that such paradoxes present no difficulty to a mind adequately trained in logic?"

"I'm with Aristotle. Every serious thinker should hone his intellect on Zeno's whetstone."

"We'll expect you by three o'clock," Articulis said, backing out of the room in a series of steps so short and smooth they constituted a credible demonstration of why the swift-heeled Achilles, tangled in the laws of geometry, would never win the great footrace. "Bring a thirst for merlot and an appetite for perplexity."

Articulis's directions were free of ambiguity, and I reached my destination with no difficulty, parking outside the main gate. Secluded in a sleepy valley, nestled beneath a thick mantle of fog, the crumbling Monastery of Tertullian seemed closer in character to a fallen citadel or a haunted castle than a spiritual retreat. The place even had a moat, a stagnant curl of mossy water enfolding the broken walls like a leprous arm. Perhaps this stinking green lagoon was once a tributary of the Hudson, but it had long since been amputated and left to fester on its own.

Crossing the bridge, I could not help imagining that, as in the Gallows Paradox, a guard would now appear and ask me to state my business. But instead I was greeted by a dour, bespectacled, clubfooted dwarf who used a croquet mallet as a cane. He introduced himself as Constantine, "major-domo of the monastery, and minor-domo as well," then guided me through the portal into the lush and labyrinthine vineyard on which the community's finances depended.

On all sides the trellises held great skeins of vines, each as dense and convoluted as the Gordian knot. Clusters of purple grapes peeked out from among the leaves, soaking up the sun like the naked lymph nodes of a flayed giant. Here and there a student in a Vassar, Bard, or rock band T-shirt stood poised on a stepladder, picking the harvest with an eye to meeting the fall semester's tuition bill.

"Don't let this go to your head, Professor, but I believe God has sent you to us," Constantine said as we reached the center of the maze, where a wrought-iron bench stood flanked by marble angels. "A plague has come to our community, and Abbot Articulis has taken the burden entirely on himself. Now he has you to share his troubles."

Uncertain how to respond, I made a paradoxical remark, pointing to a Vassar student and saying, "That elephant is about to charge."

We continued our journey, always making left turns, the strategy for solving any connected maze except one designed by Escher, until at last we walked free of the vineyard. Before us stood the abbey, a dilapidated two-story affair, stricken with creepers. As Constantine sidled back into the labyrinth, Articulis emerged from the building and descended the stone steps, clutching to his chest an antique, leather-bound volume that I assumed was a Bible. We exchanged innocuous and anodyne pleasantries. His handshake was earthy and vigorous. He flashed the cover of his book—not Holy Writ after all but rather a *Confessions of Tertullian*—then gestured toward the adjacent chapel, its windows displaying as much empty leading as stained glass, the bell tower faced with exfoliating stucco.

"Upon your arrival, you doubtless noticed that our community occupies an island." Taking my arm, the abbot led me across the monastery grounds and into the cool air of the chapel. "One thousand years ago, on the blackest of Black Fridays, the world suffered a momentous rupture—a crack in the Teilhardian lithosphere."

"You don't say."

"In the primeval reaches of the Hudson Valley, a basin then populated largely by Algonquins and Mohawks, the divine pipework sprang a leak."

"My goodness."

A spiral staircase presented itself. We ventured upward through the bore of the tower, round and round the moldering bell rope, eventually disembarking into an open-air turret dominated by an enormous bronze bell laden with spiderwebs and lacking a clapper. Articulis guided me to the nearest Gothic window. Cirrus clouds hung in the sky like cuneiform characters. Below us spread the malevolent lake, coiled around the monastery like an immense anaconda.

"Left unchecked, the tarn will ooze across the entire lithosphere, menacing the biosphere with poison, pestilence, and pandemonium," Articulis said, indicating the moat with a rigid finger. "At the moment, only a few denizens of the noosphere, my brave band of ordained monks and nuns, stand in opposition to the rift. Through their religious devotions they keep the tarn at bay."

"That doesn't sound very plausible," I noted, the dust of NYU rationality still clinging to my shoes.

Articulis laughed and said, "*'Certum est, quia impossibile.'*" He brushed the cover of the *Confessions*. "No, I'm being needlessly clever. It is certain because of what I find in these pages. Tertullian not only foresaw the rift, he founded a religious community and charged it with containing the exudate when it appeared fifteen hundred years later. The man was a devotee of riddles. Indeed, it was he who gave Christianity its counterintuitive Trinity, *'tres Personae, una Substantia.'* He believed that when the fateful year 1700 arrived, his monks and nuns were duty-bound to travel to the New World, make their way to the Adirondacks, build a monastery on the site of the fault, and begin to cultivate the Five Primal Paradoxes. If they held these contradictions in their minds night and day, decade after decade, century after century, then the leak would never grow so copious as to threaten the planet."

I'd say one thing for the discourse available in Hudson Valley monasteries—it effortlessly eclipsed the polysyllabic chatter that occurred at NYU Philosophy Department meetings.

"Did Tertullian specify the five problems?" I asked, instantly receiving the abbot's nod. "Let me guess. I'll bet the Liar Paradox made the cut."

"Not only did our founder mandate that one, he anticipated all the flourishes Bertrand Russell would add many years later. The *Confessions* also prescribes the Ruby Paradox, the Nonsense Paradox, the Lawyer Paradox, and the Sorites Paradox."

"All good choices."

"Every one is Greek in origin, a fact that gave Tertullian pause—'What has Athens to do with Jerusalem?' he once remarked—but for the sake of the greater good he set aside his anti-pagan prejudices. Through fifty generations, our Order has pondered these fundamental puzzles. Hour by hour, minute by minute, heartbeat by heartbeat, we have eaten the paradox, drunk the paradox, breathed it, smelled it, sweated it, voided it, dreamt it."

"A recipe for lunacy, I'd say."

Articulis hummed in corroboration. "No one understood better than Tertullian that this great commission would blur the distinction between a monastery and a madhouse. And yet the Order cleaved to its task, inspired by our founder's revelation that, come the dawn of the third millennium, the fault would finally begin to heal. By the year 2015, or 2020, or perhaps 2025—Tertullian was never clear on this point—it would be as if the crack had never occurred."

"So you've beaten the Devil?" I asked, gazing through the Gothic window. A flock of vultures wheeled above the tarn in apparent prelude to feasting on the corpse of the Teilhardian biosphere.

"Not quite," Articulis said. "For it happens that in the final days of our project Lucifer has acquired an ally—five allies, actually, one for each paradox."

"Allies?"

"They are difficult to describe, but happily I needn't try, as the quintet is available for your inspection. With characteristic prescience, Tertullian foretold their advent. In the *Confessions* he called them cacodaemons."

It occurred to me that, to enjoy a conversation of this caliber, a person would normally have to organize a seminar among the dozen most accomplished schizophrenics in the five boroughs. "Are they in fact from Hell?"

"Why would you ask such a question, Donald? You don't even believe in Hell."

"True—but you do."

"Not really, no. Concerning the source of the cacos, Tertullian is most explicit. He calls them the children of Vorg—Vorg being their creator-god, an elusive deity inhabiting an inaccessible netherworld on another plane of reality. The *Confessions* predicted that when the five cacos spewed forth from the fault, they would arrive singing hymns to Vorg."

I leaned through the window. A blast of hot summer air pulsed against my brow and cheeks. The tarn's iniquity ascended to my nostrils in spiraling filaments of stench. I gagged and jerked back inside.

"A crack in the lithosphere," I muttered. "You know, Bartholomew, I almost believe you."

"Will you help us weld the fractured world whole?"

"What I'm about to say is true," I told the abbot. "What I just said is false."

As the sun began its paradoxical descent, being a stationary object that manifestly moved, Articulis took me to a classroom in the basement of the abbey. Covered head to toe in a threadbare frock, his face obscured by the cowl, a runty monk sat slumped in a maimed leather chair, gouts of cotton stuffing streaming from its wounds. His attention was locked on a wall-mounted chalkboard displaying two sentences rendered in capital letters.

LINE 1: THE SENTENCE WRITTEN ON
 LINE 1 IS NONSENSE.
LINE 2: THE SENTENCE WRITTEN ON
 LINE 1 IS NONSENSE.

Articulis tapped the monk on the shoulder. "Brother Francis, I would like you to meet a visitor, Dr. Donald Kreigar. He has come to help us seal the tarn."

Brother Francis rose but, instead of facing me, remained fixed on Line 1 and Line 2.

"Ah, the infamous Nonsense Paradox," I said, attempting to strike up a conversation. "In assailing the self-referentiality of Line 1, the author of Line 2 has offered a cogent and credible definition of nonsense—and yet Line 2 is the very sentence it so justly criticizes."

Francis said nothing.

"Is he under a vow of silence?" I asked.

"A pledge of paradox," Articulis corrected me. "Speaking would compromise his ability to nurture the contradiction." The abbot stepped forward, interposing himself between the monk and his conundrum. "Dr. Kreigar would like to see your caco."

Without saying a word, Francis slid back his cowl. His face, a pale, wizened, bulbous-nosed affair, seemed almost attractive compared with the slimy, legless, roach-brown vermin attached to his left temple. In shape the parasite suggested a horseshoe crab, in size it evoked a spatula, and in spirit it echoed a cancerous tumor. My immediate impulse was to locate a pair of canvas gloves, pull the thing off the monk, and mash it beneath my shoe—but when I proposed this remedy to Articulis, he countered with Tertullian.

"The *Confessions* claims that a cacodaemon cannot be forcibly extracted without killing its host. We have no reason to doubt this assertion. Were Brother Francis to die, not only would the Order lose a beloved child of God, the Nonsense Paradox would lose its strongest avatar on Earth. And yet, as things stand, Francis will soon be unable to serve the lithosphere, for the caco is sapping his strength and impeding his powers of concentration."

"If I were ever colonized by one of these fiends," I told Articulis, "my powers of concentration would be the least of the casualties. I would also lose my ability to control my bowels, retain my breakfast, and sustain my reason."

Among the strangest of the caco's aspects was the noises it made, a series of staccato gasps testifying to the satisfaction it took in absorbing the Nonsense Paradox, every seventh exhalation accompanied by a sound that fell on my astonished ears as "Vorg."

"It seems to be praising its god," I said.

"Exactly," Articulis said. "Vorg, Vorg, Vorg—just as Tertullian foresaw."

"This plague must be combated," I said.

"Combated, exactly—with all our philosophical resources. We don't know whether the cacos are immortal, or what their weaknesses might be. We know only that they feed on paradox the way a butterfly feeds on nectar or a tick on blood. Last week I hit upon a strategy—tentative, untested, but a strategy all the same. I shall give you the details presently, but first you must witness the full scope of the infestation."

We bid farewell to Brother Francis, ascended to the first floor, and entered the library, sphere of Sister Margaret, whose calm demeanor and placid apple face belied the apocalyptic quality of her devotions. Two ornately carved jewel boxes rested before her on the reading table. I recognized the accoutrements of the Ruby Paradox, sometimes called Newcomb's Paradox after the refinements wrought in modern times by William Newcomb of the Lawrence Livermore Laboratory. By the rules of the game, Sister Margaret was permitted to open both Box A and Box B, or else just Box B. She could not open only Box A. Whatever resided inside any box Margaret opened was hers to keep, but she could not retain the contents of any box she declined to open.

"Sister Margaret, please remove your wimple," Articulis commanded.

Silently she complied, never lifting her eyes from the jewel boxes. Her caco jutted from her occipital area like a hair bun, emitting moans of psychosexual ecstasy and panegyrics to Vorg.

The abbot proceeded to expound on the Christianized iteration of the Ruby Paradox practiced at the Monastery of Tertullian. Heaven's canniest angel, Gabriel, whose prophecies are almost always accurate, has placed in Box A a single gold coin, valuable enough to pay for refacing the monastery's bell tower. If Gabriel has predicted that Sister Margaret will open only Box B, he has also deposited an enormous ruby, worth a thousand gold coins, in Box B. With such a sum, Sister Margaret could fulfill her lifelong dream of building an orphanage in Kabul. However, if Gabriel has predicted that Margaret will open both boxes, then he has put nothing in Box B.

Paradoxically, there was a decisive case for Margaret opening both receptacles, and an equally decisive case for her opening only Box B. Think about it. As I explained in chapter two of *Adventures in Self-Reference,* the classic Prisoner's Dilemma turns on the same schizoid logic. The recently apprehended criminal will find himself constructing a sound argument for confessing and an equally sound argument for remaining silent.

Next Articulis took me upstairs to Brother Jonathan's cell, a clean and ill-lighted place, spare as a crypt. His caco sat atop his cranium like a hideous brown yarmulke. Articulis explained that Brother Jonathan passed every waking hour meditating on the Liar Paradox, which, owing to its Scriptural heritage, enjoyed particular prestige within the Order. Speaking of the Jewish Cretans in his brief Epistle to Titus, Saint Paul warns his proxy, "One of themselves, even a prophet of their own, said, 'The Cretans are always liars, evil beasts, slow bellies.' This witness is true. Wherefore rebuke them sharply." Beyond Paul's usual anti-Semitism—not without reason have I become a Tillichean dialectical humanist—we find in these verses a cogent though evidently unconscious formulation of the Liar Paradox.

Not only was Jonathan engaged in an intense inward consideration of Russell's Antinomy, he'd also written the basic formulation in an unbroken hundred-character line along the vertical surfaces of his cell, twenty-five characters per wall.

> THE CLASS OF ALL CLASSES THAT ARE NOT MEMBERS OF THEMSELVES IS A MEMBER OF ITSELF IF AND ONLY IF IT IS NOT A MEMBER OF ITSELF.

Standing in the center of the room, the monk pivoted slowly on his heel, repeatedly pondering the paradox, reifying the vicious cycle by dint of his own continuous rotations. A buzz of sensual contentment arose from his caco. According to legend, puzzles of this sort had caused the death of at least one ancient logician, Philetas of Cos—a story I now believed: Philetas had indeed succumbed to his own thoughts.

"Alas, Russell's discovery of set paradoxes did not mark the end of his troubles," I noted.

"Gödel's Incompleteness Theorem," Articulis said with a knowing nod. "In any formal logical system predicated on the natural numbers, there exists at least one statement that can be neither proved nor disproved within the given structure."

We exited the abbey and started across the courtyard, casting long El Greco shadows on the weed-choked grounds. A late afternoon breeze enveloped us, filling my nostrils with the heady scent of ripe grapes. Our destination, Articulis informed me, was the cloister, where we would meet Sister Ruth, keeper of the Lawyer Paradox.

Consider sly Protagoras, who trains attorneys and each year makes an unusual contract with his pupils. "You may attend all my lectures without any money changing hands," he tells the class, "but you must pay me ten drachmas if you win your first case." One particular pupil, Euathlus, takes Protagoras to court with the aim of getting free tuition, arguing that if he wins the case, then the teacher's fee must be waived, since that is the object of the suit. If Euathlus loses, however, Protagoras's fee must still be waived, since this is the pupil's first case. So far, so good.

Reaching the arcade, we beheld a diminutive nun circumnavigating the quadrangle, east to west, north to south, west to east, south to north, her glassy eyes contemplating some unseen and ever receding focal point. Articulis told Sister Ruth to remove her wimple. Without breaking stride, she did as instructed, revealing a parasite suckling obscenely on her left parietal. The beast, an albino, emitted the usual sounds of cacodaemonic satisfaction.

As Ruth passed me for the third time, I realized that she was muttering, over and over, now and forever, Protagoras's argument to the judge.

"If you find in favor of Euathlus, he owes me ten drachmas, as this is his first case, but if you resolve the dispute to my advantage, Euathlus still owes me ten drachmas, since that is the content of your decision ... If you find in favor of Euathlus, he owes me ten drachmas, as this is his first case, but if you resolve the dispute to my advantage, Euathlus still owes me ten drachmas, since that is the content of your decision ... If you find in favor of Euathlus ..."

Our final stop was the vineyard. The student pickers had gone home for the day, leaving the labyrinth to Brother Thomas, a blowsy, roly-poly man, his enormous eyes resting in their sockets like cupped eggs. The monk wandered aimlessly through the maze, enacting his assigned conundrum, a version of the Sorites Paradox, *sorites* being Greek for "heap." Stained with red grape juice and affixed to Thomas's right temple like an ancillary brain, his parasite feasted greedily.

Consult chapter six of *Adventures in Self-Reference,* and you'll learn that the Sorites Paradox belongs to a class of antinomies predicated on the pervasiveness of vagueness in the world. Consider a sand dune. Take away one grain. Is what remains still a heap of sand? Almost certainly. As a general rule, we may assert that if two sand heaps differ in number by just one grain, then both are dunes—or else neither is a dune. Alas, this seemingly innocuous principle leads to the unacceptable conclusion that all collections of sand, even single-grain collections, are heaps.

Not surprisingly, Brother Thomas employed the omnipresent grapes in contemplating the paradox. When is a bunch not a bunch? he wondered aloud. An arbor not an arbor? A vineyard not a vineyard? A harvest not a harvest?

"No doubt my philosopher has deduced the strategy by which I hope to defeat the cacos," Articulis said as, abandoning Thomas, we meandered among the trellises.

"You intend to turn their appetites against them," I said.

"Exactly."

"This will require a baited trap."

"Quite so," Articulis said. "The snare in question is now walking beside you." Reaching the core of the maze, we eased ourselves onto the wrought-iron bench. "Give me an impregnable paradox, Donald, something so tempting from a cacodaemonic perspective that they'll all desert their hosts for me."

My temples throbbed as if a pair of parasites had attached themselves to my head. "An impregnable paradox."

"Impregnable, delectable, ironclad, and unique."

A wave of nausea rolled through the whole of my digestive system. "I really want to help, but, you see—what am I trying to say?—I've never faced a challenge of this magnitude. I'm an academic. This smacks of the real world. I don't like it."

"And yet you're clearly the man for the job."

I reached toward a low-hanging cluster, plucked a grape, and popped it in my mouth. "Do you think they'd be lured by Zeno's quarrels with space, time, and motion?"

Quitting the bench, Articulis rose to full height and presented me with a tortuous smile. "The *Confessions* explicitly states, quote, 'Zeno the Pagan will prove useless in healing the crack,' and therefore I must assume a caco would find those puzzles equally unexciting. Tertullian is likewise unimpressed by the Grid Paradox, the Lottery Paradox, and the Paradox of the Ravens. He also anticipated and dismissed Moore's Paradox—'It's raining outside but I don't believe it is'—as lacking genuine eschatological muscle."

"I won't even ask about the Barber Paradox."

In a remote Sicilian village, the barber shaves every man who does not shave himself. Who shaves the barber? Although the problem has some features in common with Russell's Antinomy, it's not especially difficult to resolve. The barber doesn't shave. The barber is a woman. My favorite answer: the barber doesn't exist.

"Tertullian says nothing about the Barber Paradox, but I can't imagine it would beguile our parasites," Articulis said, starting toward the abbey. "Dinner will be served at eight o'clock. If the cacos continue to feed for another month, or perhaps just another fortnight, I fear our community will die of depletion"—my client vanished, enshrouded by the dusk—"which means the Devil wins after all."

As darkness crept over the Adirondacks, I headed for Sister Ruth's domain, the cloister. Lost in thought, I shuffled along the arcade at the methodical pace of the hooded figures in Escher's *Ascending and Descending*. Step by step, I boxed the courtyard, north, east, south, west. Every ten minutes or so, the nun and I passed like ships in the night, each of our preoccupied minds oblivious to its transient neighbor.

It came to me that I'd entered into a kind of contest with Tertullian. The two of us had become long-distance rivals, facing one another across the valley of the shadow of death. Whatever venerable absurdity I might put forward by way of helping Abbot Articulis and, by extension, the rest of *homo sapiens,* Tertullian had almost certainly anticipated the problem and ruled it out. What I needed was a conundrum that couldn't possibly have occurred to even the smartest third-century theologian—a wholly contemporary paradox, notorious for having tried the patience and taxed the sanity of modernity's shrewdest thinkers.

By some poetic coincidence, stars bloomed over Rhinebeck just as the required riddle took shape in my brain. Stepping into the quadrangle I scanned the celestial dome with its countless suns, each twinkling point a piece of my epiphany. The answer to our needs, in every possible meaning of that perplexing predicate, was heaven sent.

I repaired to the library, seeking to verify my revelation. The cosmology section was larger than I expected, featuring not only eccentric Christians like Teilhard and Bergson but the secular likes of Michael Hart, Stephen Hawking, Nikolai Kardashev, Freeman Dyson, and M.

D. Papagiannis. I perused each relevant paragraph with the frustrated frenzy of Achilles attempting to catch the tortoise, madly scribbling notes on the flyleaf of Shklovskii and Sagan's *Intelligent Life in the Universe*. Fixed on her jewel boxes, Sister Margaret ignored my presence. Even after the nun left for dinner, I continued my self-incarceration, until I finally had enough material for a credible presentation to Articulis.

"Shazam!" I shouted, striding into the gloomy, tenebrous, candle-lit refectory.

The abbot sat at the head of the table, monks to his left, nuns to his right. Not a caco was in sight, the infestation being entirely hidden beneath wimples and cowls. At that moment the parasites' murmurings were redolent of discontent—a sensible enough reaction: although the five hosts were still cultivating paradoxes, they had to devote a modicum of mentation to eating their stew and drinking their wine, with a concomitant reduction in the quality of the cacos' nourishment.

"The Fermi Paradox!" I cried.

"Tell me more," Articulis said.

"Why is it that, in such a vast cosmos, with two hundred and fifty billion stars in our galaxy alone, of which one hundred billion may be orbited by Earth-like planets, we have found no evidence of intelligent alien life? Why this Great Silence?"

"Continue," Articulis said.

Consulting my jottings on the flyleaf of *Intelligent Life in the Universe,* I told the abbot that astronomers had to date detected over 300 exoplanets—worlds circling sunlike stars outside our solar system—and the tally was increasing every year. Many astrobiologists believed that somewhere between one thousand and one million advanced civilizations may have already arisen in the Milky Way, for an average of 500,500. And yet: no extraterrestrial radio signals, no signs of galactic colonization, no plausible UFO narratives, no credible archaeological evidence of past visitations, no von Neumann probes, no Bracewell probes, no Dyson spheres, no Matrioshka brains. Nothing, nada, zero, zilch, bupkis.

"It's a genuine paradox," I continued, "complete with an absurd conclusion: five hundred thousand five hundred advanced civilizations have thus far eluded our senses because we should have detected them by now. As Enrico Fermi famously put it, 'Where is everybody?'"

Dressed in a splotched white apron, a hulking member of Constantine's staff appeared at my side holding a fissured ceramic tureen. He introduced himself as Jeremiah, then proceeded to serve me a steaming glob of boiled venison using a ladle the size of a caco.

"I'm impressed," Articulis said.

"I've been serving you this sludge for the past twenty years, and *tonight* you're impressed?" the cook said.

Articulis scowled and squeezed my hand. "Give me your indulgence while I play the contrarian. Like Tertullian, I subscribe to the doctrine of Original Sin. Perhaps the answer to the Fermi Paradox is simply that intelligent life, upon discovering thermonuclear weapons, inevitably destroys itself. Or maybe all those hypothetical advanced civilizations, in their mad pursuit of absolute security, have succeeded in annihilating one another."

"Line 1: The sentence written on Line 1 is nonsense," Brother Francis said.

"Like many renegade Catholics, I'm a Darwinist," Articulis continued. "A Teilhardian and teleological Darwinist to be sure, convinced that evolution is drawing us toward an Omega Point, but still a Darwinist. We can dispense with the Fermi Paradox simply by assuming that the biological processes found on Earth do not obtain elsewhere. Perhaps the odds are formidably

stacked against the transition from prokaryotic cells to
eukaryotic cells. Or maybe the move from single-celled
to multicellular life is difficult in the extreme."

"I wonder if I should open Box B only?" Sister Margaret said.

"Perhaps Earth has been deliberately sealed off as
a kind of wildlife refuge," Articulis persisted. "Perhaps
we're under a moral quarantine, doomed to isolation
until we eliminate poverty or outlaw warfare. Perhaps
the aliens are deliberately concealing themselves, knowing from bitter experience that extraterrestrial contact
inevitably leads to disaster."

"The class of all classes that are not members of
themselves is a member of itself if and only if•it is not a
member of itself," Brother Jonathan said.

"Maybe the aliens are so intelligent they have no
more reason to communicate with us than they do with
petunias," Articulis went on. "Maybe their minds defy
our notions of conscious rationality. Maybe they're
philosophically and spiritually advanced but don't make
machines and never will."

"If you find in favor of Euathlus, he owes me ten
drachmas, as this is his first case," Sister Ruth said.

The abbot was up to speed now. With uncanny per-
spicacity he reeled off a litany of possible resolutions,
most of which I'd already scrawled on the *Intelligent Life*
flyleaf. The aliens are already here, but they're keeping
out of sight. We haven't been searching long enough. We
aren't listening properly. Advanced civilizations broadcast radio signals for only brief intervals in their histories. Such societies are too distant in space and time to
contact us using their existing technologies.

Now Jeremiah got into the act. "You know what I
think? I think they've uploaded themselves into computers and don't give a fig about space travel."

"If there are sixty grapes in a bunch," Brother Thomas said, "does that mean fifty-nine grapes likewise constitute a bunch?"

"My favorite refutation is pure science fiction," I said. "Our universe is a simulation created by aliens who deliberately left it devoid of extraterrestrial intelligence."

"There, you see—even *you* don't believe it's a serious contradiction," Articulis said.

"No, I merely believe that the only substantive threat to Fermi's Paradox is the simulated-universe hypothesis, an argument for which the burden of proof clearly lies with its devotees. The remaining challenges all leave the conundrum in place. You see, Bartholomew, for any given advanced alien civilization C_1, that is, an extraterrestrial society whose unavailability to our empiricism is easily explained, there is always C_2, a civilization that by any rational measure should have become manifest by now. If in our perversity we choose to dismiss C_2 with a plausible unavailability scenario, we must still deal with C_3, a different civilization that should have revealed itself already. If we take the trouble to build a case against C_3, we have to cope with C_4, not to mention C_5, C_6, C_7, C_8, C_9, C_{10}—all the way up to $C_{500,500}$. I don't know about you, but somewhere around $C_{250,000}$ I would begin to admit there's a problem here. It takes just one community of celestial eager beavers to break the Great Silence— just one, that's all. What's going on, Bartholomew? Are we truly alone? How could that be?"

The abbot knitted his brow, smacked his lips, and took a long swallow of Château Pelagius. "All right, Donald, let's give it a try. You've not quite won me over, but for the moment you've allayed my doubts."

"Excuse me, Dr. Kreigar, but aren't you overlooking the most obvious solution of all?" Jeremiah asked. "Isn't the best answer staring us in the face?"

The instant I heard the word "obvious," a razor-toothed chill coursed along my spine. I winced internally. The cook's tacit argument was cogent, lucid, and supremely rational—and I had no riposte.

"Poe," I said.

"What?" Jeremiah said.

"The Purloined Object Effect," I muttered feebly. "I call it Poe because he wrote a story about the phenomenon. Some secrets hide in plain sight. The tarn didn't give rise to the cacos—they came from outer space. The parasites themselves have broken the Great Silence."

"I don't read much, but that's what I meant," Jeremiah said.

An interval of quietude descended upon the refectory—not as profound as the Great Silence, but palpable nevertheless.

"We have nothing to lose by proceeding as if Jeremiah is wrong," Articulis said at last. "Ergo, I shall brew myself a pot of coffee and spend the night pondering the Fermi Paradox. If the cacos are aliens, the problem will hold no interest for them, since they are its resolution. Otherwise, God willing, our visitors will come after me, determined to draw sustenance from a particularly erotic conundrum."

"God willing," Jeremiah echoed.

"God willing," I said.

"If you resolve the dispute to my advantage, Euathlus still owes me ten drachmas, since that is the content of your decision," Sister Ruth said.

"If there are fifty-nine grapes in a bunch," Brother Thomas said, "does that mean fifty-eight also constitute a bunch?"

"All Cretans are liars, the Cretan insisted," Brother Jonathan said.

Sobered by the Purloined Object Effect, I sought

to become intoxicated with Château Pelagius. The first glass failed to meet my criteria for drunkenness, as did the second, but by the third measure Achilles overtook the tortoise, Euathlus received free tuition, the barber got his shave, and nobody gave a damn when a heap stopped being a heap. I was now so rickety that my journey to the dormitory required Jeremiah to stand behind me, grasp my arms, and gingerly walk me up the stairs and along the corridor. I collapsed on the straw pallet, my brain reeling with wine and paradox. A moment later I was dreaming of *The Day the Earth Stood Still,* that ingenious allegory of solipsistic contact, humankind invading itself with its own crippled conscience, the iridescent angel of our better nature emerging from the gleaming vulva and imploring the world's leaders to heed his warning, for otherwise humanity will be chastised by the afterbirth, whose destructive power is without limit.

I awoke shortly after dawn and set about extricating myself from a nightmare, my Michael Rennie reverie having been supplanted by a dream in which, per Jeremiah's intuition, the cacodaemons had revealed themselves as tourists from the Oort cloud. Scrambling into my street clothes, I dashed down the hall to Brother Jonathan's cell. Still asleep, the monk lay sprawled across his pallet, snoring and smiling, dressed only in a nightshirt. His cranium was free of hair and—*mirabile dictu*—shorn of the Liar Paradox caco. Could it be? Was it possible? Had Enrico Fermi inadvertently saved the world?

Overflowing with love for the nonexistent occupants of our sterile galaxy, I descended to the library and, approaching the reading table, sat down across from Sister Margaret. She glanced up from her devotions, offered me a nod, then returned to cathecting the Ruby Paradox.

Her bare head held wisps of hair as ethereal as corn silk. Her shorn wimple lay beside the jewel boxes, marred now by a gaping hole rimmed with bits of torn thread. I rose and, circling the nun, inspected her occipital. Having broken free of Margaret's cloth, her caco was now gone, called to a higher paradox.

I lurched out of the library and charged down the basement stairs, praying that Brother Francis's parasite had also found satisfaction in the Great Silence. The monk sat before his blackboard, eyes fixed on a negation absurdly synonymous with the proposition it negated. Breathlessly I snuck up behind Francis, then gently slid back his hood to reveal a naked left temple where once the Nonsense Paradox caco had feasted.

Upon returning to the main floor, I realized that my respect for Tertullian now rivaled my appreciation for Bertrand Russell. That clever theologian had gotten everything right. Not only had he accurately prophesied the coming of the parasites, he'd intuited their terrestrial provenance. I rushed outside. A soft moan filled the morning air, the mellifluous correlative of cacodaemonic bliss. I followed the sound to its predictable source, Bartholomew Articulis. He sat on the wrought-iron bench in the center of the vineyard, a caco clamped to his left temple, a second to his crown, a third to his occipital. Constantine stood behind the bench, hovering protectively over his employer.

"Not a single von Neumann probe," Articulis muttered. "No Bracewell probes or Dyson spheres."

Catching sight of me, the dwarf raised a finger to his lips—a superfluous gesture, for I already knew it would be disastrous to distract the abbot.

"Vorg," sang the caco trio. "Vorg . . . Vorg . . . Vorg . . ."

"Success," Constantine whispered.

"No colonizations, visitations, or plausible abductions," Articulis hissed.

Even as the abbot sustained the Fermi Paradox, the two remaining cacos appeared in the clearing, wriggling across the grass like primeval slugs, thickening the dew with glistening slime. I recognized Brother Thomas's caco from the grape stains on its dorsal side, Sister Ruth's from its pallor. Reaching Articulis's feet, the cacos began their ascent, slithering up his legs and across his torso.

"No radio contact," said the unflinching abbot.

At last the Sorites Paradox caco came to rest on Articulis's left parietal, then set about nourishing itself. Seconds later the Lawyer Paradox caco reached the abbot's right temple.

"How long will it be, I wonder, before he goes mad?" I asked, *sotto voce*.

"This is a monastery," Constantine replied. "Providence is on our side. I know in my heart that Abbot Articulis will remain healthy until the rift is healed. God didn't bring the Order this far only to abandon it on the shores of the tarn."

"Vorg," trilled the happy cacos. "Vorg . . . Vorg . . . Vorg . . ."

"Perhaps I should stay here today," I said. "Shall I cancel my three o'clock class?"

Constantine shook his head and said, "If I need you, I'll send for you, but right now I'm abrim with hope. I must thank you for helping us defeat these malicious imps."

At a loss for words, I merely said, "This sentence is not about itself, but about whether it is about itself."

"I must admit, I've never cared for you Tillichean ground-of-being types," the dwarf said. "It all seems to me like atheism by another name. But God works in mysterious ways. He may even work through assistant professors. Tonight I shall remember you in my prayers."

As you might imagine, after my stay with the Tertullianists I had considerable difficulty adjusting to life back at the Bertrand Russell Institute of Paradox Studies. For all its gritty vistas and gnarly particulars, its noises, odors, tastes, and textures, the East Village now struck me as an unreal place, absurd in a way that made the Monastery of Tertullian seem merely implausible. Throughout the rest of July, my poor blameless Philosophy 412 students endured the nadir of higher education, their professor having become an erratic tyrant who assaulted them with incoherent tirades, arbitrarily canceled office hours, and every day upped the page count for their final paper.

I even tortured the class with the notorious Examination Paradox, claiming that I would give them a surprise multiple-choice test sometime the following week. The catch, I sadistically insisted, is that any teacher who wields such a threat cannot possibly make good on it. Friday will not bring the alleged surprise, for if the previous four days have been examination-free, then the test will inevitably fill the one remaining slot. The same reasoning applies to Thursday. Since the previous three days have been examination-free, and because Friday has already been ruled out, springing the test on day four would hardly qualify as unexpected. Through this chain of logic we can likewise assert that neither Wednesday nor Tuesday nor Monday allows the teacher to fulfill his desire.

Given my irrational condition, I was actually relieved when Constantine phoned and begged me to return to the monastery. Alas, the Fermi Paradox had proven less robust than Articulis had hoped, but he had no intention of surrendering to the cacos. If I could possibly manage it, I must come to Rhinebeck immediately and furnish the Tertullianists with a superior antinomy. I promised the dwarf I would leave posthaste.

At three o'clock I marched into my Philosophy 412 class and announced that the unexpected examination had been canceled, the course itself terminated, then cheerily informed them they were all getting As. Returning to my office, I told Mrs. Graham that I planned to spend the rest of the summer in the Adirondacks, healing a crack in the lithosphere.

"An academic conference?" she asked.

"Something like the opposite," I replied, wondering what I meant. "I am the thought you are thinking now."

"The day you stop talking crazy," Mrs. Graham said, "I'll know you've gone insane."

Two hours later I stood on the shores of the tarn, inhaling the miasmic vapors. It might have been a trick of the dying light—a visual paradox, if you will—but it seemed that the pestilential fluid had receded by several inches. Unless I was deluding myself, the battle had swung in favor of the Tertullianists, even though the Fermi Paradox was now evidently on the ropes.

I passed through the gates and entered the vineyard, soon reaching the center. Brother Thomas sat on the bench, considering his heaps, oblivious to everything save the problem of ill-defined boundaries. Absently he rolled back his hood, no doubt with the unconscious intention of savoring the evening breeze. For me the gesture proved impossibly distressing. The monk's grape-stained caco had returned, once again drawing sustenance through his right temple.

I broke free of the maze, then dashed toward the cloister, drawn by a glimpse of Sister Ruth. She negotiated the quadrangle with measured strides, all the while cultivating the Lawyer Paradox. "If you find in favor of Euathlus, he owes me ten drachmas, as this is his first case," she muttered. A malign bulge protruded from the left parietal area of her wimple, testament to a recrudescent caco.

Constantine came hobbling across the grounds, his pointed hat and lederhosen giving him the appearance of a garden gnome. Fighting tears, suppressing sobs, he guided me into the abbey and up the stairs to the dormitory floor. An instant later I found myself in Articulis's cell, his recumbent form stretched out along his pallet. The abbot's head was free of cacos, but his face betrayed a pervasive anguish. Sweat speckled his forehead like condensation on a glass of iced tea.

"Did you bring another paradox?" he inquired through clenched teeth.

"Yes," I said, lying.

"A good one?"

"Tremendous."

"Thank God." Articulis released a rasping cough, the sort of wheezing hack that was less its own event than the symptom of a dire condition. "Last night a sixth parasite came among us. Tertullian neglected to foretell its advent, but I cannot deny the evidence of my senses. By cacodaemonic standards this new creature is apparently a great sage—though its appetites are not exotic. Even as we speak, it feeds contentedly on the Liar Paradox."

"Before attaching itself to Brother Jonathan, our Übercaco made a presentation to its fellows," Constantine said, wiping Articulis's fevered brow with a cold damp cloth. "In honor of Tertullian, the sage spoke in Latin. There is no Vorg, it revealed. The creator-god, like all creator-gods, is a fiction. Our galaxy is bereft of transcendent beings, but it does contain billions of spacefaring vagabonds, the category to which every caco belongs."

"Evidently they believed their sage," I said.

"Every word," Articulis said.

"And so the Fermi Paradox has collapsed."

"Never to rise again."

Closing his eyes, Articulis rolled onto his chest and pressed his moist face into the naked pillow. The shaft of a goose feather poked through the ticking. The abbot groaned, abducted from the moment by fever, pain, and weariness, his torments now bearing him to some muzzy borderland between sentience and sleep.

Constantine took me aside and explained that, on learning the truth of their origins, the cacos became furious with Articulis, convinced that he'd deliberately deluded them. Before abandoning the abbot and wriggling away to their accustomed hosts, the invaders had avenged themselves, planting their stingers in his flesh and filling his veins with venom.

Articulis, awakening, cried out for water. I filled his glass from a clay pitcher and placed it to his lips. "Tell me, Bartholomew, do you believe the sage's argument? Is every creator-god a fiction?"

Articulis took a protracted swallow. "For me, God the Father will always be real. I know my Redeemer liveth. The Omega Point beckons." His sentences came slowly, each syllable purchased at the price of a spasm. "But until humanity attains that celestial apex, our Order must continue its great commission." A seismic shudder possessed the abbot, a fleshquake rolling from his cranium to his knees. "My monks and nuns are all still at their posts, fighting the good fight, and as soon as I'm rid of this poison, I'll tutor myself in your new paradox, then proceed to ponder—"

Ponder. An appropriate last word for so thoughtful

a man. We applied the usual tests, feeling for his pulse, pricking his heel, holding a mirror to his nostrils. Constantine drew a sheet over the abbot's imposing frame, whereupon the two of us, Tertullianist and Tillichean, prayed for the soul of our departed friend.

Shortly after sunrise, I helped the dwarf bury Articulis in the monastery graveyard, home to the hundreds of fault fighters who'd gone before him. The soft July ground yielded readily to our spades. At noon I visited the library. My search proved fruitful, providing me with a paradox such as Tertullian would never have anticipated in his wildest dreams.

For the next four hours I sat in the refectory, cultivating the conundrum in the garden of my brain. Sister Margaret was the first to arrive. No sooner had she taken her place before a steaming bowl of venison stew than the caco detached itself from her occipital and started in the direction of its new Omega Point, myself, inching along the dining table like some ghastly casserole come horribly to life, leaving lambent threads of slime behind. Slithering up my abdomen, chest, cheek, brow, the parasite at last came to rest atop my head. The alien was predictably cold-blooded, assuming it had a circulatory system, but this sensation was easily offset by the hot flush of conquest I now experienced. I'd lured the beast, by God. I'd seduced it with my genius for absurdity.

Brother Thomas appeared next, followed by Brother Francis, then Sister Ruth. In a matter of minutes my occipital region, right parietal, and left temple had each received a caco. Now Brother Jonathan entered the refectory, bearing his customary parasite on his crown. Sucking on the Liar Paradox, the Übercaco sprouted from his right temple, a lewd glistening invader, fatter than its fellows. I was not surprised when the lesser alien abandoned its host, twisting and flopping toward me until at last it found a home on my left parietal. The Übercaco remained in place, drawing affirmation from that vast set of antinomies by which a dissembler may dissemble to obscure his dissemblance. But my brain harbored a paradox more pleasing still—or so I hoped.

Imagine a box, large enough to contain a cat plus an outlandish contraption consisting of a hammer, a flask of deadly gas, a nugget of radium, and a Geiger counter. For this particular radium sample it happens that, over the span of one hour, there is a fifty-fifty chance that the nucleus of a single atom will decay. Detected by the Geiger counter, this event will trip the hammer, which will in turn break the flask, thus releasing the poison gas and killing the cat. Note that our *Gedanken* demonstration perversely couples the macroworld of discernible reality to the microworld of quantum mechanics, that probabilistic plane on which, under certain circumstances, we may legitimately claim that the collapse of the wave function occurs in consequence of the observer's consciousness. We are thus forced to the unacceptable conclusion that, until the instant the experimenter opens the box and peers inside, the cat is simultaneously alive and dead, trapped in an absurd superposition of eigenstates.

Concentrating ferociously, breathing as deliberately as a mother giving birth, I fixed Schrödinger's Paradox in my mind, its paraphernalia growing more delicious with each passing second. The radium sample glowed. The flask coruscated. The Geiger counter acquired a silver aura. The hammer became a Platonic archetype. The cat's pelt transmuted into a sleek numinous rainbow.

After an excruciating interval the Übercaco abandoned Brother Thomas and undertook the journey to my brow, in time coming to rest on my right temple. Jeremiah entered and began to serve everyone Château

Pelagius from a one-liter bottle. As he filled my goblet, I decided that my powers of concentration would not suffer in consequence of a few swallows. Thus it came to pass that, as the Tertullianists savored their wine, ate their stew, and battled the crack, I drank a toast to Schrödinger's impossible cat.

It has been plausibly asserted that losing always feels worse than winning feels good. But allow me to suggest that nothing could possibly feel as terrible as saving the world feels terrific. Of course, I couldn't have done it without the help of three monks and two nuns, all of whom, to the degree that their vocations permit triumphalist emotions, doubtless share my pride and participate in my joy.

The victory turned on our willingness to nurture the six absurdities or die in the attempt. We persisted, and we won. After a mere three weeks of contemplation, we beheld the tarn evaporate completely and the parent rift seal itself. The cacos hung around for another ten days, then finally took leave of my cranium, bound for some brighter star with better puzzles. And so it happens that, held to a standard of tangible evidence, the strange events related herein might as well never have occurred—a judgment that, the more you think about it, the faster it flips its facets: a verbal Necker cube.

Upon my return to the university, I made a point of keeping silent. Any attempt to relate these adventures to my colleagues might have greased the wheels of Dr. Virginia Sayles's hostility, and before long she would have required me to undergo a psychiatric evaluation, subsequently manipulating the results so that they seemed to demand my institutionalization. Appearances to the contrary, becoming a mental patient is rarely an astute career move in academia.

A question hovers in the air. Why should a man like myself, an aesthete who would rather achieve tenure than a state of grace, have risked his sanity in appeasing a voracious band of extraterrestrial parasites? Why should he place the common good before his self-interest? I really don't know. The mystery stumps me. Call it a paradox.

There remains only the matter of the boxed cat. You will be pleased to hear that Snowball lived. She recently gave birth. The kittens' names are Bartholomew, Francis, Margaret, Jonathan, Ruth, and Thomas. How can I pronounce with such confidence on Snowball's fate? Simple. Every word in the narrative you have just read is false, as befits a composition by yours truly, Donald Kreigar, assistant professor and competent philosopher, who never opens his mouth or picks up his pen except to tell a lie.

About the Authors

Michael Arsenault loves to write stories. He's won no awards, signed no lucrative contracts, and never really prospered from his work. Still he perseveres, secure in the knowledge that, like all the greatest artists, his genius will be discovered after his death. Which is kind of a bummer, when you think about it. (Feel free to send notes of encouragement to michael.b.arsenault@ gmail.com, otherwise he might be tempted to become a janitor.)

Pat Cadigan is the author of fifteen books, including two making-of movie books on *Lost in Space* and *The Mummy,* four media tie-ins, three short-fiction collections, one young adult book, and the Arthur C. Clarke Award-winning novels *Synners* (1991) and *Fools* (1994). Her work has been translated into French, Spanish, Italian, German, Polish, Russian, Portuguese, Japanese, and Czech. She tweets as Cadigan, faces Facebook as Pat Cadigan, lives out loud on LiveJournal as fastfwd, and still finds time to roam around London with her husband, the Original Chris Fowler.

Paul Di Filippo has been writing for some thirty years now and hopes to continue for a like number. He lives in Providence, Rhode Island, with Deborah Newton, Brownie the cocker spaniel, and Penny Century the calico cat. Paul participates in a group blog, The Inferior 4+1 at community.livejournal.com/theinferior4.

Sheila Finch is the author of seven science fiction novels and short stories that have appeared in *Fantasy & Science Fiction, Amazing, Asimov's, Fantasy Book,* and numerous anthologies. A collection of her "lingster" stories recently appeared as *The Guild of Xenolinguists.* Sheila taught creative writing at El Camino College for thirty years and at workshops around California. She also writes about teaching creative writing, and currently a series of her short essays on the subject appear online at the SFWA website: www.NebulaAwards.com. Her work has won several awards, including the Nebula Award for Best Novella, the San Diego Book Award for Juvenile Fiction, and the Compton Crook Award for Best First Novel. Sheila's website can be found at www .sff.net/people/sheila-finch.

Matthew Hughes writes science fantasy. His stories have appeared in *Asimov's, Fantasy & Science Fiction, Postscripts,* and *Interzone.* His latest novels are *Template, The Other,* and *Hespira: A Tale of Henghis Hapthorn.* Matthew's website can be found at www.archonate .com.

Alex Irvine's most recent novels are *Buyout* and *The Narrows.* He is the author of nonfiction books including *The Vertigo Encyclopedia* and *Supernatural: John Winchester's Journal,* as well as comic series *Daredevil Noir* and *Hellstorm, Son of Satan: Equinox.* He teaches at the

University of Maine. Alex blogs at alexirvine.blogspot
.com.

Jay Lake is a winner of the John W. Campbell Award for
Best New Writer and a multiple nominee for the Hugo
and World Fantasy awards. "Permanent Fatal Errors"
is part of Jay's *Sunspin* cycle of stories, others of which
may be found in *The New Space Opera 2* and his 2010
collection *The Sky That Wraps*. Lake's other 2010 books
include *Pinion* and *The Baby Killers*. His short fiction
appears regularly worldwide. Jay's website can be found
at www.jlake.com.

David Langford has published over thirty books, about
eighty short stories, and hundreds of magazine columns
since his fiction debut in 1975. His awards include the
Skylark, the European SF Award (shared with co-authors
Peter Nicholls and Brian Stableford) and twenty-eight
Hugos—some of the latter awarded for his SF newslet-
ter *Ansible,* launched in 1979 and currently appearing
monthly at: news.ansible.co.uk. Langford's most popular novel is the nuclear farce *The Leaky Establishment*
(1984), based on his years as a weapons physicist. His
straight stories are collected as *Different Kinds of Darkness* (2004), and his notorious parodies and pastiches
as *He Do the Time Police in Different Voices* (2003); his
most recent collection, of columns, essays, reviews, and a
few short-short stories, is *Starcombing* (2009). His large
Victorian house in Reading, England, contains numerous computers and far too many books.

Paul McAuley worked as a research biologist in various
universities, including Oxford and UCLA, and for six
years was a lecturer in botany at St. Andrews University, before becoming a full-time writer. His latest novels

are *The Quiet War* and *Gardens of the Sun*. He lives in North London. Paul's blog, Earth and Other Unlikely Worlds, can be found at unlikelyworlds.blogspot.com.

Yves Meynard was born in 1964 and has been active in Québec science fiction circles since 1986. He served as literary editor for the magazine *Solaris* from 1994 to 2001. He has published over forty stories in French and English and seventeen books, including three short-story collections, nine YA novels, two short novels, and one huge space opera. Several of these works were written in collaboration with Jean-Louis Trudel under the common pen name of Laurent McAllister. His fantasy novel in English, *The Book of Knights*, a finalist for the 2000 Mythopoeic Award for Best Novel, was translated into French as *Le Livre des chevaliers*. He holds a Ph.D. in computer science from the Université de Montréal and earns a living as a software developer. Yves's website can be found at pages.videotron.com/ymeynard.

James Morrow has been writing fiction ever since, as a seven-year-old living in the Philadelphia suburbs, he dictated "The Story of the Dog Family" to his mother, who dutifully typed it up and bound the pages with yarn. Upon reaching adulthood, he proceeded to write nine novels and enough short stories to fill two collections. To date Jim's most conspicuous effort is a postmodern historical epic called *The Last Witchfinder*, praised by the *New York Times* for fusing "storytelling, showmanship, and provocative book-club bait." He followed it with a thematic sequel, *The Philosopher's Apprentice*, which NPR called "an ingenious riff on *Frankenstein*," and a standalone novella, *Shambling Towards Hiroshima*, set in 1945 and dramatizing the U.S. Navy's attempt to leverage a Japanese surrender via a biological weapon that strangely anticipates Godzilla. A two-time winner of both the World Fantasy Award and the Nebula Award, Jim maintains a website at www.jamesmorrow.net.

Mike Resnick is, according to *Locus,* the all-time leading award winner, living or dead, for short science fiction. He is the winner of five Hugos, plus other major awards in the USA, France, Spain, Croatia, Poland, and Japan. He is the author of sixty novels, over 240 stories, and two screenplays, and has edited more than forty anthologies. His work has appeared in twenty-three languages. You can find Mike on Facebook.

Lezli Robyn is an Australian writer who wrote and sold her first two stories to *Clarkesworld* and *Jim Baen's Universe* in the closing months of 2008. In the thirteen months since then she has made sixteen further story sales, selling to markets such as *Asimov's, Analog*, Tor's 50th Anniversary *Twilight Zone* anthology, Hadley Rille's anthology *Origins,* celebrating the 150th anniversary of Darwin's *The Origin of Species,* and other science fiction markets as distant as China, Russia, Poland, Italy, and Bulgaria—alone or in collaboration with Mike Resnick. Lezli is currently working on her first novel and a YA trilogy with Mike Resnick.

Kristine Kathryn Rusch is a bestselling, award-winning writer of genre fiction, whose latest book, *Diving into the Wreck*, has garnered excellent reviews. She also writes mystery as Kris Nelscott and funny paranormal romances as Kristine Grayson (the next of those, *The Charming Way,* will appear in spring 2011). She's the first writer to have a science fiction crime story in the prestigious *Best American Mystery Stories* and *The Year's Best*

Science Fiction anthology. That same year, she won the Asimov's Readers Choice Award and The Ellery Queen Mystery Magazine Readers Choice Award. Her short story collection, *Recovering Apollo 8 and Other Stories,* has just appeared. She got the idea for "The Dark Man" while in Rome with Adrian Nikolas Phoenix, who was researching a novel set near the Spanish Steps. Find out more about Rusch's work (and those of her pen names) at www.kristinekathrynrusch.com.

Felicity Shoulders was born in Portland, Oregon, nine months after the eruption of Mt. St. Helens. She holds an MFA in writing from Pacific University. Her fiction has appeared in *Asimov's* and *CALYX, A Journal of Art and Literature by Women*. Her website can be found at felicityshoulders.com.

Ray Vukcevich's fiction has appeared in many magazines and anthologies and has been collected in *Meet Me in the Moon Room* from Small Beer Press. Find his tweets, links to online stories, interviews, and more at www.rayvuk.com.

Ian Watson's most recent story collection may well be the only full-length genre fiction book written in collaboration with a writer of a different mother tongue: the transgressive and satiric *The Beloved of My Beloved* (2009) with Italian surrealist Roberto Quaglia, two stories from which have been anthologized in volumes of *The Mammoth Book of Best New Erotica*. Ian also wrote the screen story for Steven Spielberg's *A.I. Artificial Intelligence*, based on almost a year's work eyeball to eyeball with Stanley Kubrick. With Ian Whates, he has just co-edited *The Mammoth Book of Alternate Histories*. He lives in a very small village in rural England midway between Oxford and Stratford. Ian's website can be found at www.ianwatson.info.

Leslie What is a Nebula Award-winning author whose writing has appeared in *Utne Reader, Midstream, Vestal Review, Asimov's, Witpunk, Fugue, Parabola, Best New Horror, Lady Churchill's Rosebud Wristlet,* and others. Her collection, *Crazy Love* (2008) earned starred reviews from *Booklist* and *Publishers Weekly* and was a finalist for the Oregon Book Award. She teaches writing at UCLA Extension and is a writer-in-schools in Lane County, Oregon. Visit Whatworld at www.lesliewhat .net.

About the Editors

Nick Gevers is an editor at the major UK independent press PS Publishing (www.pspublishing.co.uk), where he co-edits, with Peter Crowther, the twice-yearly *Postscripts* anthology, the latest volumes of which are *Enemy of the Good, Edison's Frankenstein,* and *The Company He Keeps.* His other SF and fantasy anthologies include *Infinity Plus* (with Keith Brooke), *Other Earths* (with Jay Lake), *Extraordinary Engines,* and *The Book of Dreams.* A noted critic and interviewer in the SF field, Gevers lives in Cape Town, South Africa.

Marty Halpern freelances as an all-around wielder of red ink. While acquiring for Golden Gryphon Press (1999–2007) he was a two-time finalist for the World Fantasy Award: Special Award, Professional. Marty has co-edited two previous anthologies: *The Silver Gryphon* (with Gary Turner) and *Witpunk* (with Claude Lalumière). In addition to working directly with writers, Marty currently freelances for Ace Books, Fantastic Books, Night Shade Books, Tachyon Publications, and *Realms of Fantasy* magazine. You can follow him on Twitter (martyhalpern) or read his (occasional) blog posts at More Red Ink: http://martyhalpern.blogspot .com.